CHOSEN PREY

Caleb was hungry. He approached the girl in the square and smelled the moistness of her, an earthy scent that was stimulating to him only inasmuch as he would derive an almost perverse pleasure in destroying what it meant: the girl was fecund with life and her role in the continuation of life. She smiled at him as he approached, not recognizing from a distance of ten feet or so that he was not a possible lover, but a destroyer. That he had not come to sow her ripe womb, but to lay her barren with salt and fire and miles of black crosses. She might have caught a glimpse of that and been momentarily startled if he'd come upon her suddenly; instead, he let her see him as a human being: his black coat open, hands thrust behind his back, dark hair swept from a face whose paleness gave him the look of a devastatingly handsome crusader who, if not for his privileged social standing of wealth and power, could have been a celebrity idol.

"Let me see," he said, nodding toward the black sketchbook she clutched to her chest.

"Oh, it's not very good." She blushed.

"Please," he said. "I'd really like to see."

"Okay," she said shyly.

Caleb opened the book and moved quickly through the first sketches. Then he put the sketchbook down.

"Come with me," he said softly and took her hand. "Come."

And she went without question, as they all did when they were chosen. . . .

BOOK YOUR PLACE ON OUR WEBSITE
AND MAKE THE
READING CONNECTION!

We've created a customized website just for our very special readers, where you can get the inside scoop on everything that's going on with Zebra, Pinnacle and Kensington books.

When you come online, you'll have the exciting opportunity to:

- View covers of upcoming books

- Read sample chapters

- Learn about our future publishing schedule (listed by publication month *and author*)

- Find out when your favorite authors will be visiting a city near you

- Search for and order backlist books from our online catalog

- Check out author bios and background information

- Send e-mail to your favorite authors

- Meet the Kensington staff online

- Join us in weekly chats with authors, readers and other guests

- Get writing guidelines

- AND MUCH MORE!

Visit our website at
http://www.kensingtonbooks.com

AFTER
HUMAN

MICHAEL
CROSS

PINNACLE BOOKS
Kensington Publishing Corp.
http://www.kensingtonbooks.com

. . . to everyone who doesn't give a shit

"Existence is plagiarism."
—*EM Cioran*

"I wish the people had a single throat."
—*Caligula*

...before you begin

Warning: you are about to open an unknown file. If you don't know who sent you the attached, or you are unsure about your system's protection, be cautious about downloading the information enclosed. There is a very good chance that it contains objectionable material or a virus that can damage your mind.

If you decide to proceed, it may prove helpful to be aware of the following:

Everything that happens here is true, is really happening, will happen, or has already happened, without exception, but in a sideways kind of way, impossible to see directly, which is to say, without imagination.

There is, of course, no such thing as a vampire: the idea of a "vampire," once a metaphor in the arsenal of the underclass, has been co-opted in a more or less deliberate campaign of disinformation meant to belittle and discredit any real investigation into the hierarchical "feeding" schema inherent in our personal, social, political, and planetary existence. That popular writers and filmmakers unwittingly, for the most part, participate in this oppression is unfortunate, and, apparently, unavoidable. Our domination is so complete that even protest is rendered mindless entertainment.

Furthermore, there is no such thing as "real" people: the concept of "real people" was invented, variously, in the ninth and late twelfth centuries, primarily as a literary and commercial device. Don't feel badly about any of the people that die in the following pages. As the Hindus say, there is no slayer and no one slain.

Two things to keep in mind:

1. You are alive because something else is dying.
2. Something else is alive because you are dying.

Finally, this is not a novel.
Read in a certain context: this is your life.
Your scene has already been shot.
There is nothing left for you to do.
This is the end.

1. endangered species

Blood, blood everywhere. On the walls, in big garish splashes like the creation of some berserk post-modern artist, pooled on the teak floors, even inside the refrigerator where one of those who'd done this had left bloody handprints in search of a snack. There wasn't a room in the mansion that wasn't marked. Seventeen bodies so far, including the B-movie actress found naked at the bottom of the empty swimming pool out back. The party at the Long Island home of a prominent plastic surgeon had turned into a nightmare. So far they had not turned up anyone famous among the bodies, not anyone they could recognize on the site anyway. That was something to be thankful for, at least. There was one man, however, without a face, pending identification.

It was bad enough that these were monied people, men and women of influence, or those closely associated with them. They wouldn't be able to keep this one out of the public eye, not entirely anyway, although they would certainly blur the picture. So long as his terrors had been confined to teen runaways, bored housewives, and philandering husbands it had been perfectly excusable. Even when he had graduated to bars, offices, and the occasional family home in places like Winchester and Fontana it had been "doctorable," given the right spin.

Nikka stood outside under the portico, out of the cold rain, and lit one of her long cigarettes, but, of course, with no intention of smoking it. He was getting more dangerous or more reckless, depending on how you looked at it. He either wanted to be stopped or believed he couldn't be stopped.

Either way, he had become a malignant entity.

She was wearing a long black leather coat, black leather gloves, black leather boots. Her lips were arterial red and carefully drawn between high cheekbones on an unlined face that didn't see the sun. She understood perfectly well the importance of her iconographic image and secretly enjoyed being photographed for the media and for the many historical documents in which she appeared.

A large, powerful man jogged up the walkway toward her, pulling the collar of his coat over his head. He stood at the foot of the stairs, looking up, in an attitude of stylized reverence. His face was coarse and brutal. He was wearing an earpiece connecting him to God only knew who, or what, or where.

"Yes, Agent Mahoney?"

Her tone was bored, indifferent. She might have been an actress in a movie. Everyone knew that Mahoney was her right hand.

"We've secured the area, Chief."

"Good. Final count?"

"Twenty-one."

"Survivors?"

"None."

"Good. Names?"

"Only the girl in the pool."

Nikka nodded. That was a nightmare averted. A B-movie actress could be disposed of in any number of ways. A Gwyneth Paltrow, for instance, could not.

"Get an ID on that faceless man. We don't want any nasty surprises. And get back to me immediately."

"Yes, ma'am."

Mahoney smiled and Nikka could see the relief in the big man's brutal face. There was appreciative laughter from some of the assistants who had followed her out into the vestibule of night. Among them her personal image manager stood on the bottom step beneath a waiting black umbrella. Her eunuch makeup artist, Tonee, followed Nikka up the walk dabbing texturizing cream onto his mistress's perfect face so that she would look absolutely stunning when she faced the media glow beyond the gates of the mansion and told the world exactly what it wanted to hear.

Is it possible to live too long? he wondered. There must have been a time when he wasn't alive. But he'd be damned if he could remember it. He'd existed forever, as far as he knew. And he would continue to exist, forever, without end, unless he decided to end it himself, or made an error of some gross and uncorrectable kind. There were certain very definite ways that he could be terminated. They weren't secret; they had been published fairly openly for many centuries. Yet he had survived witchhunts, pogroms, wars, personal vendettas, and cataclysms both natural and unnatural. He had done so by adhering to one simple law: change. You could live forever, but you could not remain the same forever. There were many who couldn't—or wouldn't—understand that. They were only memories now. Others like them would be memories eventually. He had mutated over the millennia like a virus always one step ahead of the vaccine. Lately, in the last two hundred years or so, the changes necessary had come at a dizzying speed. So, so many had fallen. And yet he remained, strong, undefeated, like death itself.

The whip cracked loudly, but Nikka wasn't looking at the moment. The light touch of her Asian Reiki boy was playing around her closed, tense eyes. Nikka enjoyed the Japanese bioenergetic art because unlike ordinary massage, it didn't require any physical contact. She was sitting in a chair of space-age alloy chrome and white rhinoceros leather that had been ergonomically designed especially to accommodate her unique lumbar configuration. Every three months or so she had her vertebrae scanned to record any slight change that might necessitate a modification in the chair.

There was another crack of the whip and a soft pretty moan from the blond club T-girl she knew hung by her wrists on the polished onyx platform. Jaleel, her favorite whip master, was doing the honors tonight. She liked the traditional contrast of his huge, heavily muscled black body next to that of the slight, petite, pale flesh of this silly, hormone-enhanced champagne stripper. Jaleel had worked in the seraglio of a Middle Eastern oil tycoon until the vicissitudes of allegiances in that turbulent part of the world had forced the wealthy Arab's murder. Jaleel had been one of the spoils of war, so to speak, a favor from a top-ranking Pentagon official. Nikka had seen his work at a dinner, years ago, when the State Department was trying to work out the release of some hostage or other.

This underground lair, impervious to any foreseen disaster, including viral contagion and nuclear war, was Nikka's gift to herself. She had designed and built this sanctuary from the world as recompense for a life lived far too much in the world. She was not unaware of the similarity that the place had to the tomb of an Egyptian queen, a dark necropolis protected by curses, in which she alone roamed, and those select slaves she required to attend her, even in semideath.

She had money, lots of it, an obscene and sinful amount of it, a card hardwired into the World Bank, unlimited wealth, quite literally. What do you want when you have everything in the world—or the means to acquire it?

You want, of course, those few things that money cannot buy. She was beyond, naturally, such pedestrian concerns as love and happiness, and all that pre-twenty-first-century propaganda. You want, Nikka thought, a challenge. You want a reason to go on living. Is that what this was?

The business on Long Island troubled her.

They got out of hand, occasionally. It was something you had to reasonably expect, being what they were. That's why she existed, after all, and why she was granted a power and an autonomy that would have made many of history's worst dictators jealous. She had the authority to question anyone; and the obligation to answer no one and nothing beyond her own merciless perfectionism.

She kept them under control, like an immune system destroying cancerous cells. It was her job to destroy them before they got out of hand. Usually, they were minor problems, localized malignancies, a simple matter of quick extraction before any symptoms arose. No one ever knew the world was poisoned. Life went on.

And on.

And on.

Is that what this was? A mere annoyance? Asymptomatic?

She sensed Mahoney beside her. Fact is, she had sensed him coming down the pneumatic a half hour before. He would go through the routine X-ray search and sterilization procedures that everyone coming or going into the necropolis did. He was scanned not only for germs and weapons, but for the beginnings of any undiagnosed organic disease, microbic or structural, that might have compromised his system. She herself submitted to these tests, so dedicated was she to ensuring that death have no inroad into this place of death. The show had ended at an imperceptible signal of dismissal from Nikka. The whip master and yet another still perfectly edible blond boy hurried off into one of the lair's many antechambers. The little freak would be paid, perhaps, or killed; his disposal was a matter of convenience and otherwise unimportant.

Meanwhile, the commando stood there, knelt, really, but with the devout impatience of a man of action using every ounce of his will to remain patient. Nikka smiled inwardly to herself and waited the beat of nineteen of her extraordinarily slow heartbeats. She opened eyes that were seen exclusively in this underworld realm. It might have been a look of a woman just waking from a deeply satisfying sexual encounter if Nikka still had sex in any of the usual ways.

"Have we put a face on our faceless man?"

"Yes."

"And?"

"Arbak Shaara."

"The son of the exiled oil sheik?"

"The same."

Another oil-rich Muslim. Nikka would be well satisfied when they finally mass-produced an affordable energy alternative to oil and one could then fly, by black helicopter, over miles and miles of beautiful, lifeless lunar desert that would one day be the entire Middle East. She was tired of running around after Arabs.

"Well, he can be made to disappear if there is a problem. Put him in a wrecked car somewhere. Or at the bottom of a lake after a diving accident. Whatever."

"There is a problem," Mahoney said. "But it won't be that easy to solve."

"Oh?" Nikka said. She clicked her eyes onto her most loyal assassin with the precision of a finely calibrated measuring device. In those eyes, the brutal man saw the first flicker of real interest he had seen in a half dozen years.

"Seems he was dating, on and off, Princess Alison Faye."

Her eyes didn't move, nor did the pupils contract or dilate even a fraction. Mahoney noticed things like this. He had no allegiance to anyone or anything outside of becoming the quickest and surest method of dispatch between Nikka and whatever she aimed him at. That was part of the reason he was so good at doing what he did. Only, he thought, grimly satisfied with himself, a part.

"How on, how off?"

"She's missing," Mahoney said, smugly.

"Hmmm . . . that won't go away, now, will it?"

"I should think not," he said, permitting himself the syntactic sarcasm.

Nikka permitted the slightest of pauses by way of appreciation. She didn't bother to look down at the effeminate boy kneeling between her long pale, untouched legs. "Stop."

She wanted to think a moment, and even the specially designed pleasure device, soundless as it was, in the deeply contemplative state she was in now, made an intolerable white noise. She had come to a decision. Mahoney could see that, and although he didn't like it, there would be no argument. He tried not to show any emotion when she gave the order, taking his cue from her, but, as usual, he failed. She wasn't taking any chances with this one, not this time.

"Get him," she said. "Immediately."

Once upon a time, they were gods. But that time was over long ago. It was hard to believe now, considering the way they lived, existing in the shadows, hunted down, killed in abandoned warehouses, old hotels, alleys, bus stops. How many of them were destroyed on a rented bed in an anonymous room at three o'clock in the afternoon? It was sickening to think that this is the way that gods died.

Caleb sat at a table at an outdoor café on the Montevideo. He watched with a vague distaste the people walking passed. Human beings disgusted him. Vain, arrogant, materialistic, rude, and selfish, they lived little better than the animals from which they descended and the machines they invented. He had seen it coming, centuries ago.

They had laughed at him—all of them. His kind had been arrogant, too, but it was an arrogance of a different sort. The arrogance of gods, it was. They never believed it would be possible for humans to live without them. An ironic idea, perhaps, or so it seemed now. It had seemed perfectly logical then.

Still, Caleb had noted the change and he'd tried to warn them. He warned them that the time was approaching when man would throw them all off and attempt to live on their own. It was an absurd idea, of course. It was mad, impossible, and for just those reasons no one believed him . . . and for just those reasons it had come to pass.

Humans were impossible. Mad and absurd.

And very dangerous.

It was hard, even for him, to believe that they had survived on their own for so long. But they had. They had turned the tide and driven his kind from the places of power. Toppled them from wherever they found them. Hunted them down. Killed them. And their blood lust wouldn't stop until every last one of his kind were destroyed. That was the human way.

He watched them walking past now. They seemed relatively harmless. Stupid and inane. They walked to their pointless jobs, their shabby love affairs, their ridiculous pastimes. They talked to each other about the most appalling trivialities, ate food they barely took the time to taste, and laughed while all the time they were rapidly dying. They acted as if they would live forever and not for what would be scarcely a handful of heartbeats in the cosmic scheme of eternity.

Not even a handful of heartbeats . . .

Once in a while, when one of them died, they seemed to remember. It would all appear then as it was for a time, meaningless to them. Caleb, at those times, relished the look of horror and hopelessness on their faces. He would sometimes lurk in churches or funeral homes during a memorial service for exactly that purpose. It was then, he thought, that humans were, at least for a time, nearly bearable. It was then, he thought, they could be beautiful.

But they always returned to their mad insanity. This terrible purposeless crusade they perversely called life. Life. As if they could ever guess what life really was.

Almost, they almost always returned. . . .

He watched a man at the next table, fat and old, white tufts of hair coming out of his large ears. The man was eating a plate of penne ziti with a light red wine sauce. He had put far too much cheese on the dish. His choice of wine, a vin rose, was an effront. This man had been arguing with someone on a cell phone for ten minutes, something about a shipment of wool fabric. The whole while he was shoving the food into his mouth. Now, he was reading the newspaper as he ate, keeping his eyes on a story about an Internet merger while he sipped his wine.

He was going to die, soon. Sixty-three, from the stink of him. Five more years. Ten. He had only that many more springs to see. Only that many more . . . and then oblivion.

Why was he reading a newspaper article about Internet mergers? What importance could that possibly have in the face of extinction? Why was he arguing about wool fabric?

He wasn't even worth killing, this fat old sack of sour blood. Imagine that, not even being worth killing. Caleb looked out over the square.

This man and the world around him were nothing—nothing but dust.

This man—he was already dead.

And yet, humans were dangerous. Humans just like this stupid fat old man. Humans "especially" like this stupid fat old man. Somewhere, deep down in their cells, they must know that they were dying. Maybe that is what made them so crazy. Maybe that is what made them so lethal.

Caleb knew, better than most, just how lethal they could be. There was a girl in the square in a pale blue sundress, a wide-brimmed hat, and dark glasses. She was looking up at a building and then at a tour map. She seemed to have become separated from her group. Caleb watched her. He liked the shape of her calves and the golden brown of her skin. He guessed, from the bone structure of her face, that she would retain her good looks postmortem.

There were still things in this world to appreciate, he thought, wryly. Like good wine, for instance.

He sipped a glass of della Stregha 1845. He understood that nowadays it was an almost impossible vintage to acquire. Only prime ministers, computer software tycoons, and the occasional celebrity had the means and connections to acquire its rare taste. The della Streghas, it was said, sacrificed the most beautiful virgin on their estates for each vintage. You had to be a connoisseur to detect the taste, of course. For the profane, it was just a titillating and chic rumor. But for someone like Caleb . . . ah, it was unmistakable.

He closed his eyes for a moment, savoring the wine . . . and in that instant he saw it all. The cross in the middle of a fallow field, the pitiless sun, the pale girl in the plain muslin smock, and all those crows. All those crows.

On his tongue, he tasted her pain and confusion. He tasted her faith. He tasted her final resignation. He smelled the sweat on her suffering, anorectic figure, a body type that would not be fully appreciated for another hundred and fifty years or so, not until the advent of teenage pop singers. He gazed appreciatively at a face more celestially beautiful than any painted by Botticelli or Raphael. It was a face whose clear-eyed serenity it would have seemed a sacrilege to sully with the sordid earthiness of human copulation. She was not for marrying or childbearing. She was not meant to be touched by mortal man. She had been chosen, not by the master of the della Stregha estate for this sacrifice, but by fate itself, a fate that even the youngest village child immediately recognized.

He saw her, slumped, stained, the blood dripping off her twitching toes. And the villagers leaving her broken body in the field and returning to their cottages in silence. There would be no returning to work until the following morning. That day would be a holiday.

In those times people still believed in the gods.

Caleb swallowed the wine and opened eyes that forever looked out at nothing. It was the same view no matter where he was in the world: Cairo, Hamburg, Oslo, Tokyo, New York City. He could see through all of it. And it bored him. Sometimes, he thought, if it weren't for his hatred, he would have no reason to go on at all.

He had seen it happen over and over, like the seasons, one empire following another. One people smashing another's idols. The old gods falling. He'd been there to see the death of Shamash and the final murder of Osiris; he'd seen the disgrace of the elder Olympians and the corruption of Shiva and Shakti. He'd stood witness at the murder of a hundred minor gods and goddesses in the back alleys of unrecorded history and he watched as the new ones took their seats in the old temples and were worshipped in their place. He stood in the royal courts of the Babylonians and the Syrians, the Hittites and the Chinese dynasties, he accepted the sacrifices of Jew and Shinto and African tribesman alike. He'd been there when Rome ruled the world and human emperors declared themselves gods and the divine appeared to be dead. Yet from within that chaos of human degradation and godlessness there rose a prophet from Nazareth and a new god was raised up for the next two thousand years.

Was it any wonder they thought it would go on forever? Up until now, it had gone on forever. From the first time man had crouched in the dirt and gathered up mud and shaped it into the shape of the great mother, he had always believed. Ever since he first saw lightning flash or an animal die, men had believed in gods.

That time was over.

He had taken a long time to die, God did. Somewhere in the 1500s, Caleb reckoned, that's when the deathblow had been struck. Four hundred years of dying. It had been a long time. Sometimes he would rise up, wounded, as if he could still stand on his feet. Then he would fall again, harder, more bloodied than the time before. It had happened before, this death of a god, but this time, there was no other god to take his place.

He was the last god and Caleb knew it.

The world wars of the last century finished him off once and for all. Computers, vaccinations, space travel, television, drugs, test tube babies, the hydrogen bomb.

The horrors of Hitler, Stalin, and the assorted lesser dictators. The countless millions slaughtered. Man had become God—a god more terrifying than any god before him.

There would be none to come after.

Caleb was hungry. He approached the girl in the square and smelled the moistness of her, an earthy scent that was stimulating to him only inasmuch as he would derive an almost perverse pleasure in destroying what it meant: the girl was fecund with life and her role in the continuation of life. She smiled at him as he approached, not recognizing from a distance of ten feet or so that he was not a possible lover, but a destroyer. That he had not come to sow her ripe womb, but to lay her barren with salt and fire and miles of black crosses. She might have caught a glimpse of that and been momentarily startled if he'd come upon her suddenly; instead, he let her see him as a human being: his black coat open, hands thrust behind his back, dark hair swept from a face whose paleness gave him the look of a devastatingly handsome crusader who, if not for his privileged social standing of wealth and power, could have been a celebrity idol.

He spoke to her in flawless Italian, which she understood not at all, seeming a little desperate, and using her hands to aid her in communicating that her knowledge of the language was severely limited.

"Ah," Caleb said with a slight nod, in equally flawless English. "I understand perfectly." He enjoyed the look of relief and pleasure that came to the girl's face, which suddenly unfolded, the least and more superficial of unfoldings that were to come.

She was traveling abroad from America with a group

of student artists to soak in the history and ambience of Italy. She had broken away, she said, to escape the rigid and relentless program of their instructor, who maneuvered them around the province with the efficiency of a plant manager checking off items in an inspection of a chicken-processing factory. Caleb laughed and learned her name was Ashley, which she hated, and called herself Juliet instead.

"That is a beautiful name," he said, and meant it. "There aren't many women with that name anymore. It suits you better than the silly one you were given at birth."

She seemed delighted and lifted her hair for him, a mass of raw sienna curls shot through with sunbeams, loosely tied back, but still partially concealing a throat that she now exposed in an unconscious gesture of such sublime submission that it drew every predatory instinct in Caleb to a one-focused intensity. She was still young, nineteen, three years past her prime, but that was to be expected in this regressive day and age; healthy, her body under the long thin peasant skirt, tight cotton bodice, and faded jean jacket was entirely natural, not artificially altered or enhanced in any way.

"Let me see," he said, nodding toward the black sketchbook she clutched to her chest as if it contained the revelation of the secrets of her heart.

"Oh, it's not very good." She blushed beneath the tan, but Caleb could tell anyway, sensing, under the creamy smooth, all-over brown, the incrementally increased warmth of her gently seasoned flesh. He lowered his head slightly, and smiled, in a gesture natural to alpha wolves when conveying peacefulness, and popularized some years ago, Caleb noted, by an actor he'd seen by chance, someone named Clooney. "Please," he said. "I'd really like to see."

"Okay," she said shyly and with additional comments

about her lack of experience, her problem with shadowing, her greater affinity for abstraction, etc.

Caleb opened the book and moved quickly through the first sketches, awkward attempts to depict various still-life clichés: bottles, flowers, a painfully arranged setup of oranges. Dead, dead, dead, dead. His fingers riffled through them all, bored and disgusted. And then he saw the faces: waitresses, cabdrivers, homeless, and, finally, the one he stopped at: a woman on the verge of losing her beauty.

"Ah," he said. "Ah."

"Those aren't for class."

"Yes." He nodded, and did not lift his eyes from the page on which the aging woman looked out, her pleading rage staring at a world that saw her less and less each passing day. "I can tell."

"They aren't very good, I know. We aren't supposed to go to portrait until much later." And she took the sketchbook back and flipped the pages past a few more faces to the sketches of various pieces of typical Italian architecture: cathedrals, cafés, palazzi, bridges, arches that her class had no doubt trudged passed so far. She held out the book and he took it once again, staring at the sketchbook.

"Awful," he murmured, and she nodded a little sadly and laughed. "Perfectly goddamned awful. Give me your pencil."

She handed him a short piece of black conte crayon and he made a few casual strokes over a depiction of an aqueduct, sketching in a slight correction of the perspective and loosening the lines. As he sketched he felt her breath on his neck as she leaned over to watch, the touch of her hair on his cheek, and all of it scented, vaguely, of zinnia and almond. He handed the sketchbook back, slightly distracted, and nodded toward it. "Like that."

The girl looked at it and then up at Caleb. "That's wonderful. It has . . . life now."

"Yes," Caleb said dryly.

"Are you an artist?"

"No," he said. "Just someone who sees."

The wind, and there had been none up to now, but rain was on the way, had picked up and riffled the pages that her thumb did not hold down, and Caleb could see each page as it passed, although at least fifty-three passed in the space of a half second, and he slid his forefinger between two, and held it down. It was a sketch done quickly, but the rendering was unmistakable.

"Oh." the girl blushed again, and this time looked stricken. "I'm sorry."

It was a café scene, tables and patrons, waiters and wine bottles, a few sparrows pecking fallen crumbs. There was an awning and conversation and others dining alone or reading, or gazing out in the dying sunlight over the cobbles of the square and one man, sitting, lost deep in thought, sipping a wine that drew his gaze away to a scene on a day in the late summer of 1845. That she had drawn him wasn't what interested Caleb in particular, although the rendering, though distant and archetypal, was strikingly faithful enough. No, what interested Caleb and sharpened his hunger, and roused his interest in her, was that she must have seen him long before he'd seen her. And even so, Caleb had not felt the sharp prick of her pencil as she touched the outline of his omniscience.

"Come with me," he said softly and took her hand. "Come."

And she went without question, as they all did when they were chosen. That evening, as a steady rain fell outside his rooms in the Villa Generalli he pretended to make love to her and, afterward, while she lay unconscious, his hunger raging, slipped out into the steamy streets. He found a pretty shop girl who, returning home from work at the perfume counter of a department store, had stopped for a drink in a tavern. Caleb seduced her, took her back to her apartment, and killed her.

Death, when it came, was never easy for them. It came with outrage and intolerable pain and finally a numbed resignation that no matter what they had previously believed or trusted about life, about death, it was all a lie. Sometimes, after it was over, their mouths stayed open, the question twisting bloodless lips, but no breath left to ask it, as if it could be answered anyway. The truth was, the question had no answer, so Caleb often reflected and reflected now, as he withdrew his penis from inside yet another once pretty girl's corpse, still warm, which he had been pretending to fuck the entire time, mimicking a passion that was for him only a form of foreplay, as was everything else.

It wasn't, of course, always like this. There had been so many beautiful deaths in the past, excruciating yes, but transfigured at the moment of crisis into something that might almost have been a work of art, if a work of art could be something that lasts but two seconds, maybe four, and seen by only one, the one whose inspiration perpetrated it, and whose need obliterated it almost simultaneously. Yes, Caleb thought, that was all a work of art was—or should be.

Sometimes, for wholly arbitrary reasons, he thought of human life as a fashion show, and the audience composed of members of his race. He had seen so many girls and boys step from out of the curtain of oblivion and walk down the runway to their doom, their faces composed and smiling, trembling inside, and coming apart so sweetly beneath his kiss. They were sustained against terror and flight by the magnificent lie of their imminent apotheosis, of an orgasm so brilliant that death wasn't death but a life that would last forever.

Of course, no such thing had ever existed. There was no resurrection, no return from the dead, no life forever. It was all a fairy tale, a come-on, a line of seductive bullshit like any other: sometimes it was a slick advertising campaign for Jaguars or Mastercards, or maybe it was a line from a new pop song, or something said by someone in a movie. The simple fact was that Caleb couldn't transform a human being into a god any more than he could get a stick to talk or stop a stone from dropping if he let it go. This world was governed by its own laws and only the ones that were made by man could be broken.

But the hope that his kind could work such miracles had sustained the human race for thousands of years. And that is what kept them obedient and fruitful and relatively happy, happy enough to go on, in spite of the famines, plagues, and wars that descended upon them again and again throughout history with a cruelty so savage, so random, it had to be attributed to the will of God, or it would have been intolerable.

Their "faith," as the delusion had come to be called, was nothing more than a psychological opiate that allowed them to accept the most catastrophic of fates with relative equanimity. Caleb had seen animals in the wild, buffalo came to mind, brought down and eaten alive by wolves, so numbed by shock and loss they seemed to feel nothing at all, and the process by which humans lived was not a great deal different. There was nothing in the end but acceptance, and the degree of pain suffered was in a direct ratio to how long it took for an individual to resign him- or herself to the inevitable, no matter how unacceptable.

It was unfortunate all around, he reflected, that they

no longer believed anymore, and that faith was so difficult to come by nowadays. They died all the more abjectly for that, and their suffering was not transformed to erotic bliss, but full of hopeless fighting, mad adrenaline, rage, broken bones, dislocated joints, massive internal damage, and, of course, such pain and terror as there was no cry so awful that could ever begin to express their sense of outrage, alienation, and betrayal.

The girl lying on her back on the stained and tangled sheets before him, spine arched unnaturally inward, broken actually, lopsided hips thrust immodestly up to reveal a ravaged secret, arms popped from sockets, calves straining against pain, her throat unzipped, was little more than a case in point. In her death throes, she had broken her sternum and neck, ruptured several vital internal organs, suffered a massive and messy rectal hemorrhage, and dislocated her jaw and left ankle. She'd had a stroke, apparently, that affected the appearance of the left side of her face, and her teeth, stained red, were bared. One eye, almost unaccountably, was missing. She had not died as beautifully as he had hoped, and this was almost always a disappointment. It had all become a rather sordid business, this nonsense of survival, and Caleb had begun losing his taste for it, albeit slowly, in the last couple of centuries. But, after all, what was he to do?

He slipped the miniature cell from the breast pocket of his coat and speed-dialed the service whose sole job it was to clean up the untidy mess that his occasional hungers left behind. He spoke on a secured channel, via satellite through a series of coded clicks, to an operator who recorded his precise coordinates and who would dispatch a team of "busboys" to the apartment after a discreet but efficient delay, as in any five-star restaurant, of some ten seconds or so, more or less, after his departure.

He replaced the cell, which folded up to the size of a matchbook, approximately, in his pocket and took the stairs to the street. He could sense by the quality of the light that dawn was just under twenty-seven minutes away. He started walking briskly toward the river beneath the ancient housefronts full of sleeping mortals and nodded to a drunken student he might have killed if it had been any another morning. He thought, quite randomly, of something Nero once said and slipped a wintergreen Altoids in his mouth to mask the scent of sweat and ureic acid on his breath although, it occurred to him, that he seldom even pretended to breathe, anymore.

"They're lying," Vince said. He stood in front of the big-screen television that dominated the cold flat like a five-hundred-channel altar. It was the only piece of furniture that hadn't once been someone else's garbage. Geek had stolen it, or it had been donated by some mysterious benefactor, the same one, presumably, who'd provided the jet to London, but who that might be, Vince had no clue.

On the screen the chief of the Central Division of Protection, an agency, incidentally, that he'd never heard of before, was talking in a ritualistic manner that seemed almost void of content. Her calm, impassive, strikingly beautiful face had the unanswerable authority and appeal of a propaganda poster, or the inscrutable high priestess of a suicide cult. The scene behind her was shot in broad daylight, she was not standing in front of the mansion, and the crime she described bore no resemblance to what had happened.

"Of course they're lying," Io said. "But you can't look away, can you?"

Vince, angry and ashamed, turned toward the slender, white-haired young man reclining in a ratty yellow armchair. He was wearing a mini-T, his flat tummy exposed, a French-cut bikini in royal-blue silk, one pale lean leg over the arm of the chair. He was blowing on the fingernails of his left hand, while a nude girl, alive or dead, it was hard to tell from behind, painted the nails of his other hand.

"I don't think we should have taken her," Vince said.

The kidnapped princess hadn't said a word since they'd abducted her from the bloodbath at the mansion. She looked like she'd been shocked into a state of almost complete objectification, like a mannequin that could be looked at, moved, or taken apart on a whim.

"Why not?" Io asked sharply, not angrily, but annoyed, as if someone had questioned him about using the color orange in, well, anything.

Vince looked from Io to the girl and back again. Someone had removed her bloody pants and had given her an oversized men's shirt to wear, which remained unbuttoned, showing off her sexy black underwear. She smelled of blood and urine and no one had bothered to wash her face, which was stained by black eyeshadow, mud, and more dried blood. She looked like the orphan of a holocaust, or a zombie in a very hip new rock video.

Vince was gripped with the dizzying unreality of it all. He had watched her grow up, in parallel worlds, of course, and had seen her picture on the covers of newspapers, books, magazines, on television and computers ever since he could remember. He felt like he knew her, almost, as if she were a younger sister, but still distant enough to be a source of sexual fascination. "Don't worry," he had told her on the private jet, where she sat staring down at the clouds. "We won't hurt you."

He had no idea if this was true or not, but he said it anyway, because that is what one said in such a situation.

He was pretty certain they weren't going to hurt her; if that was the intention, wouldn't they have done so, already? Still, she had just seen them casually slaughter twenty or thirty people. It was silly to tell her not to worry.

Hell, Vince was worried.

"They'll look for her."

"So?"

"I mean they won't stop until they catch us."

"That is the point—to capture their attention. Do you think the end of the world can be brought about without anyone noticing?"

"I thought you said the end of the world had already come?"

"It has. I am just letting everyone know it."

Io was inconsistent, as usual. He always claimed that he was inconsistent on purpose, that it was a form of revolt, a method of radical deconstruction, whatever he meant by that.

"It seems too soon, that's all."

"How long do you think we should wait? The world has been waiting—I have been waiting for five hundred years."

Vince was used to this kind of talk. Io often interchanged himself with the world. He was megalomaniacal, but in a coy way that left one wondering if it wasn't all some kind of joke that you weren't getting.

"I'm just not sure it makes sense. . . ."

"Sense, sense." Io jumped out of the chair. "Why are you still talking about making sense?" He stormed to the corner where the girl was sitting and yanked her across the floor by her arm. She didn't resist or even try to get up. Vince wanted to intercede but he didn't: the suddenness, the fury of Io's movements, like his speech, his sex, his thoughts, blocked all spontaneous response, numbed, paralyzed. He was crouched behind her now, holding her head to one side by the hair, exposing her neck and in particular an artery that suddenly seemed all too prominent, all too vulnerable.

He was holding a small blade, or rather, he was suddenly wearing a kind of ring equipped with a blade that seemed to be made of titanium. It curved at the end, like a cruel metallic fingernail. Vince had seen him—and the rest of them—"trash" victims before. He had seen them do it casually, without so much as interrupting a conversation, as if opening a can of diet soda.

"I'll kill her right now, just to prove my senselessness, to illustrate my total identification with chaos. I'll kill her even before the story properly begins, for no other reason than to defy sense."

"Io, please . . . for crissakes."

The white-haired boy froze for a second, and then his lips parted in a sexy grin. "I should," he said evenly, "just for that dumb remark alone, strangle her with a foot or two of her own extracted intestine." And for a second or two, Vince thought he would do just that. But then Io closed the hand with the ring and pushed the girl over. She lay there, unmoving, in a fetal position and one of the nine or so cats in the room sauntered over to sniff at her, curious.

"But I won't kill her," Io said, taking his throne once again in the ratty armchair. "And do you know why?"

"Why?" Vince said, knowing that if he didn't ask, Io would never answer the question.

"Behind you," Io said, "on the wall, there is a spider. If it had walked up . . ." He drew a finger across his throat. "You see, dear Vince, I am a roll of the dice! Oh, my, look," he said, suddenly examining his hand with a pretty pout. "All this philosophizing has smudged my polish."

Nikka was in her coffin, speeding through the
night. That was what she called the black armored customized limousine in which she sat, alone in the backseat,
her naked body as untouchable as liquid nitrogen. She
gazed out the tinted window, the weapon-proof glass as
close as she got to the real world nowadays, and felt as if
she were visiting life from another dimension.

The fact was that the life she lived now, though more
fulfilling than any she might have imagined, really didn't
belong to her at all; it was the product, it sometimes
seemed, of someone else's imagination. In this life, she
touched no one—and no one touched her: she was perfect, self-contained, invincible. She was like one of those
perpetual-motion devices that once given a single initial
impetus would keep on going, without the need of any
further aid, or inspiration.

She'd had another life once: she caught glimpses of
it on occasion, at odd times usually, in the middle of
dictating a memo, pausing for the voice-recognition
software to catch up, or while coming out of anesthe-
sia. She remembered a man and even a child and she
was reasonably certain that they were connected to
her, but in exactly what way, she couldn't be certain.
There were other oddities, too; an irrational fear of
water, a repulsion for a certain kind of running light,
and a level of ambiguity toward oral sensation that
would have seemed abnormal in anyone less studiously
and determinedly abnormal. And there was pain—a
brief, searing, inconclusive pain that stood between
her and whatever had been separated from her on the
other side of the selective amnesia that she interposed
between her personal history and her world duty. Whatever lay on the other side of that wall was too horrible
to think about and so Nikka followed the simplest and

most straightforward of strategies: she didn't think about it. She might have been a woman who one day walked out into the ocean and kept on walking until she disappeared into the waves. She might have been; but she wasn't.

"Show me something ugly," Nikka said.

Her driver was a government killer she had rescued from a disgrace so unredeemable his only option had been suicide—or to find a manner of living that ensured that he'd never have to look a living soul in the face again. He lived as solitary as a monk, in a self-imposed isolation even greater than that of his mistress, his only function to ferry her on these 3:00 A.M. jaunts. At her command, he steered the coffin north through the most hellish parts of the city.

Nikka gazed out the window momentarily distracted by crumbling buildings, demonic graffiti, uncollected detritus, and the forlorn piles of humanity leaking onto broken pavements. What city was this—what difference did it make?

The route had been preplanned, of course; it was one of several computer-generated tours and selected at random each night by a self-activated logarithm in order to thwart assassins from other departments, as well as assorted terrorists and revolutionaries. Within these preplanned routes there were enough variations so that the random permutations were virtually endless and the journeys would seem unique each night if Nikka lived for a thousand years.

It was, perhaps, not even a real city that she passed through at the moment, but a simulation so authentic as to be indistinguishable from the real thing—an archetypal city of man's soul. She had hoped to see some spontaneous violence tonight of one sort or another. Sometimes an "event" was planned for her, a shooting, or beating, or rape. But Nikka found that these staged happenings, as bloody and fatal as they usually were, did not bring the same excitement and frissons as the ones that happened "accidentally," although she had left strict instructions that she never be told the difference, because she knew there wasn't any.

For some reason, Nikka thought of Mahoney and how she had plucked that killer, too, out of obscurity and saved him from death, although of a different kind than the driver's. She had surrounded herself with men, hard men, men who'd lost their souls and had no consciences. These men formed an inner circle of charmed monoliths that forbade the approach of both friends and enemies. Nikka had obsessively rid herself of any feminine influences and cleansed her physical and psychic space to contain her own pure female energy in its most unadulterated and most potent form.

"Excuse me, Ms. Seven."

"Yes."

"We are being followed."

There was, of course, no other car in sight. The source could have been any number of remote surveillance systems, a satellite, perhaps, or an implanted bio-bug, or even a psychic in trance a continent away. The car's defense system had picked it up, but Nikka was sensitive enough herself to detect the intimate, dictatorial, invisible sense of violation that was the unmistakable symptom of being "seen." She knew, however, that it was no ordinary satellite or bug or psychic watching her. She had been under observation for some time now. She did not yet know by whom, nor why, but she sank back in the seat of the coffin and let the disgustingly familiar sensation of being watched flood over her, and reached down between her legs, and touched herself.

"Show me," she said to the driver, feeling an intimacy

that she hadn't felt since she didn't remember when, "something that breaks the heart."

Arthur Schopenauer brought them together.

They met, of all unlikely places, in a chat room dedicated to the nineteenth-century German philosopher, famous, in part, for statements of such black pessimism that even two decades out of graduate school, Vince had not forgotten them. "Human life must be some kind of error," Schopenauer had written. "Life is bad, and goes on getting worse and worse until the worst of all possibly happens." Vince had checked his e-mail, answered what needed to be answered, and made his usual survey of porn sites. He had four bottles of Xanax and a bottle of cheap wine opened on his desk. He was well on his way to his nightly rendezvous with oblivion. The link to Schopenauer was at the bottom of a Web page posted by an intelligent masochist with tastes that ran from neo-Nazi punk rock to transvestism, tastes that were not as alien to Vince as he would have liked.

He was past forty, balding, grown a potbelly. He had a crappy job in which he'd grown too comfortable, lived in a dump, had no real-life friends, no wife, no girlfriend, no life, really, outside the one he could access with a modem. He'd woken up in the middle of life to realize not only that he'd wasted the first half of it, but that the second half would be lived out in an endless series of chat rooms, message boards, and cyber-sex sessions in which he usually pretended he was someone else and, perhaps most disturbing of all, that was perfectly all right with Vince.

He wondered what he had done before the Internet. He must have had some kind of life, or so he assumed, but he'd be damned if he could remember much of it. It was irrelevant, actually. Fact was, he felt more alive sitting in front of this keyboard until 3:00 A.M. every night than he did at any other time. He could be anyone, do anything, experience everything. Life, shit, who needed it? He lit up an old joint that he found next to a disk container and watched the discussion rolling inside the chat window on his monitor. The smoke in his lungs tasted like a ghost of the life he might have led if only he had been born someone else entirely.

   [private message from Io01 to Senika55]: How come so silent?

Vince hadn't noticed the message until it had moved halfway up the chat screen. He'd been zoning out, thinking of something else, of the new photo retouches he'd briefly glanced at from SlasherT. Good stuff, really edgy. He must be using the new Poser software. He typed back, the joint between his lips, inhaling.

   [private message from Senika55 to Io01]: Chat here a little technical for me.
   [Io01 to Senika55]: The matter is really very simple, isn't it? Live or die?
   [Senika55 to Io01]: Yeah, simple.
   [Io01 to Senika55]: So what is it, Vince?

Vince was about to log off. He didn't need any tedious interchange with some wisecracking troll when he felt the back of his neck go chicken-flesh and he slid up out of his slouch. There was no way his name should be in that chat window, no damn way at all. Shit, had he been hacked?

   [Senika55 to Io01]: Who the fuck is this? Derek? Greg?
   [Io01 to Senika55]: I'm not anyone you know.

Vince. Not yet. But I do believe you'll want to
know me.

[Senika55 to Io01]: If I don't know you, how the
fuck do you know my name?

[Io01 to Senika55]: Why, you're an internet
celebrity of sorts. Aren't you Mr. Manning? I've
been enjoying your website for quite some time.
Very interesting . . .

It was all some kind of joke, Vince thought, had to be,
but the mention of that website, that wasn't good, because no one knew about that, no one who knew his real
name, anyway.

[Senika55 to Io01]: What are you supposed to be
. . . an internet cop?

[Io01 to Senika55]: Is there such a thing?

[Senika55 to Io01]: I don't know. Are you one?

[Io01 to Senika55]: Do you believe in life after
death, Vince?

[Senika55 to Io01]: Who are you kidding, dude?

[Io01 to Senika55]: Do you believe your life has
any meaning?

[Senika55 to Io01]: meaning what?

[Io01 to Senika55]: Do you know why you suffer?

[Senika55 to Io 01]: because it's 3am and I can't
even find anyone to even pretend they're giving
me head?

[Io01 to Senika55]: ever hear of Buddha?

[Senika55 to Io1]: Football player, right?

[Io01 to Senika55]: Buddha says we suffer because
we don't accept that things don't last. Well Buddha was wrong.

[Senika55 to Io01]: *You* tell him that.

[Io01 to Senika55]: death lasts. Get it?

[Senika55 to Io01]: yeah, baby, I get it. What I
don't get, tho, is why you're telling me this.

[Io01 to Senika55]: Can you be in Germany on the
15th?

[Senika55 to Io01]: Why?

[Io01 to Senika55]: I want to give you an exclusive.

[Senika55 to Io01]: An exclusive on what?

[Io01 to Senika55]: The end of the world, sweetheart.

[Senika55 to Io01]: I think I'm busy.

[Io01 to Senika55]: Be there. I'll leave you a ticket.
Check your email. One time opportunity. It will
change your life. xo

[Exit Io01]

Vince was looking down, typing the words, "I don't
want to change—" and looked back up in time to see
that Io01 was no longer in the chat room.

"Shit-head," Vince mumbled.

The virus scan he ran turned up negative. That was a
fucking relief. Maybe it was just some computer geek
having a little fun with him. Vince turned off the computer, took a last toke on the stale joint, and rubbed his
face, already bristling with a beard he'd have to shave off
in less than four hours. He got up and stretched his
limbs, cold and stiff, and stumbled to the couch, before
the three milligrams of Xanax he had popped sometime
during the above exchange kicked in.

The next morning, scanning through his e-mail as
usual, he found a notice from United Airlines confirming
a first-class ticket for Düsseldorf on the fifteenth.

There is no weather at fifteen thousand feet.
That is what Vince thought as he sat in his first-class

seat and looked down on a violent purple thunder-
storm a mile below him. He sipped a very weak scotch
and managed not to read a single sentence of the
glossy popular magazine he'd bought at an airport
news shop and that sat in his lap all the way across the
Atlantic Ocean. He had decided to go to Germany,
after all. It had not been, in the end, that hard a decision to make. The ticket, he reasoned, had already
been purchased for him, he'd never been to Europe,
and he had nothing he would regret saying good-bye
to for the time being—or, for that matter, forever. He
put in for an emergency leave at work the very next
day, packed lightly, and splurged on a cab to the airport. He was a man with a secret that somebody knew
and he wanted to know who knew it. There was
enough gray area in the law to allow for interpretation,
and while he was no legal expert Vince was fairly certain that what he was doing was not technically illegal;
however, there was no guarantee that it couldn't be
construed as being illegal, if there was an inquiry, and
depending on who did the inquiring. The fact that he
had been positively linked to the Web site at all was a
source of some mild concern to Vince. His life could
be made inconvenient if his pastime became generally
known in certain quarters but, chances were, only inconvenient, and yet his life, such as it was, Vince knew
all too well, could not bear much more inconvenience.
Still, none of this was the real reason why Vince had
decided to drop everything and fly to Germany on this
rainy Friday morning. The real reason was far more
frightening, so frightening in fact, that Vince refused
to see it at all, and it sped toward him, even as he sat in
a first-class seat sipping a weak scotch on a United Airlines flight to Düsseldorf, silently, from an unseen
location, like an assassin's bullet.

They met in the flesh three days later in a Hamburg glam bar. Io unmistakable in his first costume change of the evening, silver blue parachute pants tucked into purple platform jackboots, black T-shirt advertising an underground Jack Maniac comic, one eye ringed in dark kohl to symbolize Odinic vision. His hair was bleached, nose pierced, and on the one thin, white, femme biceps he exposed there was a tattoo of an Egyptian ankh and stenciled above it, in Bookman Old Style font, the words "dead chic."

He was sipping, or pretending to sip, a Hydrogen Winter and speaking in a completely vague way to a small group of pink Nazis, fake heroin addicts, and anarchic Catholic libertarians, each of whom seemed to be vying to attract, more or less unsuccessfully, his sexual attention, which seemed to be diffused and unfocused, spreading itself over the entire scene in the club, like an alien fertilizer. His surveying gaze rested on Vince, who was hanging back by a broken amp, fake-sipping an Electric Spine, and trying not to look directly at Io, but off to the left, equally vague.

His peripheral vision poor, Vince nevertheless saw the thin body disengage itself from the circle of admirers and move toward him, only very subtly, letting the surrounding music inform his fluid movements in nothing that could be called dancing, God forbid, but was more accurately an instinctive way of using sound as camouflage. His arrival startled Vince; even though the latter had seen him coming, knew him coming, there was a suddenness to the event, like a snake strike, that caused the breath to catch in Vince's throat.

Up close, Io was shockingly more beautiful than Vince had originally imagined, stunning actually, with a bone structure and lushness of mouth that caused Vince to blush without any definite thought at all. "You knew it was me," he said, lamely.

"I knew it was someone . . . interesting," Io said. His eyes, unmistakably disguised behind false lenses, were nonetheless too dangerous to look at. They reminded Vince of thin ice over countless miles of nowhere.

"I'm not really." Vince shrugged hopelessly, apologetically. "Interesting."

Io looked off into limbo, bored. "Who . . ." and then he hissed, purposely ridiculous, ". . . isss?"

Vince took a real sip of his drink, gulping involuntarily, and stared hard, to keep his eyes off the floor, at the place between the two cords at the base of Io's beautiful white throat. He dared a glance upward. "I think maybe you may be."

"Are you trying to seduce me?" Io winked one of his impossible eyes. He had a rip in his black T-shirt, and a rouged, stimulated nipple, double-pierced, showed through on a soft, smooth, slightly plump chest. "Oh, look," he said, delighted, "I've embarrassed you. How adorable. There's no need to be ashamed, darling." He laid a thin, pale hand on Vince's arm and gravity seemed, for a moment, to cease. "I hope you find your tongue soon. I'm going to need it." There was either a long pause here, or Vince just imagined there was, but, finally Io said, ". . . I want you to interview me."

Vince wasn't sure he'd heard correctly. "Interview you . . . for what?"

"Your Web site, silly."

"That . . ." Vince said, and didn't know how to finish the sentence. "About that," he tried again, and failed once more. He gave up, pleadingly.

"I'm tired of shouting," Io said. "Let's go someplace."

Vince finished his Electric Spine in one last convulsive

swallow. He would have followed Io anywhere but he asked anyway: "Where?"

"Someplace . . ." his eyes took a thousand years to blink. ". . . else."

"I am a student of the apocalypse," Io said later, "any apocalypse." He was rimming his nostrils with red fluorescent meth crystals in a club so dark and edgy Vince wondered if it was a club at all, or just some abandoned rathskeller used as a shelter from the cold and cops by thugs, addicts, hookers, and freaks. Io caught Vince glancing furtively around the dim environs of the place as if trying to peer into the edge of consciousness.

"My people," Io said with a grin. "In a hospital, Rimbaud, after they'd amputated his leg, delirious with fever, confided to me in one of his last moments of lucidity, that *A Season in Hell*, like practically everything else he wrote, was pure nonsense."

Io, Vince had already discovered, had a curious habit of speaking of the dead as if remembering actual conversations, attributing questionable, historically inaccurate statements supposedly addressed specifically to him. Vince took it to be a deliberate attempt at provocation.

"Himmler." Io giggled once. "liked to paint swastikas on my toenails."

And on it went, the semiprofound mixed with the ridiculous, absurdity with threat. Vince found the old-young boy by turns cool and passionate, verbose and laconic, smirking and innocent. They ended up on a water mattress in the platinum penthouse bedroom of one of Io's ex-girlfriends, or the husband or lover or father of one of his ex-girlfriends; as he was and would be so often, Io was vague to the point of unreality. Whatever he used to style his hair glowed neon in the black light.

"Are you a faggot?" he asked, dreamily, inhaling a noxious blue smoke from a bong, going through the motions of smoking it, anyway. It was a strange question to ask, and answer, buried to the balls in Io's pretty white ass as Vince was at the moment; and Vince, achingly close to orgasm, managed to cry out one plaintive word as he came: "No," but to what question asked or unasked it was really the answer to, he had no idea.

"Look," Io said, much later, after they had dressed and left the penthouse, pointing down the slope at their feet, where hundreds and hundreds of tombstones were half dissolved in the early morning twilight like regurgitated pills, "at all the dead."

He passed Vince a cocaine-laced joint and Vince inhaled the drug along with the chill and the fading stars and the quiet that emanates from miles of lifelessness where life used to be.

"Do you know what I see?" he continued. "I see boxes of bones, openmouthed, the void laugh. The dead outnumber the living, they wait in the heart of every town, units of an army only waiting for the call to mobilization . . ." Io's voice trailed away, almost wistfully, and Vince thought, for an instant perhaps, that a rumor of a genuine expression might flicker in those forbidden eyes, and he dared a glance at Io's dark glasses, but saw only a reflection of dead miles. "There is only one question." Io exhaled narcotic smoke. "Do you know what it is?"

"No," Vince whispered, inhaling Io's question, which hung in the chill air between them, literally, taking the amorphous blue form of the exhaled smoke.

"My God, why hast thou forsaken me?" Io said. "That is the only question. When you're on the cross, split in agony, and your life has been betrayed of all meaning, that is the question you ask. You can't ask it sitting in an armchair sipping port on a Sunday afternoon, or while waiting for a convivial dinner appointment at eight, or in between vacations on the cape. And every single answer is a lie."

Vince felt his hands trembling as he sucked desperately on the dead joint and he might have checked his pockets for a match or lighter, except he didn't trust himself to move.

"I sense in you someone ready to ask that question," Io said. "And with the courage . . ." He let the question hang for a moment. ". . . not to answer."

"What," Vince asked, a lifetime of shame folding inward, walls and walls between him and something unmentionable collapsing, "can I possibly mean to you?"

"I want you to be my evangelist. I want you to write my gospel. I want you to use your Web site."

"It's just a porn site . . . full of . . ." Vince still could not say it.

"I know what it is," Io said, and one side of his beautiful face, suddenly the color of a purple twilight, seemed the beautiful profile of a decayed angel, who had stared straight into the glare of an atomic blast. "You average twelve thousand hits a day. From far lesser disenfranchised masses, amazing revolutions in consciousness were achieved."

Io turned toward Vince with the imminence of a sun rising, the sun in fact rising over the plain of the forever dead, and nothing meaning anything for all eternity. "Drop your burden and follow me." He mouthed a slow kiss with his mouth painted the color of frozen blueberries.

"Are you the Savior?" the question slipped from Vince as ludicrous and childish and innocent as a white unicorn.

Io lit a wooden match that released an odor of peppermint and relit the joint that Vince brought to his own lips, trembling, blanched, as sitting there, waiting in the morning graveyard for an answer that would never come, a crow perched on a child's tombstone ten feet away; and, everything undone inside him, totally wasted, Vince felt with an eerie quality of calm that he was falling, inevitably and tragically, in love with whatever it was that was destined to erase his name from all existence out of sheer purposeless spite.

"Is he dead yet?" Nikka asked, lounging dramatically on a chaise and enjoying the shape of a black olive between her lips while watching shots of herself playing endlessly on CNN. As was her custom, she was having one victim from her vast offshore seraglio ritually sacrificed to her, as she did every night, to symbolize the death and rebirth of herself, every day of her immortal life.

"Not yet, Star-One," her high priest intoned, using one of her hundred and one ceremonial names, the only one besides Nikka herself allowed to speak in the ceremonial chamber. He had leaned forward a little in a stylized gesture to stare into the face of the suffering victim. "But soon."

Nikka, somewhat bored, or perhaps otherwise preoccupied, had only scanned the printout. Tonight's victim was originally male, of course, thirty-two, five-feet-ten, fair-skinned, dark hair parted on the left, green eyes, an Aquarius. There was a photo, reproduced, from a former life. He looked nothing like that anymore.

Nikka yawned.

According to custom, his body hair had been removed, and he'd been fed a diet of low-fat whole grains, oats and bran and brown rice, primarily, and all of it laced with high concentrations of estrogen, Premarin, and other powerful female hormonal extracts. As a result, he had lost whatever muscle bulk he might have had when he'd been kidnapped five months ago. He now displayed a pleasing overall smoothness of body and facial contour, including secondary female characteristics, such as rudimentary breasts. Even more striking, he possessed an ultradocile nature that partly accounted for the placidity with which he knelt on the ornamental pillow and waited serenely unconcerned as he was being ritualistically slow-strangled by the temple executioner, an ex-mercenary with an eerily reconstructed jaw and phoenix headress-mask.

"What could have been its name?" Nikka asked, mainly to amuse herself, or, at least, to try and amuse herself from the general tedium of the whole procedure.

"Alexandria," the high priest sang, but Nikka already knew that. They were always named Alexandria. The victim was gurgling now, its airway all but closed, smooth arms hanging useless at its sides, hands making small, meaningless, "frustrated" gestures.

The high priest was reading from a copy of the same printout that Nikka held; only his had been stained onto a sheet of specially manufactured papyrus that was anachronistically mounted on a clear plastic clipboard. Nikka hadn't been paying attention to anything he was saying. She was thinking, vaguely, about satellites. When she listened again, this is what she heard the high priest say: "Its preslave name was Mark Alan Adler."

"My," Nikka said, bored out of her mind. "What could it have done?"

"A financial analyst," the high priest droned, in a kind of nasal, pseudo-liturgical chant.

Incense had been lit and the scent of rose petals tramped by a team of white stallions ridden by blind teenage prom queens seated backward, naked, wrists bound, in the falling snow, filled the chamber. The victim's eyes, bulging slightly, were running with tears, which smudged his tear-proof eyeliner, and he made

darling little efforts to pant, causing the bells on his
pierced nipples to ring in D and D minor, left and right,
respectively. Nikka could see his whole rib cage expanding and contracting like a white punishment corset with
three hundred stitches.

"He was married for six years and had a child, aged
four and a half, a girl." The high priest droned on and
on: bank accounts, hobbies, alumni associations, favorite
movies, computer passwords, and some love poems he'd
written to Nikka during his langorous imprisonment in
the harem, waiting for a sexual encounter that never
came. He was taken outside a 7-Eleven in Barstow, Mis-
souri buying a quart of 2 percent milk, a loaf of rye
bread, a bottle of children's cough syrup, and a package
of jacks. There was also a box of dog biscuits in the bag
he carried, although he did not own a dog.

The victim's face was purplish now, his pierced tongue
pushing out past his collagen-enhanced pout, and his
curvy body, slick with sweat, was trembling rather violently, the bell jingling in merry crisis. A violet froth
wreathed his bruised mouth, as he tried, and failed, to
breathe, and he was still blowing more violet bubbles,
but slowly, and more slowly, as he started to fade.

Nikka duly noted all of this, appreciated it for what it
was worth, but instead found her attention focused on
the victim's chemically shrunken genitals and asked herself the same question over and over: "Didn't I request
that from now on the ritual was to require that the private parts of sacrifices to my chamber were to be gilded
in gold leaf so as to appear abstracted, idealized?"

Nikka rolled onto her back and stared distractedly up at
the giant monitor mounted to the space-ship joists, which
showed a clip of her speaking before a special assembly of
the United Nations. An angled shot of representatives
from Norway, New Zealand, and Peru interrupting some

totally irrelevant and insincere statement she was making with spontaneous applause. *This is my life,* Nikka thought, a series of photo-ops shown repeatedly, news clips rerun at all hours, all over the world, quotes attributed to her in newspapers, spots as an "expert" on TV news magazines, history texts, and entertainment programs.

Am I alive? she wondered, without urgency, but because it seemed required here. *Or am I a figment of the world's imagination?*

She didn't wait for her mind to provide a corresponding answer, but left the inquiry unfinished, probing the darkness of all that is unknown, and will remain unknown. Instead another question followed.

Can I be killed?

She left this question unanswered as well, having asked it, countless times before, and always, leaving the thought unfinished, she felt more natural, and more energized, living, as she always did, in a state of electric suspense. To enhance this sense, to raise it to a degree that it occasionally attracted her attention, she had made very unusual arrangements that intersected, but not in a totally self-dramatizing way, a tendency toward suicide.

Nikka turned her head simply to provide her brain with a different set of signals, a purely prelogic sensual consideration, and she noted, impassively, that, appropriately, while she had been absorbed in thoughts of herself, her sacrifice had been sacrificed.

Its body lay with its back facing her, its disposition vaguely suggesting the clichéd fetal position, long, posthormonal bleached hair swept discreetly over the discolored, contorted face, leaving only a suggestive length of smooth jawline, ending just short of the rounded, feminized chin. Along the spine, tatooed on each side of the spine, Nikka read the long columns of meaningless personal hieroglyphics she had designed in a dream hibernation, and read them all the way down to the boy's coccyx, and the tempting top of the shadowed cleavage between the smooth, firm, plump white mounds where his ass began. The body lay there beside the ornamental pillow, strategically lit to complement the natural disposition of its limbs, from above and the sides, and Nikka spent long moments especially to appreciate the delicate shadows beneath each small, curled toe.

"Is it ready . . . for the amber ministrations?" Nikka asked, apparently no one, using one of the many euphemisms she employed to further distract herself from any direct action she might ever accidentally take.

"Yes," the answer came, sounding suitably impersonal, but without being authoritarian, seemingly originating from nowhere; and by suspending disbelief, she could almost believe that it was the voice of the masculine aspect of her dual divinity, although she knew all too well the voice was piped in right on cue through hidden quadrophonic speakers, by a trained actor, exceedingly famous, who had "died," quite spectacularly, some years ago.

Nikka sighed, preparing to rise, and then lay back again, looking off to the side, at a video clip of an appearance she'd made at a meeting of the European Commonwealth, maybe six years ago. "I am so . . ."

She listened for a sound, any sound, and satisfied that there was none, that there was a perfect artificial silence, she simply left it that way.

Caleb watched the man slurping calamari across from him with a mixture of distaste and disbelief. They were sitting at a sprawling villa in Sicily, where Caleb had been summoned to the kind of meeting that always vaguely sickened him, the kind upon which his continued existence depended. The villa was owned by a man so legendarily successful at the arts of intimidation, corruption, and murder that in spite of the fact that his fortune originated entirely in drugs, weapon sales, gambling, and worse, one had no choice but to call him a "businessman."

There was a fountain, gaudy and overdone, depicting three pretty, naked maidens stabbing each other to death in a danse macabre just outside the portico where they, or rather, he, ate lunch, but it wasn't the businessman who sat across from Caleb, but that bastard Mahoney. The commando looked up from his plate of inky-looking squid, napkin tucked gauchely into his collar, protecting a JC Penney shirt that might have cost half of what Caleb's right shoelace cost.

Mahoney grinned, as if he knew what Caleb was thinking, as if he knew exactly how much Caleb hated this, as if he was perfectly aware of the irony of it all, which, of course, the ex-commando most definitely was. He let the pale orange oil of the overly garlicked dish glisten on his square chin for far too long, an unbearably long period of time, and then slowly, with great deliberation, lifted the bottom of the napkin tucked into his collar and dabbed it only partially dry.

A nude girl, dark-haired, tanned, and lean, but not especially beautiful, came to the table, holding a clay pitcher of wine. She refilled Mahoney's glass, bowed slightly, and smiled gently in acknowledgment when he fingered her shaved cleft, and then retreated back to where she came, ready for any request, anything from another spoonful of parmesan, for instance, or a casual order to cut herself on the right breast just below the nipple.

Mahoney lifted the glass to Caleb, winked, and drank. He nodded toward the place where the girl now stood, partially hidden, behind gauzy summer curtains, waiting.

"The daughter of a midlevel minister in Rome. He can't repay a favor; it's a minor thing, but . . ." Mahoney shrugged. "It amuses the master of the place. You know how it is."

Caleb touched his fingers to a previously untouched bottle of chilled mineral water. Mahoney watched the almost aborted movement and grinned again, this time far more slowly, and Caleb was certain that the man had misinterpreted the gesture, which meant nothing, but not the way Mahoney might have guessed. Caleb watched, disinterestedly, a fly walking along the livid scar on the man's forehead, an old battle wound, no doubt, and the two of them understood that Mahoney would never lift his hand to brush it away.

"This," Caleb said, and he let the buzzing of the fly, which had traveled from the scar to the plate of calamari and back to the scar again, fill the long interval of a silence neither man felt at all compelled to break if it lasted the course of a normal human lifetime, "is all very tiresome, Mr. Mahoney."

The commando had his head down near his plate of squid, but he kept his eyes on Caleb, and the amusement the vampire saw in those twin holes leading to the black core of his dead heart was forced. Mahoney hated him, plain and simple, and not with any ordinary hatred, but with an apocalyptic violence, an explosiveness that would destroy the whole world in a single unthinking flash, that even Caleb could respect. There was a thermonuclear fury in the man that was hardly contained, and yet it was contained, but only against the day when it would be released in a shock wave of destruction that was beyond anyone's ability to imagine; but a brief memory of Hiroshima, after the bomb, a moonlike landscape, dust, emptiness, nothing, was a suggestive metaphor.

That it was part of his job, perhaps the main part, to

accommodate Caleb, to coordinate the cleanup of his messy "feedings," to oversee the transfer of money and properties, and to generally serve as runner between him and Nikka must have galled the commando to the point of the insanity from which he clearly suffered. If the eyes that watched over him always blinked just once, however briefly, he would have used that split second to kill Caleb where he sat, or try to kill him, however futile such an attempt might have been; and, under the right circumstances, it might not have been futile at all. But Caleb knew very well that it wasn't the watching eye, ultimately, that held the commando's rage in check. Mahoney would violate any law, even the laws of logic and common sense, if he thought it would win her approval. No, what stayed Mahoney's murderous rage, the only thing that could hold back his killing hand, Caleb mused, staring into the flawless blue sky in the direction of an invisible Saturn, was love.

Mahoney lifted his head, watched Caleb for a moment, and turned toward a view of the sea, a blue slightly darker than the sky, sparkling with ten million million needlepoints of light at the foot of the rocky promontory where they dined in the open air. Last week he had personally raped and broken the neck of the boy-lover of one of Italy's largest auto makers and thrown the slim, twitching body into the sea, along with that of a young blooded goat. The gesture had been meant as a warning, but a warning about what, and from whom, Mahoney had no idea, and, neither had the billionaire industrialist, who was forced to watch terrified, not twenty yards from the spot where Mahoney now sat, under almost normal cirumstances, sipping a wine the color of brain fluid. How many sacrifices had been made? What had he not been compelled to do? He put the glass down and continued to stare out at the sea and spoke in colloquial Czech.

"You think it all tiresome, Mr. Darr, and yet you know very well you depend on the grace of our mutual bene-factress to survive. Sometimes, it seems to me, you pretend to have forgotten that."

Caleb didn't answer for a long time. Instead he watched the oily footprints the fly had left on the man's broad, square brow. He wasn't angry at the commando's words, or offended, any more than he would have been offended by a move made by an opponent on a chess board, QB six to KR three, for instance. He looked down from his musing into the heavens and fixed Mahoney, who had turned from his lesser, but no less intense musing on the sea, with an indifferent gaze, hidden from the commando by the blackout glasses. It was a moment re-peated countless times from time immemorial and it held no meaning for Caleb, or for Mahoney, and yet so it was.

"A service provided for a service rendered, Mr. Ma-honey. I don't exist by anyone's . . ." Caleb shifted his attention, momentarily, to the slight elevation in Ma-honey's blood pressure, and then back to the man's cold eyes, flat as something pressed down with thumbs. ". . . grace." He finished the sentence and savored, briefly, the slightly spicy but altogether healthy scent of the commando's pubic area, so distinct from that of his underarms, say, or his perineum area. He won-dered at the man's genital girth; the length and potency were clear to him. "If I wasn't needed, my ex-istence, such as it is, wouldn't be suffered. I would suddenly become . . . extinct. It's the law of nature. She needs me, Mr. Mahoney. Deal with it."

The commando suddenly grew very calm, his blood pressure dropping, and a great stillness took posses-sion of both his mind and body. Caleb, who knew that such a man was at his most dangerous precisely when

he was calmest, momentarily let himself enjoy the
heightened sensory perception that inspired. Among
his most immediate impressions: the shadow cast by a
single loose thread on the edge of his exquisitely folded
napkin and the sound of a grain of earth falling from
inside a donkey's hoofprint on a slope half a mile away.
Caleb savored these impressions like the connoisseur
he was, although, jaded as he was, the truth was that
he had tasted and dismissed all these pleasures a mil-
lenium ago. It was the tone of what Mahoney said next,
the atonal music of the words themselves, rather than
the meaning, that caught whatever attention he paid
them at all, which was hardly any.

"You overstate your value, Mr. Darr."

This part of the conversation, Caleb had decided, long
before they'd arrived at the place where Mahoney would
say these very words, was long over. He thought, briefly,
of taking off his glasses, and, in the end, did not. It was
time to turn toward the conclusion, even though he
knew there would be no conclusion, ever. "Have you
come to assassinate me," remembering briefly, Marie An-
toinette on the morning of her beheading, preparing
her makeup, "or to offer me an assignment?"

"I've come with orders."

Caleb allowed a small smile, stylized, frozen. "The
problem with living so long," he said, with the weariness
of someone knowing exactly what the reply would be,
dishearteningly certain that no improvisation was likely,
or, for that matter, possible, "is that everyone has run out
of original things to say."

Mahoney, of course, did not disappoint him, and the
genius of it was, that the commando would have done
this on purpose, if he'd only known.

"That's too bad. Maybe it's time for you to leave the
stage. I can help you out with that."

"Maybe you can, Mr. Mahoney. Maybe. Until then . . ."

Mahoney made a gesture, which the girl, unmentioned, but unforgotten, answered by appearing with an atomizer and spraying a place on the table. Almost immediately, as if generated spontaneously from whatever had been sprayed on the tablecloth, thirty-six honeybees, fevered, had gathered on the wet patch. The girl, the unspoken request satisfied, whatever its significance, retreated back to the relative shelter of the gauze curtains, where she awaited, with nearly perfect immobility, any further irrational requests.

The commando made a show of being satisfied, which only caused Caleb's disgust to deepen, if that had been possible, which it hadn't.

"He is calling himself Io. He is moving through Europe right now with a small group of followers. We've been watching him for some time now, a hundred and fifty years or so. He's become . . . problematic. There was an incident in the United States recently—"

Caleb held up his hand. He'd heard this all before, a hundred times, or read it in the newspapers or in a history book, or, perhaps, he'd dreamed it. Of the many unbearable things involved in being a "vampire," and there were innumerable unbearable things, perhaps the most unbearable was the oppressive sense of constant déjà vu.

"I'm aware," he said, fighting off exhaustion.

"What you may not be aware of," Mahoney said, sharply, unable to hide his irritation at being interrupted during a presentation he'd obviously planned with a certain amount of relish, "is that he's kidnapped the fucking princess of England."

Caleb hadn't been aware of that; and, almost in spite of himself, the fact actually did interest him, but only in a distant and indistinct way, like a suggestive brushstroke in a landscape painting.

"That information," the commando said, ". . . has been red-penciled," which, as Caleb well knew, meant edited from the reality script.

Mahoney was unable to conceal a hint of smug pride and satisfaction, childish as that was, particularly insofar as he had no role whatsoever in the propaganda arm of his organization or its ability to dissemble and distort reality. The fact was that he was probably just as much a victim of its relentless disinformation as anyone else.

Mahoney searched the vampire's inscrutable face for a reaction, but Caleb decided long before the revelation that no reaction would be the reaction best suited for this particular scene. So he maintained a look of perfect sangfroid, which he felt, more or less, or told himself to feel. He did acknowledge, if only to himself, the difficulty of keeping such a monumental detail secret. His admiration that Nikka had been able to do so, against all odds, was considerable. But then he never considered her anything but the best at what she did, whatever that was exactly, and it was questionable that even Nikka knew what she did for sure, aside from concealing the truth at all costs, a truth she herself most assuredly did not believe, or even possess.

"Has the usual theoretical précis been completed?"

Mahoney nodded perfunctorily. "Provisionally."

"Meaning?"

"Provisionally."

"Summary of provisional conclusions?"

The commando looked ostentatiously, and unnecessarily, at his watch. It was a cheap radio-controlled Casio, needlessly cheap, Caleb thought distastefully, as if Mahoney was trying too hard to not prove something.

"I'd prefer not to waste both our time, Mr. Darr. I must catch a jet to Antwerp, perhaps, in less than fifty minutes."

"You have the report?"

"Homework is awaiting your return. You'll find it . . . challenging, I suspect."

Caleb once again thought of removing his glasses, folding them, and putting them in the inside left pocket of his sports jacket, but it would have been extremely underappreciated. Instead he clicked the empty glass at his place setting, the glass that had remained empty and unused the entire time, along with the rest of the setting, but that had been set down only out of courtesy and form, with the fingernail of his left forefinger. There was a little *ping* like the sound of a marble accidentally dropped on an iron catwalk and, somehow, caught before it bounces a second time.

"Then that concludes our business, Mr. Mahoney."

"For now Mr. Darr. I will be in touch, per the usual arrangement." The commando smiled grimly, and Caleb noted the beginnings of a cavity between his incisor and right front tooth. "Don't fail us, Mr. Darr. Don't even consider it."

"As per the usual, Mr. Mahoney," Caleb remarked, off-handedly, although nothing anymore would be offhanded, not, at least, for some time.

"Would you like me to roll out the red carpet?" the commando asked, nodding to the naked girl, on the flagstones by his chair.

She had appeared at some invisible command, or she had merely been instructed, when the meeting was over, to present herself, helplessly, as she was currently doing. She was lounging, on her left side, propped on one arm, holding her hair back with the other hand, the pose suggestive of a billboard model selling suntan lotion, or a new bride on honeymoon waiting for a kiss. The Aztec sacrificial dagger she had carried in her teeth was in the commando's right hand, its smooth obsidian blade, smudged with her lipstick, melting, incrementally, into the thin skin covering her carotid.

"Sir?" she whispered, sensually, forcing an inviting smile.

Caleb had already risen, turning from the entire vulgar display. He was no longer surprised that such things had become a kind of mockery, if he'd ever been surprised, but only surprised that he still recalled a time they hadn't been.

"Suit yourself, Mr. Mahoney," he said.

Of course, it would have been easy for Caleb to sense if Mahoney had opened the worthless girl or not; in fact, without taking precautions, it would have been unavoidable for him to know, yes or no, but uninterested in playing the commando's game, Caleb took the necessary precautions and purposely blocked it all from his mind, not that Mahoney would know that, or, if he did, would care. And what difference did it make, anyway, if he leisurely cut a girl's throat after lunch; it wasn't as if this kind of thing didn't happen all the time, every day, when two such men met to inaugurate an important project. Caleb thought of something the emperor Tiberius once told him when in retirement on the island of Capri and that led to a thought on color blindness and then some equations regarding black holes and before he knew it he was in the back of a limousine racing down a secret country road that would take him to the heliport and, from there, on to Rome.

Who is he? Mariana asked at dinner, the group having gathered to discuss that day's tour of some minor frescoes by painters none of them except Claire, and, of course, the instructor, had ever heard of. Juliet had been fidgeting at the sketch she'd drawn of him, trying to correct the curve of the line that described his upper lip, lending his mouth the shape of a word that had not been invented or the way one would form one's lips if about to kiss eternity. The closest she could come was the way someone might smile if there was nothing to smile about, as if, perhaps, standing at a window on the morning after the last day of the world, not horror, not regret, but just . . .

Juliet rubbed the mouth away with her white eraser, and stared briefly at Mariana without seeing her, trying in her mind to conjure him again, a man in dark clothes standing in the wind on a deserted plain, or in a crowded square, always standing in the wind, even where there was no wind at all.

"He's a man I met, two days ago . . ." and then she realized that he never told her his name, or she didn't remember if he had, although she couldn't imagine forgetting it. "I don't know his name."

"He looks familiar," Mariana said, and took a drag from a cigarette, her elbow propped on the table, blowing the smoke straight up from her bottom lip, pretending not to look at a handsome family man across the crowded dining room, who was pretending not to look at her. "Like one of those Italian movie stars who no one has ever heard of."

"I can't get the mouth right," Juliet said, trying again, failing, trying again, and finally, giving up, brushing away hopeless mouths, unborn kisses from the page, along with white crumbs, using the back of her hand. "It's hopeless."

She took the cigarette from between Mariana's fingers, inhaled, and looked down at the incomplete drawing. The eyes, she thought, what are the eyes looking at, and who doesn't he want to see what he's looking at?

Mariana lit another cigarette, tossed the match into Juliet's cold farfel, and said something about meeting an

Italian soccer player earlier that afternoon at a frozen fruit concession and then something about a parking ticket she received a month ago in Newport, Rhode Island. Later that night, in a club that started with the letter P, on a stone street whose name she didn't know, she and Mariana, and maybe Claire for a while, but definitely Beth and Danielle and Ross, were all quite drunk and laughing and occasionally flirting, and Danielle got picked up, and Ross drifted out into the night, and Claire was either there or not there, and Beth and Mariana, who never stopped smoking, were talking and kissing for drinks two guys, maybe Germans, were buying them, and Juliet heard Beth say loudly, almost aggressively at one point above the din, "What's with her?"

And Mariana, her lipstick blurred, was laughing and said, "Oh, don't mind her, all she can think about is mouths," or something that sounded like that, and everyone was laughing and then one of the German guys, who might not have been German, said something vulgar that was supposed to be funny, except it wasn't, at least Juliet didn't think so, and everyone laughed harder. She blushed and looked down at the bar and the cocktail napkin on which she'd doodled, almost unconsciously, hundreds of mouths, and she snatched it up, and shoved it deeply into her pocket and ordered another drink, although the bartender wasn't listening.

Even later that night, Juliet lay, curled on her side, staring out the window of the cold hotel room she shared with Mariana, eyes shut, trying to ignore the nauseating sounds of other people's sex coming from the next bed, where Mariana was doing it with one or both of the possibly German guys or Beth or the soccer player she mentioned meeting earlier that afternoon at the frozen fruit concession, or some combination of them, or even Claire, whose voice Juliet thought she heard, although it might have been part of a dream, or coming from the hall. She dozed and woke and dozed and woke and stumbled past the bed where Mariana was still tangled with someone's body, sometimes making love, and sometimes not, and into the bathroom where once she saw Ross, who shrugged at her sheepishly, and another time someone she didn't recognize, and she knelt on the cold stone floor and threw up undigested brandy and nicotine and rinsed her mouth in the sink and fell asleep on the floor between the bathroom and the bed, and when she woke up at 1:00 P.M. the next afternoon it was to a cell phone ringing the opening chords of Beethoven's Fifth a foot away from her face and when she answered it someone on the other end asked for someone named Barry or Boris and she looked up at Mariana coming out of the bathroom with a cigarette in one hand and a toothbrush in the other asking, "Who's that?"

"Someone who wants Barry or Boris."

Mariana shrugged and told Juliet to tell whoever it was to call back so Juliet did and hung up and three seconds later the phone rang again and they both ignored it and Mariana said, "How do you feel?" with a grin on her face and Juliet said, "Okay, I guess," but all she could really remember of the night before was having the same dream over and over, well, not really a dream because nothing happened, just an image of him, standing in the wind, a man whose mouth she couldn't stop looking at, couldn't stop wanting to be kissed with, a mouth whose expression she understood now, a mouth that disdained the touch of anything human.

That same night, Caleb commited suicide, yet again. He was in India, of all places, in a genteely run down hotel with a partial view of the Ganges, at a

place where the river was wide and slow, where so many had their bodies consigned or their ashes scattered, and now he sat by the window, staring, a tumbler of that river's water by his hand, motionless. Earlier in the evening, he'd pretended to smoke first-grade hashish with a thugee, one of Kali's devoted assassins, in a market stall with a wealthy collector of rare artifacts and a celebrated mythologist long thought to be dead. They spoke of the business of collectibles: extinct genes, missing historical murder weapons, celebrity abortions. Caleb made the final arrangements for a handsome transfer of funds and chattel scripts to disappear into one of his Japanese accounts after negotiating the delivery of a Cleopatra toe joint.

It was an old routine, this suicide that could never quite be successful, and tonight it was no different. Caleb had no clear idea why he went through the motions at all, procuring the pills, securing a rope, or better yet, a belt of braided Moroccan leather, using a dagger from the ritual arsenal of the notorious twentieth-century mage Aleister Crowley, or a revolver filled with bullets painted white by Salvador Dali. It was, perhaps, as most things were of this sort, a kind of ritual, soothing and compulsive, in addition to being altogether impotent and futile. He sat there now, with a more prosaic weapon, a .38 police special bought for fifteen dollars from an orphan in a Calcutta street alley whose mother, only fifteen feet away, lay dying messily of leprosy.

Caleb was tired: he was tired of living, tired of thinking, tired of seeing, tired of talking, tired of being, tired of being tired. It had been a long time since he'd wanted to live, as they called it, here, on earth, anything resembling life. It had been a long time since he'd even remotely wanted to pretend to breathe and eat, to drink and make love. He had no more poems to write and no more canvases to paint. He had no more Top 40 pop songs to compose or any more advances in virology to make. He had no interest in any of the current sixteen wars being waged around the world. He didn't want to run for governor of North Dakota. There were no more girls to love or boys to fuck. He was finished, the way a piece of music or a good conversation is finished, and whatever came afterward could only mar what had come before. Caleb had said everything there was to say; he had used every word in every language. He had squeezed all the meaning there was to be wrung out of life, drop by drop, and savored it, like a viper's tear, and it had poisoned him.

He was, in short, ready to die. There was, however, a problem. It seemed to Caleb that there was, always, something that could be called, at least provisionally, a problem.

The file had been delivered, as Mahoney had promised, and lay on the table beside the tumbler of cloudy Ganges water. Caleb had carried the file from Rome to Hollywood and then to India, unread, the wax seal with Nikka's familiar double-axe and invisible petrifying virgin on rampant azure intact, and he had no intention of reading it now. Instead he lifted the revolver to his chest, just to the left of his breastbone, and, without reflection, but without ostentatious casualness, simply pulled the trigger.

The bullet passed through him as if he were nothing but an old husk, which he was, splintered the back of the chair in which he was sitting, shattered a mirror somewhere he hadn't even noticed, and passed through the thin papered wall behind the mirror where it lodged in an armchair placed in front of the television in the vacant room next door. There was the usual burning smell and a small wisp of smoke curled from the neat black hole left in his custom-made French linen shirt. No blood, of course, not a drop, issued from the wound.

Caleb frowned. He put the revolver down, picked up the tumbler of Ganges water, and fake-sipped. He closed his eyes lightly and saw this: flaming pyres on dark riverbanks, wrapped bodies being pushed out into the river, glittering chunks of bone in smoky ashes, bright flower petals scattered on brown current. He opened his eyes, staring, momentarily, at the door, where someone was knocking loudly and calling out in Urdu, and he answered, in German, "Leave. There is nothing here," and then shifted his gaze out the window, where he saw a red fireworks explode, and then fall, fading, silently, hundreds of kilometers away.

He knew what it would really take to end his existence. There were methods and there were "certain people," and these were, quite naturally, known to him, and though his mind desired extinction with a one-point focus, his body did not, and it was this body, mute, dumb, unintelligent, that insisted on continuing, that flinched, instinctually, from death in spite of, perhaps because of, everything. This body, which he had come to recognize as part of himself, was not susceptible to logic, to reason, to argument. It was susceptible to nothing, for that matter, but its own continuance, no matter what: it drove Caleb with a dictatorial virulence to seize the next moment, no matter how useless, moment by moment, forever.

There would never be "enough" moments. Although he had collected them all, there was always another, even if he had ten million, already, identical to it. Caleb had evolved from a species adapted, over long eons, to survive in a world far more harsh than this one, and so he had, but never had he experienced a world more senseless than this one, and the most senseless thing of all, so he reflected now, was that he survived, more or less, entirely against his own indomitable will.

Caleb put his fingertips on the unread file, pulling it toward him slowly, as if he'd decided to open it once and for all, but he knew when he reached for it, even before he reached for it, that he had no intention of opening it yet, if ever. It was futile, as if it had all been done already, which it had or had not, and it didn't make any difference; done or not, nothing would change. So Caleb sat in the chair by the window, the file unread under his fingertips, the tumbler of cloudy Ganges water beside the revolver on the table, and a day passed, or two, or even three, but eventually he rose, picked up the unread file, and took a private jet to the desert.

Bees, hundreds of thousands of them, covered the walls, the ceiling, the floors of the hexagonal chamber in which Nikka sat, alone, naked, and hieratical, humming an empty syllable, eyes abstracted, hands in a complex and stylized mudra, signifying, quite literally, nothing at all. The chamber was warm, subtropical, an eternal summer, as the bodies of the swarming bees gave off a hibernating heat, a high-pitched swelter in which Nikka felt entirely at home, grounded, unperturbed, and secure, as if at the center of her own personal cosmos, which, she never doubted, she was.

The body of the latest Alexandria, whichever one, strangled or poisoned or electrocuted, was already partially embalmed, wax sealing lips, obscuring features, filling anus and naval, bees doing their furious work, depositing wax in nostrils, under eyelids, between each toe. The bees clung to the side of the chamber, pulsating, the entire chamber pulsating, no up and no down, everything humming, including Nikka, at peace, whole, at one, at last, and at all times, always.

There is nothing for Nikka to do, nothing she can do, and she has no thoughts, not one, and it's at these moments she understands the beauty of her flawless and unassailable uselessness and yet the absolute essential quality of her presence. She is content to be, sitting in this chamber, the mute queen and mother of no issue, the virgin generator of it all, the mystic motor and the center of creation, humming. She is this, and only this, a symbol, if that, an icon, an advertisement, a sublimation, an inducement, a catalyst, a stimulus; she is simply that which is and needs to be for anything, whatsoever, to happen.

And the bees pay homage, ceaselessly humming, flying past her, but never touching her flawless face, her perfect hair, the composure of one never to be disturbed, the unattainable that all labor, tragically, to attain and never do. The pollen dusts her exquisite lips, flecking them with gold, but she never licks. It is wrong to say she smiles or feels at peace; it is wrong to say she is fulfilled or lost in contemplation, or in a state of permanent enlightenment. It is wrong to say anything at all, and impossible, anyway, to talk or think, above the humming din, the hum that fills the cosmos beyond words and light and life and death. Instead she's left in the midst of such devotion, the impression, as she sits there, divorced from everything, that, perhaps not quite paradoxically, she really isn't there at all.

2. crusader

Don't interfere, that's always the first rule, and if you can't avoid interfering, do the opposite of what you were going to do, and pretend it didn't happen. Don't use personal pronouns. Don't touch anything; if possible, don't go anywhere in person: fingerprints, skin flakes, fallen hairs, all leave detailed directions back to whatever point A from which you originated, no matter how oblique and abstracted.

The subject knows the watcher is watching: that will always be assumed. There is no way to avoid that. The eye is not invisible, nor the eye beam, and there is no such thing as slipping unseen into the paranoiac field that surrounds a potential target, especially a target as high-profile as the target currently under consideration; and all targets, worth targeting at this point in the proceedings, are high-profile targets. Such a high-profile target has a paranoiac field as expansive as the entire cosmos. There is simply no vantage point, no Texas Book Depository or hotel kitchen that escapes surveillance, where anyone feels safe, where an attack is not suspected, or even expected.

Fact: for every attack that doesn't occur there is a vague sense of disappointment on the part of all concerned, ie., the potential target, the would-be agent, the expectant audience.

Fact: for every attack that doesn't occur there is that much more heightened expectancy that the next time it will occur, ie., that much more chance that it will be detected, aborted, or otherwise altered.

And yet, in spite of this cautionary advice, the job is not impossible. Fact is: it is more than likely. One might even say: it is inevitable. The aura of invulnerability surrounding those on "the list" is, of course, a pure myth, a publicity campaign to enhance celebrity status, or cultic appeal to an always rising class of generally disaffected youth, and serves, in general in all cases, to ennoble those who moor society to a stability long enough to ensure maximum parasitic activity.

This is what you have been taught in the training camps, technical schools, and adult education courses. Don't forget it. This is what you have been told in the churches, support groups, and outreach programs. Don't forget it. This is what you hear on the nightly news at 5:00, 9:00, 10:00, and 11:00 P.M. This is what, contrary to what you might have thought, it has been made plain that you have really believed during your time in the rehabilitation facility and this is how you protect the world from those whom, motivated by irrational reasons of their own, the world needs protecting.

Miscellaneous: use the left side of the street, avoid dreams, stay on-line, record nothing, don't remain silent but be careful not to say anything.

Finally: value nothing, and nothing less than your life. In short:

You watch and you wait and you report back to the authorities whether you think they hear you or not. You follow the orders that come, either ceaselessly or periodically or not at all, from the earphone or the implant in your medulla oblongata.

You watch and you wait for the order to strike.

You are certain this order is coming soon, but whether

it does or not, you must proceed under the assumption that it is. You must be ready.

You will know the order when it comes, if it comes: see above.

You won't be imagining any of it. It is unmistakable, if you don't take the time to mistake it, whatever form "it" takes.

Don't question.

Have faith—or not. That you believe in what you do is of no importance, neither particular nor general to anyone, including yourself.

Act.

Commit an act of faith.

In the middle of nowhere, the U.S. Army surplus jeep came to an abrupt stop, and Caleb stepped out into the sand and sun of a barren landscape unrelieved by shadow and stretching out flat in all directions for as far as the eye can see. The driver, who had said nothing during the entire ride, which lasted approximately two hours from the parachute drop, said nothing now, and no sooner had Caleb disembarked than he hit the gas, made a wide turn, and sped away in the direction from which he came, whichever direction that might have been, all directions in the desert looking exactly the same.

The church, which stood improbably among all this desolation, was built five centuries ago, and rebuilt, or partially rebuilt, several times since, dating back to the time of the Crusades. It was a time when it seemed important to plant God's cross everywhere, to claim every last outpost for his glory, to stake each square foot, no matter how forlorn and useless, in his name. Caleb walked on the pathless dust in front of the church and through the crumbling stone gate, unguarded, and into the abandoned courtyard of ruined shacks and rotting wood where snakes and scorpions hid from the midday heat, and all the chickens had long since disappeared.

There was a statue of John the Baptist, pitted by centuries of blowing sand, crumbling like all the other stone in the courtyard. He was pointing with a smashed hand, in an indeterminate way, toward the desert or the church or the sky or at Caleb himself. He was pointing, in effect, nowhere at all, and the fingers, broken off, left the hand looking like a stone fist, raised in speechless rage against eternity for the promise and faith unfulfilled and unrewarded, for no savior, anywhere, was coming.

This is all that's coming, Caleb thought, as he passed the Baptist, *this is all that's left: me.*

The door, wood and iron, had been smashed, by time or weather or vandals, each of them striking a blow, but it still hung, more or less, from, heavy, rusted hinges. Caleb shoved the door open and stepped inside. A good part of the ceiling lay on the floor, which was littered with torn breviaries, machine gun bullets, animal bones, ruins of small fires, and all of it covered by the fine plaster dust of pulverized holy statues. The church was being used as a roosting place by vultures who perched on the backs of ruined pews, on the altar, on the remains of the high walls, which had been invaded, partially, by a kind of fiercely hardy desert vine that had found a niche here, and a bit of shade.

He walked down the center aisle between the pews, stepping over unexploded mortar shells, broken CDs, movie posters, used condoms, and AA batteries. Out of the corner of his eye, Caleb saw a tall, fawn-colored animal, starved and guilty, maybe a dog or a hyena or some impossible cross between the two, lope from behind a headless statue of the Virgin Mary, which had been defaced with childish bathroom humor and a large mop pail.

Caleb stopped some yards in front of the large wooden cross behind the altar, or what was left of the altar, the remains of a long-eaten meal still lying there, next to a rain-plastered novel whose pages were unreadable, and made a vague genuflection, neither the sign of the cross, nor a profane gesture, but something in between the two.

This was the Jesus that he preferred: a long, angular body and a face that was thin, ascetic, fierce. Those muscles straining in his legs, that look on his face—it wasn't a semiecstatic swoon meant to blur the line between sex and death. This wasn't one of those feminized boy Jesuses with dainty hands and pretty feet, his loincloth slipping down seductively over dancers' hipbones. This Jesus was suffering: this was a human body nailed, goddammit, to a cross of wood and suffocating as it collapsed, trying, futilely, to raise itself up on pulped feet to gulp another mouthful of air: this was a creature, mortal and yet doomed to know its own mortality, crying out to whatever force or combination of forces, purposeful or random, was responsible for its existence. This was man before he became a God at the very extreme of suffering and asking the same question he'd asked from the first time the lightning struck the rock or someone died: My God, why hast thou forsaken me?

This was a dying man asking the ultimate question.

And getting no answer.

"So you've come at last. It's been a long time."

Caleb stared up at the forlorn, bearded face of the dead prophet. "It is all, somehow, unavoidable."

"You knew, didn't you?"

Caleb nodded. "I had my suspicions."

"And yet you didn't try to stop him."

"There were a lot of would-be gods at the time. Any one of them might have been the one. He was a dark horse, but I remember speaking of him to a young Gaius. Before, of course, he went insane."

"Who could have guessed, eh?"

"It was ingenious really, and could only have come about by accident. The idea that men became God by giving up the very world to which they'd been born. No more fighting, no more striving. Just surrender."

"Surrender . . . ah . . . absurdity."

"Of course. And to explain the absurd one must have faith, for faith lets one believe what is entirely irrational and accept what is unacceptable and dispenses with any explanation whatsoever. He made a strength of weakness, a victory of surrender, a god of man."

"He turned out to be the greatest savior of our kind. And yet . . . the herald of our doom."

"We need . . ." Caleb paused to brush away a fly that was somewhere, but not here, not now. ". . . to talk."

"I'm always waiting."

"I want to fuck you," the man said, but he said it in Italian, and not in those exact words, but others that meant the same thing, leaving nothing to misunderstanding, even though she didn't understand a word. Juliet was smoking some other man's cigarette, not this man's, some other man's who'd tried to pick her up and failed, or had not failed, Juliet could not remember. She was drunk, or drugged, that wasn't clear either, nor did it matter, so long as she felt nothing, which she didn't, except the urge to feel a little less. The man beside her at the bar was telling her that she was beautiful, or words to that effect; he was speaking

English, or trying to speak English, but both of them knew that whatever he was saying was totally unimportant. They were communicating on a level beyond words, if they were communicating at all, but whether yes or no, Juliet understood what he expected when he slid off the bar stool and she followed him outside into the night where it was raining yet again, or still, whichever one, it seemed entirely appropriate.

"Follow this way," he called back, grinning, strong white teeth in an unshaven face, some kind of coat that looked associated with the sea.

She had left that afternoon, telling no one, waiting for Mariana to leave before getting out of bed from which she had feigned a flu or headache, whatever required drawn curtains and undisturbed rest. She had dressed hurriedly and slipped out into the twilight, pretending she hadn't heard Claire calling to her in the hallway and that she didn't recognize whoever took the elevator with her to the lobby, whether she knew him or her, or not. She went to the streets that had not been highlighted on their tour maps, the small and crooked streets, which had no names, and found them one after another, a man like the man now urging her to hurry up the street, looking both ways, as if guilty of something, smiling the whole time, nervous, and hungry.

"Come, come," he said, motioning with his hand. "It's not far, we're almost there."

What she was looking for tonight, or the other nights, she couldn't say, although she might have said it was him, the man in the square, whose mouth she couldn't draw, who pretended to make love to her, she might have said that, but she didn't. What she was looking for was what she'd been looking for all her life, as was everyone, but unlike everyone, she had found it, or thought she had, and lost it again. What she did tonight was not as unusual as she might have wished, or pretended, even to herself, it was only more reckless, perhaps, and more pointed toward catastrophe, or ecstasy, or, as the two were entwined in her particular fantasy, both.

Juliet might have stopped to take her shoes off, to lean against a wall or street lamp, but it was unnecessary. She had lost her stockings somewhere, and her bra, but the leather jacket she still had, but nothing as silly as an umbrella, and she was drenched. She followed the man down a sort of short alley that opened to a dreary square where a bicycle without wheels was standing upside down on saddle and handlebars as if someone had meant to fix it a hundred years ago and just forgot. There were other things to see: a pile of bricks, a folding chair, a window box of plastic geraniums, and much else, but Juliet was thinking, instead, of the long black limousine she'd seen parked across the street from the entranceway to the short alley she'd just turned into, an idling limo with blacked-out windows, and things happening inside that were better not to imagine.

It seemed impossible not to note such a car, idling improbably on a street such as the one they had just exited; its presence seemed suspicious in the extreme, ominous, forbidding, suggesting some kind of imminent interference; but the man Juliet followed paid it no attention whatsoever, hadn't seemed to notice it at all, which made her wonder if somehow there weren't some collusion between the two, or if the car had only been a figment of her imagination, because, after all, she had been seeing it all over the place of late.

She looked out the window of whatever room they were in, whatever room in the nondescript building was his, and the street below was empty, save for the rain. The limousine that she had seen, or imagined she had seen, was gone, but whether the street she was looking at was the street from which they'd arrived, it was impossible to say, and turning back to the man who had led her here, Juliet knew it was equally impossible to ask.

"Get away from the window," he said, but again she was only guessing at what he really was saying. He grabbed her by the arm and pulled her toward the bed, or what she thought was the direction of the bed, the room having been too dark upon entering, as it was now, to see much of anything, except the window. He stepped past her and went to the window himself. He looked out it briefly, made to pull down the shade, but there was no shade to pull down. He looked out the window again, felt for the nonexistent shade again, peered up to the top of the window, back at her, out the window, back at her, and cursed.

He kept on cursing as he came at her, gesticulating, flecks of spit hitting her face, which, she tended to think, was generally void of expression, although whatever expression she didn't wear, whatever she didn't say, seemed to be provoking him into a greater rage, which may only have been his own mounting sexual excitement, or justification, or both, for what was to come next, and none of it having anything to do with her. He was blaming her for something and Juliet was aware that whatever it was she had supposedly done wrong, it wasn't her fault at all, but had been done or not done by someone else in this man's life, and if she felt anything at all at the moment it was nothing but a completely unsurprising and overwhelming sense of boredom.

He hit her, suddenly and rather unnecessarily, but altogether predictably, with the back of his hand, a blow that dropped her on the bed, which was there, after all, and left the inside of her head ringing. She sat there, neither stunned nor alert, but tasting blood and thinking, well, at least that was something, wasn't it? He hit her again, as if to answer the question, and once more, as if she hadn't heard his answer the first time. She grunted softly, or rather her body grunted, when he planted his fist in her stomach, driving the air from her, and she felt, from a great distance, his hands, hands made dumb by eating too long alone and tying ropes in the cold morning, pull at her clothes in a way that suggested he might have been hurriedly dressing her, after an act of which he was ashamed, as much as undressing her before the same such act.

There was the taste of motor oil or what motor oil smelled like, and sunlight through the branches of a willow when you're lying on your back looking up at the sky. There was the sound of a music box your mother might have had on her dresser when you were eight and the white silk of a hundred mortarboards at an outdoor graduation from something or there was your father taking the dog away in a blanket for the last time and a conversation about a *Vogue* fashion on the plane to Italy a week earlier that might have taken place a thousand years ago and not included you at all. There was a pain that was not the pain you were feeling now but one that hurt more and a mouth with an expression that seemed to include all those things and a knowledge of some secret you never admit but imagine that's what someone would look like if he were about to say the words. . . .

"Is it over?" she asked numbly, not talking about what was going on at all, but what she was talking about, in what context this question belonged, she had no idea, no idea whatsover. "Is it over?"

"Crazy bitch," she heard him answer in hybrid English. "Stupid cunt," but his voice sounded shaky, scared, and his threats that she tell no one, or he'd kill her, maim her, disfigure her, muttered hurriedly as he dressed, were more for form than anything else, and somehow he knew this, and that is what made him scared. He ran from the room, finally, one boot in his hand, and she heard the uneven clomping of his steps as he ran from the building into the rain.

Some time later, many hours later, perhaps, she rose from the bed, finding herself more dressed than not, and left the room, careful to lock the door behind her. It was not quite dawn on the street outside the building, the rain having lightened but still falling, and Juliet noted the black limousine parked at the curb a half block behind her, idling, and though she was tangentially aware that its presence portended great significance, she wasn't tempted, at all, to turn and look back and realized that, having left her leather jacket, she had provided someone, somewhere with an artifact, although she wasn't sure what that meant, or why she specifically used the word "artifact," and not "evidence."

"So that is what sadness looks like," Nikka said, shutting off the tape recorder, always running, which captured her oracular pronouncements and gnomic utterances. Somewhere, however, a second tape, backing up the one she controlled, continued to run. She spoke to no one, and to the ages, and there was a difference, but it was negligible. The black limousine, her coffin, pulled slowly away from the curb, and the film outside the window seemed to start moving again, even though Nikka knew very well that she wasn't going anywhere at all. "Shall I follow her?" the driver said, or thought he said, having said nothing at all. "Are you talking to me," Nikka answered, somewhat confused, "or are you asking whoever is following me?" Her driver, unaccustomed to these subtleties, chose not to answer, and hoping to avoid being caught lying in any later cross-examinations, simply said, "As you wish." And Nikka, understanding that this was neither an answer nor an evasion, but the manner in which someone might end a prayer to God, touched her hand to the black glass of the limousine as it sped in a direction opposite the one in which the girl was resolutely walking, in the direction opposite of everything, and thought, quite unoriginally, "God is dead."

Juliet returned to the hotel, somehow. It was more accurate to say she found herself back in the room she shared with Mariana, but how she got there she couldn't say, only that she was there in the hotel bathtub, while Mariana gently bathed her. The latter had been upset upon first seeing Juliet and inclined to call the police, but had eventually come to be persuaded that Juliet was quite all right and, bruises aside, had not received any treatment that, if not quite understandable, she hadn't welcomed. They ended up in Mariana's bed, where they made a kind of love, a thing they'd done less than five times, in varying degrees of sobriety and passion, always to no orgasm. Afterward, assuring her friend that she needed a walk and a cigarette and would be back in ten minutes, Juliet dressed and left the hotel the last time, in a manner of speaking, she'd ever be seen alive again.

"Forgive me, Father," Caleb said quietly, "for I am about to sin."

He was kneeling in a confessional that had been designed in another time for smaller men, a dank little closet of penance that smelled of urine and old dollar bills and beetles under wet boards. For centuries Caleb had come to this church in the middle of the Spanish desert to be absolved of his sins, or to go through the motions of pretending to be absolved of them, and it was here that he returned every time he began a new assignment of any import, even though he knew that no one had the authority to forgive him for what he did, least of all a killer of the magnitude of Father Xeno.

The priest on the other side of the grated window made abstract gestures with his hands that approximated sacerdotal blessings, but may, accompanied as they were by rapid staccato movements of the eyes, just as well have been the symptoms of hallucinatory delirium, a kind of strangling motion, violent in the extreme.

Father Xeno had left Europe in the fourteenth century, leaving behind a continent and a people ravaged by plague, and setting his face toward a healthy land of handsome savages embarking on one of the greatest civilizations the world has ever known. He had lived among the Aztecs during the heyday of high sacrifice when tens of thousands would be put to death in the most lavish spectacles of devotion. The gods they sought to nourish were divinely maniacal and eternally unsatisfied, and Father Xeno stalked in the shadows of these deities with unpronounceable names and uncompromisingly terrifying aspect, hardly bothering to disguise who he was, or what, but jealous all the same of the stone idols standing gruesome in the merciless and unblinking sun.

Even now the old priest's eyes flicked with visions of victims, skinned and headless, tumbling in slow motion down the hundred stairs, his own hands raised, and cupping therein a human heart, warm and fluttering, the most precious meat.

He had been there, too, when the Spanish came, Cortes and his ships, filled with soldiers and pestilence; and with an instinct for greater, if short-term slaughter, and an acumen for reading the turning tides of history, he betrayed the indigenous people to the foreign invaders with the greatest relish and watched, as by the tens and tens of thousands, they were slaughtered in a sacrifice even greater than the greatest of sacrifices they could imagine.

Those were the days, he'd later muse, drinking wine out of a skull as he sat on the top of a Franco-era tank, staring out at the vanishing point, the simulated stigmata wounds on his palms and insteps where he'd driven the nails himself, every morning and evening before devotions.

He had returned to Europe sometime in the sixteenth century and found both the continent and himself much changed in the intervening centuries. The plague had killed off the majority of Europe and with it the faith in Christ, or for that matter, faith in much of anything more holy than the breath a man carried in his lungs. Xeno had seen what Caleb had seen, the twilight of the gods, and the dawn of the end, but he'd taken a different direction than Caleb, and had sought in his own frenzied and homicidal way to defend a futile faith in an absolute God, while Caleb had become an outcast, pure and simple, a poacher in the wastelands of anything forbidden.

Caleb ignored the insane priest's conniptions and spoke loosely of the atrocities he had witnessed during the Chou dynasty, but not the ones recorded by historians. He spoke of his activities during the revolution, the Russian or French, it made no difference, one revolution or another; the point was the memory he had of taking a duchess from behind, her breasts in his hands as he tore apart her throat and an insane peasant ate the flesh from her thighs.

"I had her beheaded the next morning," Caleb said,

and wondered, absently, if this had really happened last week in Manhattan, and not the eighteenth century, if it had happened at all. "The whole aristocracy was rife with vampires," he added, almost as an afterthought, which it was.

"You trouble yourself too much with conscience," Father Xeno said, and it seemed an odd thing for a priest to say, let alone for a priest to say during a confession.

Caleb laughed, but, naturally, without humor. "I have killed more vampires than the humans have . . ."

If there was a way to finish that sentence, Caleb didn't know it, or care to exercise it.

"You exaggerate, Caleb."

"But not by much."

"There is no point to the line of thought you follow, or any line of thought, as you well know. It ends, all of it, in extinction."

"Surely, though, there must be a special place in hell for one who slaughters his own kind."

"Tell me about it."

"In Hong Kong, a vampire feeding off prostitutes . . . a sordid business . . . but these prostitutes were valuable, you see . . . an internationally renowned Buddhist meditation master . . . and a diplomat . . ."

"Yes, yes," Father Xeno said, "an old one. I've heard it a thousand times," and he laughed that laugh peculiar to human ears, but not to their race, that laugh that was what laughter was meant to be—a meditation on the blackest square of space—before humans aped it and made it sound like a donkey's bray, and directed it at other people's common misfortunes, losing their hats or tripping, for instance, as well as television sitcoms.

"You understand me then."

"We are what we are what we are," the old priest sing-songed, tunelessly, to what sounded like a song by someone who used to be named Mandy Moore. "Let me tell you a story," Father Xeno said. "The parable of the worm and the bleeding virgin," but that's all he said and the parable went untold, to Caleb's relief.

"I want you to have me killed," Caleb said, visualizing stars exploding unseen in space. "You can have it done. The Church has its deliverers."

"You know that is impossible, well, not impossible."

"You can do it."

"No, I can't. You don't want to die. And you know it."

"That's not true."

"You must come to me wanting death with all your mind and body. Can you tell me that is true? Can you? Confess to me, Caleb."

"It's true. So help me, God."

"You liar," Father Xeno said, and seemed suddenly distracted, the sound of a snake in the courtyard, having caught his attention, both his and Caleb's, as it locked its eyes on a mouse, suddenly paralyzed with fright. "You must go and find Io."

Caleb tore his attention away from the frozen tableau of snake and mouse. "You know him?"

"The veil has been rent, Caleb. The veil has been rent. Go find Io. Go to the Overseer."

"I was afraid you would say that. There's nothing I want to do less."

"It wouldn't be a confession if that weren't the case," Father Xeno said and began the parable of the daffodil and Gatling gun, which he did tell, but he told it to an empty confessional, for Caleb, already absolved of the future, had disappeared.

"None of this is real," Vince said, trying to spoon-feed the kidnapped princess some beef-flavored water, but her teeth were clenched tight, and it was quite hopeless, although he kept trying, alternately knocking the plastic spoon against her teeth and wiping what spilled untasted down her chin and neck with a wad of napkins.

She hadn't eaten since they'd taken her from the mansion, which had been days now, possibly a week or two, Vince had lost track of time. He ran through the list of possible things to say: that everything would be all right, that she wouldn't be hurt, that it had nothing to do with her personally, that the people at the mansion had been part of a larger problem, that it would all make sense to her very soon. Vince wasn't being altogether calculating or insincere: he had told himself the exact same lies for as long now as he could remember.

Finally, after exhausting every other possibility, he shared with her the last and most preposterous explanation of all, the final refuge save insanity in a world of total irrationality:

"None of this is real," he repeated, as much to himself as to the princess, who seemed to be staring hard at empty space in order better not to see it.

She had changed a lot from the media pictures of her, even the ones taken only days or weeks ago. Someone, perhaps Vince himself, had bought a magazine with a picture of her on the front, a supermarket tabloid with a story "celebrating" her triumph over the twin difficulties of bulimia and a childhood lived under constant media scrutiny and the personal and public trials of her royal parents' many infidelities, addictions, compulsions, and criminal acts. The magazine was dated next week and had photographs of the smiling princess joking around with a teen matinee idol at a movie premiere the night before when she had been lying on her side, thumb in her mouth, as Vince himself sponge-bathed the obscene cartoons Io had drawn on her back with a black felt calligraphic marker.

How did they do it? Doubles? A multimedia production acted parallel to "reality" episode by episode? Was such a thing possible? Was it impossible? Wasn't it more probable than not? Didn't people need a myth to live by? Perhaps that was what was recorded in the papers, magazines, TV news shows, movies, numerous exposes—a story more real than reality, a story that gave meaning and order to reality, like the stations of the cross, so to speak, leading to the climax of crucifixion. Vince looked back at the slick magazine tabloid and the carefully staged candid photo of the sexy princess with the stylish belly shirt, long skirt, and platform sandals. Everyone, supposedly, was having their hair done in the bobbed curly style she was sporting in the picture, but which she had long abandoned, even by the night of the multiple murders.

Vince had argued for the scanty clothes she now wore, Io preferring to keep her naked, as he did all the humans in his entourage, save Vince, and when the issue of the toilet inevitably came up, diapered. Although he hadn't been able to talk Io out of the diaper, Vince had wrangled permission to dress the catatonic girl, albeit in the only thing the boy vampire would allow: black and pink lingerie of the most outrageously obvious variety, the style, if not the actual items, that Io himself wore when he was in one of his "Tie me, beat me, humiliate me please, Daddy" moods.

Vince had been trying to protect the girl's dignity, or protect himself from his own shame and guilt, or trying to bring her back to herself, although he could hardly think why any of these reasons, more so the last, could make any difference whatsoever. She might have been wearing anything, or indeed, nothing, as far as she seemed concerned or aware, and Vince was reminded of his earlier comparison of the princess to a mannequin, and now even a corpse, as he dressed or undressed her unresponsive body, manipulating her arms and legs, moving a famous body that she seemed to have vacated entirely, showing no emotion at all, not so much as a flicker of modesty or shame, not even when he changed her diaper.

"None of this is real," Vince had reassured himself, walking through the compound on Long Island, recording every outrage with his digital camera for later download, and it wasn't just a trope; the level of violence he saw could not be real: the theatrically ripped open torsos, the entrails draped over banisters and treadmill arms, a head casually placed out of the way on an upper shelf while someone examined some vintage Civil War miniatures—none of it was believable, not for a single moment.

He was reminded of the first time he had seen Io kill someone. They were in a hotel room in what was probably Nagasaki after a day of desecrating Shinto mountain shrines and perversely ignoring the fact that the second atomic bomb had been detonated here. Io was holding court, as usual, over some arcane topic, how a hair regenerated seemingly from nothing, for example, even when it had been previously plucked out by the root.

They had picked up two pretty Japanese transvestites outside an anime festival, or perhaps they were actual women, at least so one of them claimed, a sister and a brother, although which was which was virtually impossible to determine. Io had set them to playing with each other, interrupting them—and himself—constantly with critiques of their performance: mistimed hair sweeps, awkward fingerings, careless toe positions, a missed opportunity to stare off into the next century, etc. His degrading and frustrating commentary, interspersed with cries of "Cut!" at which point the two comfort creatures were required to stop instantly whatever they were doing, even if doing so defied gravity or other laws of physics, had the pair alternately in tears and practicing greater and greater perversities to please their exacting and forever displeased patron.

"Human sexuality," Io announced, with faux exasperation, "has exhausted itself. Even taboo has become commonplace."

Vince had been snapping digital photos of the girl calling herself Miki, spitting wearily into the face of her sister, a girl calling herself Kimiko, as the latter, her expressionless face covered in silver-blue android makeup, sang to her sister softly while offhandedly dripping carbolic acid from a pipette onto the poor girl's shaved and yet still indeterminate genitals, decorated liberally with hundreds of pins, alternately red-tipped and yellow, simulating a pattern that might have been drawn from one of the great battles of Western military history, Antietam, perhaps. The girl with the pipette, Miki or Kimiko, it was impossible to tell them apart, had the same treatment dealt her by her sister only moments before, the both of them made up to look like androids, the entire effect aimed at confusing one not only as to whether they were girls or boys, but whether they were even human.

"Bring her to me," Io said, making some kind of gesture toward the window in the direction of old Kyoto.

"Which one?" Vince asked, lowering the camera.

Io was talking to one of the others in the room, talking to the darkness in which one of the others was supposedly standing, it seeming impossible that Vince and Io were alone together. He turned back toward Vince, briefly. "Does it really matter? You choose."

Vince crossed the room to where the transvestite playthings sat teasing each other with plastic water guns filled with lighter fluid, and took the one on the left by the arm, Miki or Kimiko, he'd forgotten, quite naturally, which was which. It didn't matter, really, they were both identical: slender bodies, small breasts, doll-like faces, submissive eyes—even the shape of their fingernails were the same. Were they twins, products of plastic surgery, clones, or some new model of mass-produced sex robot?

The girl looked at him with a sad, fearful expression that Vince pretended to ignore but rose without any hesitation, except for the care necessitated by her painful lap of pins and the red areas where the acid had left cankers on her white flesh, and walked, elegantly, heel to toe, to where Io sat. She knelt before the young vampire in a stylized gesture she had peformed many times, no doubt, in front of bishops, cabinet ministers, industrialists, vice presidents, alien dignitaries. Io turned from whatever he was saying to whoever, stroked the long ink-black hair of the slave, and quite casually pulled her head to the side and back and to the left or right and kissed her throat in that special way that when he lifted his blond spiky head his mouth was decorated with a red carnation and the tv girl had a matching flower on her long white throat, only hers was spurting blood.

"Pictures, pictures," Io said, making a camera-clicking motion with his thumb and forefinger, when he saw Vince staring at him slack-jawed. "I'm thinking . . . oh, I don't know . . . a thousand white moths."

Vince had no idea what Io meant by the moths. He

was startled by the blood flowing down the girl's throat, splashing onto the floor, already forming a puddle beneath her still obediently kneeling figure, like a spotlight.

"What are you waiting for, darling?" Io said, looking faux aghast.

"That looks . . . real."

"Look at it through your camera, baby doll. It will look differently through the viewfinder, I'm sure."

And when Vince, with trembling hands, was once again able to bring the camera to his face, it did all look differently. The other tv had crawled over, weeping, apparently with permission, to his or her sister or brother, ordered by Io to provide oral sexual service to the dying sibling, eyes fluttering rapidly, perhaps timed to ventricular fibrillations, body still kneeling, blood puddle having reached, evidently, its mortal limits. Io, meanwhile, was standing behind the scene in low-slung white hip-hugger jeans, purple Komodo dragon skin boots, thin bone-blond torso bare, arms raised in a vaguely priestlike gesture of blessing. He was staring directly at the camera and winking slowly, his mouth still a red hole, as if he'd been shot in the face to no effect.

Someone, perhaps the gray naked vampire who now lay on top of the trembling body of the second tv, feeding off her, while pretending to fuck her ass, his gray bony buttocks bucking, had painted, with the fingers of his left hand, the word "Immortal" using one of the girls' spilled blood across Io's sunken, fashion model's tummy, which, by the way, was unnecessarily decorated with a navel piercing, from which dangled the golden charm of some made-up religion.

Vince circled the tableaux, trying to lose himself in the shoot, pretending to himself that he was concerned with the lighting, which someone else, apparently, had set up with a studiously labored attempt at achieving an amateur look. The gray vampire, whose dead flesh had taken on a telltale purplish tint suggestive of the fresh young blood consumed, had effortlessly yanked the limply dying tv to a semiseated position on his pistoning dead pelvis, so that she could offer oral ministrations to the erection now emerging from Io's white jeans. She placed her painted lips over the golden phallus sheath, which may or may not have contained a genuine erection, the question of whether Io truly possessed a penis or not remaining entirely unanswered.

But the question of whether the dying tv was boy or girl was answered, perhaps, as her mouth went slack and wet with pink spittle, her smooth thighs webbed with blood and urine rivulets, her eyes unfocused and dilated, and with a last shudder, a small white spurting could be detected, spattering the face of his sister or brother, already dead. Although on closer examination, the fluid may just have been drool shaking off the body of the now dead tv, who, covered in alien spittle, was still being vigorously fake-fucked by the sucking vampire, and the whole scene suggested nothing more than utter futility, and no orgasm, anywhere, at all.

"They're dead," Vince said, as the bodies were being posed in a curious parody of God's leaning down from heaven to touch Adam's finger, as painted, of course, by Michelangelo on the ceiling of the Sistine Chapel, although the contact was instead from dead tv whore to dead tv whore, and there was no pretence that either was playing God.

"They're really dead," Vince repeated, for no good reason.

"Not really," Io said.

"But I saw them . . . I see them . . ."

"Blah, blah, blah." Io had removed the gold cock

sleeve. "This was molded from the actual erection of Ivan the Terrible."

It was Io's perfect cool that had Vince off balance, among other things.

"What do you mean, they aren't really dead?"

"Oh, honey, really. You're such a naif. It's a fake. By the way, this scene is officially over. Didn't I say 'Cut'? Oh, goodness, don't tell me film is still running."

Vince looked off to the side where, before the fade to black, some of the vampires were putting the last-minute touches on the bodies, a colored egg in an open palm, a camellia blossom between two slender silver-painted toes.

"That's a wrap, everyone. Let's clear out of here. See you all tomorrow." Io turned back to Vince. "Get a few closing shots and get them downloaded on the Web site by dawn tomorrow."

He air-kissed the gray vampire, covered in gore and scat, passing by toward the bathroom. "Great work, darling." There was a group, huddled ominously, by the wet bar. "Ciao, baby," Io said, ignoring their muttered conspiracies, and gave a glamour-puss wave, or maybe a limp-wristed Hitler salute, to his gallery of imaginary admirers as he exited the apartment holding the leashes of two white Alsatians that he'd only recently acquired.

Vince recalled all of this, but only vaguely, as he attempted to feed the princess the bowl of beef water, now gone cold and all but forgotten, but the spoon he held was empty, and he looked up into the eyes of the girl and for the first time he saw the hint of a presence, not necessarily her, but someone, at least. She looked at him, almost hopefully, although what a silly and inappropriate word that was, and that wasn't the look anyway, but that's the word that would have to do until they invented one for the look a rat has climbing out of the rubble where hundreds of others rats have been crushed, its eyes sharp and glittering, smelling spoiled pork.

She said the words as if she were answering a question on a game show for twenty thousand dollars and it had been fixed from the beginning that she'd win on this very question, and the only thing left to do was to deliver the line convincingly, as if she wasn't sure, even though she was perfectly certain all along.

"None of this," she said, waiting for the clock to wind down, the way she might have practiced it a hundred times before a mirror, as the audience sat at the edge of their seats, "none of this is real."

And the studio audience, as it always did, everywhere, went wild right on cue.

"Something's up," Mahoney said, dropping three sugar cubes, slowly, one after another, one for each syllable, into a cup of jasmine mint green tea, and watched as they sat at the bottom of the cup, not dissolving, in the already cold, pink water. He was talking to the bare-chested man with the gray snap-brim hat, the one on the right, who had taken a break to stretch his shoulders and crack his knuckles.

Mahoney was smoking a cigarette, but only so that he could put it out on the raw, quarter-sized wounds that ran up the bound arms of the nude informant bucking in the chair.

"He may be telling the truth," the man in the snap-brim said.

Mahoney picked up an ashtray filled with bloody toenails and stared at it for a moment, as if trying to remember what it was. He put them down, disinterestedly.

The man in the snap-brim shrugged. "He really doesn't seem to know anything."

Mahoney nodded, but at a conversation he was re-playing in his mind. "That may be true," he answered, eventually. "But that doesn't mean he can't tell us what we want to know."

The informant was moaning, but whether he was only acting or they had managed to push him past his limits to some new, truly authentic region of sensation, it was difficult to say, which is what made dealing with professional informants, nearly all of them accomplished masochists, virtually impossible, especially when time was of the essence, as it seemed to be now.

"Shoot him again," Mahoney said.

"He's already had five hundred ccs over the lethal limit."

"Are you a calibrated talking test tube? Are you an Inquisition-era PDR?"

The other man, also wearing a snap-brim, also bare-chested, didn't stop, even for a moment, during all this, but continued to sew live cockroaches into slits made in the informant's thighs.

"Just a little thing I do," he said, looking somewhat embarrassed when he saw Mahoney watching.

His name was Green and his partner's name was Blue, or at least that was what Mahoney called them, although he generally didn't call them anything, but spoke to both at once, or either of them, it was the same thing, or, at least, it didn't seem to make any difference. They were professional torturers, nameless, faceless, emotionless, pointless, all they did was cause pain. They knew, of course, the informant in the chair, a fellow professional in the pain game, they were all old acquaintants, and that left Mahoney feeling the odd man out, and a bit pissed off, suspecting that a lot of the in-references and shorthand talk could easily be going straight over his head.

"He may not be able to take it," Green said, preparing the hyperdermic.

"That's less of a concern to me than you might imagine. Fuck professional courtesy. I want him to tell the truth if it kills him."

Mahoney came forward, leaned over, his hands on the raw wrists of the informant, who stiffened, screamed, and wet himself again, but whether it was due to the debilitating pressure Mahoney applied to the ganglia on the insides of the man's elbows, where the commando had slid his hands, or the needle that Mr. Blue jammed into his neck, it was impossible to tell, and didn't matter.

Either way, Mahoney kissed him, full on his lying mouth, and did something he didn't even want to think about, something irrevocable, with his left hand. There was another bloodcurdling scream, the usual obscenities, and a snatch of prayer or old lullaby that might have been sung by someone's grandmother. Mahoney stood up, grinning, as if it were all going exactly as planned, and the informant, after vomiting noisily, fixed the commando with staring eyes that looked terrified, although they were not, but only seemed that way, as the lids had been removed some time before.

"Does anyone," Mahoney asked no one in particular, "does anyone have the slightest idea where my goddamn cigarette is?"

There was no answer and Mahoney picked up an ice pick that lay at his feet, looking at the tip speculatively.

"Ah," he said, "I just thought of something."

On and on and on it went just like this; after all, that was torture. At one point the informant, having lost his teeth, said something that sounded like the word "goulashes."

Mahoney, who hadn't been paying particularly close attention, asked what the man had said.

"Sounds like goulashes," Mr. Blue—or Mr. Green—had said.

"The things you put on your feet or the Hungarian stew?"

"Either."

"What does that mean?"

"It's his safe-word."

"Ignore it," Mahoney said, waving a hand in front of his face as if brushing something away. "Proceed."

The informant began giving up information indiscriminately, emptying out the memory banks, bartering anything he knew for a few moments of pain relief. This, Mahoney thought, or would have time to think later, sitting in an armchair and pausing from an issue of *Modern Railroading*, was what torture was all about. The informant told him about secret arms sales in Portugal, election fixes in California, a counterfeiting plot that could bring down the Israeli economy, congressional sexual secrets, and the location of several rogue nuclear devices. Mahoney yawned, theatrically checked his fingernails, and then really found something of interest there. When he looked up again, this is what he saw:

Half of the man's lower bowel had been coaxed through a small incision below his navel, the tube looking blue and red, something like a raw turkey neck, and tied off in several places with copper wire to cause blinding cramps. The nipples, by now, had been cut away, and the scalp peeled back, like sod, the skull exposed and ghostly. Electricity, of course, was also involved. There was the usual incongruous object shoved up the rectum; it wasn't even necessary to inquire, but Mahoney had, only because he was thorough, and he didn't remember what it was, but he remembered thinking, admiringly,

Oh, that can't be possible. The genitals were gone, long gone, although Mahoney would be damned if he remembered what had happened to them, some adaptation of an old American Indian ordeal, he supposed, as much of this routine was. He saw the informant's balls lying around somewhere, that much he knew, but then he became involved in other matters. It was simply impossible to stay on top of everything.

The informer's babbling was so intense, so intermittent, so unremittingly hysterical that Mahoney, in exasperation, ordered the man's tongue removed, and, as an added precaution, his throat cut. A short holler followed, some strangled gurglings, a blessed silence.

"Is he dead?" Mahoney asked, after a period of time passed that seemed excessive, even allowing for a miracle.

"No."

"Well, I guess that would defeat the purpose of torture, wouldn't it?"

"Yes. In every case I've been connected with."

"Will he survive?"

"My professional opinion?"

"What else?"

"No."

"Mr. Blue?"

Mr. Blue looked up from some unnecessary work with the spinal column. "Yes?"

"Same question."

"I concur with Mr. Green."

"Okay then. Begin to help him, but as ineptly as possible."

"Will do."

A subordinate of Mahoney had stepped into the interrogation room at some point, perhaps when they were injecting the informant's breasts with a special jelly of mosquito larvae and napalm, and now he came forward, lighting the fresh cigarette his master put between his lips. It was an act that had more than vague sexual undertones, especially the way it was done, but then didn't everything? Mahoney was trying to remember who the kid was, if he had fucked him or not, if he even belonged here, but he was coming up blank, which didn't surprise him, as lately everyone under fifty looked more or less the same. Whoever the kid was he asked the same question, patiently, six times. He had, Mahoney thought, potential.

"What now?" the kid said a seventh time.

"Start killing."

"Who?"

"How should I know? It doesn't matter. Anyone."

"You mean . . . indiscriminately?"

"It's crazy time."

There is no such thing as a typical day to Nikka. Each of them is atypical, and they are all, every last one of them, exactly the same.

At 0800 hours Nikka turns to the left, pauses, holding the pose for a photograph, but there is no photographer, nor anyone watching, no one she knows about anyway, although she imagines them watching. At 1523, she lays a frozen tulip against her cheek in the manner of a woman remembering a lost lover, although her mind is perfectly blank. At 0545, she listens to a real-time audio feed of a hundred thousand cheering a public appearance she may or may not have actually attended. At 2230 she says something that is not said to be heard but to be conveyed in the way her lips don't move at all and she maintains a perfect silence. At 0400 she imagines herself sitting in a platinum room about to push forward a black crystal checker, and then changing her mind.

What she has eaten today: nothing.

Total estimated caloric expenditure: 0.

She is visited by a "Colonel" Branch in an old Prague courthouse that has also served, perhaps relevantly, as a drug clinic, community outreach program, foster home, avante-garde theater, and now accommodates the administrative offices of a bureacratic entity that officially monitors bureaucratic entities, including itself. The meeting lasts less than six minutes and the colonel leaves visibly shaken, alternately consulting his watch and scanning the sky.

A man, provisionally identified as a doctor, arrives at the make-believe ranch of a supposedly disgraced televangelist, where Nikka is rumored to be in seclusion, carrying a heavy black box that may contain either enough weapon-grade plutonium to destroy California, the last supply of antibiotic for a new strain of cannibal plague, or a complete and fully functional human vulva. There is no record of the meeting ever beginning or ending, and there is some question as to whether Nikka is even at the ranch or not, although it is quite clear that everyone, including Nikka, believes that she is present.

They are followed, in different locales, by various meteorologists, astrologers, quantum physicists, hypnotists, alchemists, geneticists, crisis management specialists, anatomists, and advertising executives.

The colonel will be found four days from now in a black Ford Focus in front of a canal in Norway, a gunshot wound in each temple, and a hose running from the exhaust into the right rear passenger window. His death will be ruled a suicide, although not without the appropriate rumors of cover-up and murder at the hands of certain "dark elements behind the scenes of socialist progressive politics."

It is uncertain what fate befalls the supposed doctor, but even now six black sedans are racing up a mountain road in Virginia to his "weekend getaway." Within minutes the door to his study will be reduced to splinters and a SWAT team will race into the room where he sits at a computer viewing an illegal Internet site. Documents have already been distributed to reporters from the *Ottawa News Sentinel*, the *San Diego Union Tribune*, and the *Minneapolis Star*, and the next day the headlines will reveal the shocking revelations that may or may not be behind his sudden and mysterious disappearance. Already, all over the country, people chosen especially for their tangential and, in some cases, nonexistent connection with him, are practicing the lines "He seemed to be a nice guy. He kept to himself, mostly."

The limousine stops at Broadway and Forty-seventh and Nikka, who is standing on a concrete island between the north- and south-flowing traffic, is looking up at the electric ticker tape that reports that Microsoft is up two and five-eighths, seventeen anarchists have been hung in Malaysia, and a cure for pancreatic cancer is still considered years—if not decades—away.

Off to the left, there is a film crew recording the entire scene, which is being broadcast simultaneously to the big screen on the building towering overhead, the same building they drop the ball from every New Year's Eve, and passersby are looking up at the screen and seeing Nikka with the backdrop of a neon-lit Broadway behind her, the very street they are all standing on this very moment, but no one seems to realize this is all taking place right now.

And Nikka herself seems absorbed in the broadcast image of herself, as she stands on the street many floors below, and looks at herself looking at herself, and she makes no move to move, because she is quite content to see what she does next, knowing that if she does it herself, it will only spoil the surprise, and, besides, anything on a screen is more real than anything she can do, anyhow.

Exhibit 73MEL93C was not catalogued; it was not on any museum guide, nor was it ever seen, or meant to be. It had been housed in the Smithsonian Museum of Natural History decades before a Smithsonian Museum of Natural History even existed, although the exhibit was planned, and the eventual museum planned around it. A self-contained, specially fortified underground bunker was built to house this particular exhibit deep under the site above which the museum, like the great tomb of events that it is, would later be erected, seemingly for entirely other purposes, and which visitors would stream to by the thousands, every day.

Caleb arrived in D.C. ostensibly to speak to a secret convocation of cabinet ministers but knowing that, in reality, he was keeping an appointment that was made, if not by him, then by whatever causes two cars to collide on the interstate at such and such a time, or a child to be born now instead of later, or anything at all to happen when it does, a pencil needing sharpening, for instance. It was an appointment that existed at the moment of existence itself, which is to say, forever, and there was no way that Caleb could have avoided it even if he tried, which, in many ways, he had.

He spent some pointless hours in the museum above, strolling through the exhibit rooms, spending some extra time at an exhibit of recently collected Sumerian artifacts, reading the cuneiform on broken stone tablets, lists of forgotten kings he remembered, grain sales and reports of battles, the minutae of human life, the news not a lot different four thousand or so years ago than it was in the *New York Times* he read on the nonstop flight from Rotterdam that morning. A few new sections of the old Gilgamesh epic were on display, although they weren't new at all, but had been in various private collections for the past two thousand four hundred years, and even now the originals weren't on display, but corrupted copies that recorded an interpolated text that intentionally omitted the truly shocking passages that would save, or at least alert, humankind altogether.

Caleb listened idly, almost without contempt, to a pedantic older man put forth various statements of learned nonsense for the ostensible education of two college-age girls from the University of New Mexico and then looked at an exhibit supposedly explaining evolution for as long as he could stand it, which, more or less, carried him up to the hour of his appointment.

The Overseer was not hidden in the museum; it didn't need to be. Dwelling among countless broken pottery shards, shreds of cloth, rotted ax-thongs, lapis lazuli buttons, mosaic squares, and ladle handles, it was simply lost. The oldest museum curator working steadily day and night through the entire course of the longest human life could not work his or her way through all that was collected here to find the way to the door of its chamber. And so the bric-a-brac of the human millennia kept secret one of the great secrets of the race of those who'd been here first of all—and who knew everything that would happen from here on to the finish.

What did it mean to say the Overseer was old, when Caleb himself was bornless, when there was never a time that he didn't exist, or at least, none that he could remember, or anyone could tell him of? And yet there was something about the Overseer that went beyond, although it may well have been that it could see so far into the future that it seemed so much older than Caleb, rather than that it had seen any more of the past.

It was in a wheelchair, not because it couldn't move without it, but primarily because it had no legs or other visible means of locomotion. It watched him from behind a vid shield because it had no eyes and an elaborate transistor system fed it audio to compensate for the lack of organic ears. There was no mouth, obviously, nor any head, not even a body on which a head would rest. What was actually there, how much was really left, after all the years had taken away in return for expanding vision, was unclear, but whatever its unsettling appearance, it shielded the visitor from the even more unsettling shock that one was probably not talking to much of anything at all. Caleb was reminded of a wind that blew ripples across a still lake, smoke that took a momentary shape, tape recorders playing in empty rooms.

"Caleb Darr," the Overseer said, in a language it was impossible to identify, but which was undoubtably illegal. "One cannot drop two toothpicks lately without them spelling out your name."

"You expected me, of course."

"To the second."

"Sorry to be so predictable."

"I knew you would require me to laugh right now," the Overseer said, "so I will do so."

It laughed the way one would expect it to, and stopped neither too soon nor too late, according to how it should be, and how much time in eternity was allowed for such a laugh. The overall impression was one of the cosmos laughing back, as if it could care.

Caleb was determined not to give it cause to laugh again. "You know then, also, why I am here?"

"Do you?"

Caleb was caught up in spite of himself. He might have thought he knew why he'd come, but the truth was he didn't, not really, and that was why he was here.

"There is a problem . . . with one of the Citizens. He's not behaving and he's not doing it in a rather alarmingly extravagant manner."

"The veil, in other words, has been rent."

"Yes," Caleb said, finding it curious that the Overseer had used the same phrase that Father Xeno had used. The coincidence tickled at meaning, but left Caleb unsatisfied, despite his probings, and he realized it was only a temptation, ultimately; for the coincidence, as everything else, meant absolutely nothing. "His name is, apparently, Io."

"He's out of control, this Io," the Overseer said, but, as with any fortune-teller, it was impossible to tell whether this was said as a statement or an open-ended question to elicit more information. There had to be more to it in this case, Caleb thought, or perhaps it was just a habit, or the way these things had to be phrased, or protocol, or tradition. The alternative was unthinkable. "I've seen him."

"What does he look like?"

"A boy like the moon. Cold and barren and with no atmosphere. He has a mouth full of blood and a laugh like a human being's if a human being could laugh like one of us."

What the Overseer said next was both not memorable and totally irrelevant: a series of nonsense words and random phrases, place-names, colors, sounds, numbers, sports scores, bits of poetry and film dialogue, song lyrics, and stock quotes, followed by a disembodied shout of "heads" seven times in a row before a shout of "tails." Caleb paid attention in an intentionally distracted way on the off chance that out of the scattershot some fragment of insight might hit the mark either now or much later.

"Thank you," he said, politely, by way of acknowledgment, and to alleviate the awkwardness of the moment.

The Overseer nodded, or communicated an intent to nod, if it had been possible, physically, to nod. "What is your business with this boy?"

Caleb understood perfectly well that this question, indeed the whole conversation, was unnecessary. The Overseer knew exactly what was going to be said, and had known, from before there were words to say it. And yet the conversation was indispensible; it would only have been immature not to play along, or to question the rules of the game, which were not merely arbitrary, but calculated to be as tedious as possible. One might as well have asked the question, Why do we exist at all?

"I was hoping you could tell me that."

"You must start with what you know."

"I am meant to kill him."

"No doubt."

"But why?"

"Curious it is," the Overseer said, "that it's never enough that one's future is known, but the actor wants to know why it must be the way it must be. That is a job for philosophers, Caleb, and not oracles."

"What I want to know—"

The Overseer spouted another series of numbers, words, and odds ratios, almost all of them without reference to anything, and this lasted nearly three minutes. A moment later there was silence, which neither broke, until the Overseer broke it.

"Let me see your hand."

Caleb found the request foolish, superficial, but he held out his hand.

"Your left hand," the Overseer said.

And Caleb, realizing that he'd been asked this already, but hadn't been paying close enough attention, pulled back the left hand he already held out and put out his right, embarrassed at the parlor game antics. The Overseer grasped Caleb's wrist in a kind of polymer pincer internally heated by a blue dye, and held his arm steady, the grip inescapable, and Caleb knew that in an instant, any instant, he could lose the hand at the wrist.

"I see a woman," the Overseer said, in an almost accusatory fashion. "A rose by any other name . . . Who is she?"

There was nothing to see in Caleb's palm, smooth and entirely unlined as it was, except for a pair of deeply grooved lines on his left hand, running perpendicular to each other, and suggesting the number seven. But the Overseer wasn't looking at that hand, nor would he ever. He was looking at Caleb's blank hand, a hand that might have been holding salt.

"There is no woman," Caleb said, "and there hasn't been for . . . decades."

"Are you sure?" the Overseer said, sounding mechanically disappointed, or was it satire? but not because its intuition could possibly, under any circumstances, have been wrong.

"I'm certain," Caleb said, aware that everything he said could and would be used against him, and that he was being set up, in a roundabout way, which he couldn't see, or avoid, to contradict himself, but to what purpose he didn't know. "There is no woman."

"She is looking for you. I can feel her eyes on you and even though she can't find you, she still sees you, and that's why I can."

"Who is she?" Caleb asked, beginning to feel slightly interested, as he perceived that what the Overseer said now might end up being slightly relevant to his original question, whatever that was. He couldn't, in spite of himself, keep Nikka sneaking, like an assassin, into his consciousness.

"We're sorry but there are no results for your search." The Overseer's response was formatted, disinterested, but unfailingly polite. "Please check your spelling and syntax and try again."

Caleb sighed. "What is she?"

"She is not your destiny, Caleb, but a turning point, a signpost on the road."

"Where is she?"

"Wherever love is . . . and that is nowhere, as you know. La-di-da."

"When?"

"Within the next two moons."

"How then?"

"By design, by trial, by death."

"Whose?"

"One death will drain and one death will sustain."

"The girl in the square," Caleb said to himself, but also out loud, displacing himself to that moment in which the girl holding the sketch pad stood forever, sketching him, when he wasn't aware of her.

He had spoken to her, briefly, unimportantly, and he had pretended to fuck her, yes, he was remembering it all now, and it seemed he hadn't killed her, but killed someone else instead. It was one of those moments repeated thousands of times throughout the millennia, forgotten just like all the others, except this time, apparently, it was important, or more important than usual, which wasn't saying much.

The Overseer let go his wrist, but Caleb hadn't noticed, at least not right away, but stood there, for the time being, staring into his own empty palm, as if looking at nothing there.

"I am to find her."

"You will find each other."

"Will she lead me to Io?"

A series of dice rolls, blackjack hands, roullette wheel results followed as the Overseer channeled the activities of a casino. Someone hit a slot jackpot: all cherries. "What's about him is what's about her, only in reverse, and compounded. You have no question."

Caleb was trying to untangle the meaning of that riddle, knowing it was hopeless, and that it was just as impossible to argue that he did, indeed, have a question, many questions, when the Overseer interrupted his thoughts by saying, "There is a book in which it is written."

"In which what is written?"

"There is a book."

"What is this book?"

"*The Book of the Apocalypse Five.*"

"I've never heard of it."

"No one has except those who have. It is written there who this Io is supposed to be and what he is supposed to do. You will find this book and know the course to take. If not, then not."

"Is it my role to be successful?"

"I can't tell you that."

"You can't or you won't?"

"I won't and I can't. You know the answer to that."

"Is it that you don't want to affect the outcome?"

"The outcome has already come. There is no altering it."

Caleb nodded in a fatalistic manner. "I suppose if we didn't play our parts the tragedy wouldn't come to its rightful conclusion."

"No, it would conclude exactly as it has one way or another. It may be that all have already refused to play their parts and this is how it ends. But I doubt that. What is the difference between playing your part and not playing it when not playing your part may be playing it?"

Caleb was fighting hard to resist the obvious question, which was to ask why do this or that, why proceed at all if everything was to be exactly as it was already? which happened to be a truth that, like most truths, he didn't doubt, and like most truths, he didn't like to be reminded of, as if he could forget, which he could, by not paying very close attention. Still he couldn't resist stating the bitter conclusion he had come to so long ago that it seemed as much a part of his world as killing did, or requesting extra wasabi for his eel rolls, which he left, naturally, uneaten.

"I suppose it's something to do."

Either the Overseer lost interest, or had been turned off, or simply had no more to say, but Caleb was aware of being alone in the cramped and cluttered room, or, more accurately, marginally more alone than he was before. Behind the vid mask, the sensors, LCD displays, and artificial limbs, there was the silence and stillness of total void, and the certainty that one was in the presense of no one, nothing, only inanimate objects.

Caleb traveled back the way he had come, through small hallways and large, taking elevators and escalators, passing through carelessly marked, but not intentionally so, rooms and hallways, down, or up, a staircase or two, and headed purposefully across the grand rotunda, through crowds still waiting to view an Etruscan sandal buckle or a fragment of a Viking Hnefatafl board, and out into the street, where it was raining again, in spite of the forecast, or because of it.

Caleb hadn't been distracted by all the dialectic

misdirection. He realized, naturally, that the question he had come to ask, the only question he'd wanted answered, had gone unanswered, but even if it had been answered somehow, it had been answered with a dozen new questions he hadn't asked and couldn't answer, a dozen new questions he should have asked instead, or meant to ask, and even if he had, would not have been answered any more than the question he did ask.

Goddammit. In this way madness lay.

That was the way it was with oracles, Caleb reflected: if they served any purpose at all, which was doubtful, it was the paradoxical one of not answering questions at all, but asking them, which only went to show that however little you knew you knew a lot less than you thought, and however tangled things appeared, they were even more hopelessly complicated than you could have imagined. The only thing an oracle predicted was just how unpredictable things were.

There was a car waiting for him in the fire zone, and a driver, and without needing to give instructions, Caleb was being sped away to the airport, waved on, by police officers instructed to give VIP clearance to his car, around a group of protestors who had assembled on the mall lawn, and who, Caleb noted in passing, had been manipulated into protesting, for no apparent reason, something or other that had to do with Nikka VII.

It was downtime for Mahoney, who was performing a kind of autopsy on a cormorant in a basement outfitted for exactly this hobby. On shelves that lined the concrete walls were jars of various sizes filled with milky liquid in which floated various animals that colleagues, associates, and admirers had sent him from around the world: gibbons, skinks, perch, wombats, marmot, tube fish, ibis—it was the variety and not the rarity of the specimens that counted, and Mahoney appreciated a fine gray squirrel as much as a deep-sea angler.

He was extracting some fluid out of the adrenal glands of the dead bird opened on the table before him with the intention of adding it to an already prepared infusion containing the sexual fluids of various species, including a bull python, if such a fluid existed in the anterior region of the snake from which he had drawn it. The general idea, which was so preposterous that Mahoney never formulated it in so many words, not even to himself, was that he was searching for the cure for death.

Such a motivation was, most likely, a remnant of a fantastical boyhood idealism that combined a love of biology and an obsession with killing small animals. At the time his goal was, more or less, explicit and the twelve-year-old Mahoney worked with a simpleminded passion to formulate just the right cocktail that, injected into a dead sparrow or a neighbor's poisoned dog, might rekindle the spark of life he had willfully snuffed out. Always, in the back of young Mahoney's mind, was the resurrection of a neighborhood girl found in the dark corner of someone's garage blocks away, raped and strangled, among some sacks of fertilizer, or so the rumors were, which Mahoney had heard, standing outside rooms where his parents spoke in whispers about the visits from the police.

Now, however, he had put away such childish fantasies and his home laboratory autopsies were simply a relaxing pastime, like stamp collecting or painting birdhouses, and meant no more than an hour or two spent in solitary joy, and nothing else.

He removed a kidney, or what, touching the tip of his tongue to it, tasted like a kidney, and thought back to the interrogation that afternoon. It was the seventh he had presided over in the last three days. And yet for all the explosive revelations of Vatican sexual crimes, trilateral commission conspiracies, and alien abduction cover-ups that had spilled from the bloodied mouths of babbling informers, Mahoney hadn't heard so much as a whisper of what he was really looking after.

Someone, somewhere, was planning something.

Mahoney knew it.

He shook some heart tissue until it dissolved in a test tube, filled a long hypodermic, and then realized he didn't have a lemur.

He could sense someone out there, sneaking, plotting, ready to strike. It was someone close, as it always was, someone you didn't expect, and yet, when after it happened, in retrospect, it figured all along. It was someone trusted, it had to be, no one else could get close enough, and that meant someone had been paid their thirty pieces of silver, someone was about to betray them with a kiss.

And Mahoney, contemplating making a paste of sea horse ovaries and a large red centipede, stopped for a moment slicing thin slices of cormorant eye, and considered, not for the first time, that the person he was looking for was, of course, himself.

"Are we all in agreement?" The question hung in the airless chamber, the temperature well below absolute zero, of a bunker that might have been buried miles below the surface of either the north or the south pole of the moon Endymion, or located in an extra-dimensional spacecraft of some advanced technology, orbiting a planet like Uranus, or even Pluto.

"I believe the situation is clear," came an answer,

finally, although it hadn't really answered anything, nor had it been meant to.

"The veil has been torn," offered a third.

"But must we take action?" added a fourth.

There were some murmurs of general approval or disapproval, of unrelated consultations, of allies taking sides, of general disquiet. Perhaps, however, in the end, it was only the hum of the mainframe backing up image files, or maybe just a meaningless fan turning on or off, according to some preset schedule.

"Something must be done."

"There are problems," said the chairman, who had been silent up to that moment, or not present, it was difficult to determine, "that cannot be ignored."

"Energy is escaping . . . without sanction."

"Wasteful, wasteful."

"Something must be done," said the same voice as before, echoing itself, as usual.

"And I think we all know what it is," the chairman interjected. There was a brief patter of applause, which, naturally, wasn't really applause at all, but an acknowledgment of a shudder of collective memory that passed through the filter of their mass intelligence. "The end of an age is upon us."

"Do we have an agent in place?"

"Naturally."

"Activate him."

"There will be repercussions."

"There always are. . . ."

"True."

". . . but the status quo must be preserved."

"A balance must be restored."

"Order."

"Average."

"Peace."

"Harmony."

"Mutuality."

"Et cetera."

The humming began again. Calculations were being made. The vote was cast. In the end, as always, the decision was unanimous, and preordained, as it must be, in accordance with omniscience.

"Ms. Haskins," the chairman called, to no one, and no one answered. It was understood, however, that a woman, mid-twenties, attractive, dressed immaculately in a tailored suit and pumps, professionally styled hair, understated makeup and earrings, had entered the room. She stood there, with a notepad and pen, even though, if she really had entered this vacuum, every atom in her body would have immediately exploded. "Have the tape of this session brought to whoever and acted out as usual."

"Yes, sir."

The appropriate beat of silence was allowed, as exact as if in an old song, which this all was, in a way. Then the chairman spoke again, at seemingly the penultimate moment.

"And, Ms. Haskins . . ."

"Yes, sir."

"Have it done to the letter."

"Yes, sir."

The footsteps continued to recede into eternity, or, at least, into silence.

The room was empty again, as it had been before, as not only the girl Friday didn't exist, but neither did separate identities for those who spoke, nor even one identity. What spoke here, as close as could be determined, was a simple intelligence, which was located one place and every place and no place, the kind of illogical phenomenon that at one time had just as illogically been conceptualized, in error, as something called, in all seriousness, God.

"It's not horrible enough," Vince muttered to himself, looking at the horrible image on the computer screen, a triple or quadruple murder scene, it was difficult to tell from what was left of the loose assemblage of largely dismembered and disfigured bodies. He added more blood here, a head from someplace else, a sprawl of glistening viscera. He was trying to match the subtleties of the hideous disemboweling one teenage girl had suffered with the expression on another face without, of course, the usual unintentional comic effect, but this was difficult, especially using one of the earlier versions of Photoshop, which he was often forced to do, in a pinch.

They were moving so quickly now it was often difficult to access fully equipped computers, and Vince was still enough of an artist that the slapdash work he was sometimes forced to upload really bothered him. He had a reputation, of sorts, to defend and, quite frankly, some of the work he had produced lately looked like nothing more than crude slash retouches using a standard Microsoft paint program.

He protested along these lines to Io, who seemed blithely unconcerned, as usual, about any distinctions between reality and fantasy, but theorized, perversely, that the more unreal things became, the more one could get away with in reality.

The idea, as far as Vince could make sense of it, if indeed it made any sense, was that the criminal images Vince was producing could be used to expand consciousness, or, at the very least, get viewers to accept that such images as they saw on their computer were now a part of their reality, and to act accordingly.

The desired result: to make real whatever Io, in his hermetic madness, could imagine.

Whatever Io's insane theories, or rationalizations, one thing was clear: the hit counter for Vince's Nekrotika Web site was rolling over like the odometer of an old Buick Riviera traveling at the speed of light. It was no longer, as Io had instructed, a pay site, but that alone couldn't account for its sudden surge in popularity. The new images that Vince was working on were being uploaded daily, the site undergoing updates as often as three or four times a day, and it was never down, earlier versions being hosted on a worldwide network of servers and cross-linked to everything from the national ASPCA Web site to www.deciduoustrees.com.

Anyone, anywhere could open up an e-mail from their boyfriend, let's say, or the guy in finance on the sixteenth floor, and find themselves staring at the corpses of three naked Maui cuties pierced with poisoned arrows above a salacious line of copy. Internet watchdog groups, censors, mind-control experts, not to mention local, state, and national police departments from all over the world, were going crazy, trying to stop what was happening, but it was proving more difficult than they could have imagined: Vince had released, almost in good conscience, what was turning out to be an uber-virus. No, not merely an uber-virus, Vince thought, as he hit a sequence of keys sending a photo shoot depicting the nail-gun slaughter of a roomful of Burmese ninth graders into cyber-space, but a veritable plague.

And yet, in spite of it all, Vince considered himself a crusader, of sorts, in the struggle to liberate from the imagination humanity's darkest and most repressed images and imaginings. He was a warrior for the right to express anything, no matter how terrible, for to his way of thinking, the most essential right a human being could—and should—possess was a license to total freedom of imaginative expression. The one thing left to say, the only thing worth saying, was what no one dared to say.

What the images he prepared forced those who looked at them to acknowledge, if they hadn't already, was the bloodthirsty voyeurism of their own essential natures. He was an artist, or so he rationalized, in the true sense of the word, a mediator between man and taboo, and although he was well aware that the majority of those who visited his site did so only for sexual titillation and that, by and large, they were severely dysfunctional, and that those who saw his images by accident were genuinely shocked and disgusted, he was also aware of some kind of higher calling. What that higher calling might be, he had no idea, but the fact that Io seemed undeniably its embodiment terrified him, and drove him to constant thoughts of suicide.

He had no doubts, however, that what he was doing was significant. That his intuition was correct could be seen in the frantic efforts of the authorities who were trying to track them down through cyberspace with the aim of destroying Nekrotika, as they did, always, to pornography everywhere, putting the lie to the propaganda that it was "only" pornography, or the associate lies that it promoted violence or abuse, or corrupted minors. It was true, a site like Nekrotika did all these things and more, but that's not why the law wanted to stamp them out: the real reason was they signaled the ultimate form of total revolt.

Vince stared at an image he'd been working on for days, a shot of a girl brutally savaged by dogs after an overdose she had taken in a Smyrna hostel. He slumped back in his chair, sipping Jolt, and stared numbly at the small screen of the pirated laptop he'd been forced to utilize.

He wondered if this was how Degas felt, or Caravaggio, or Kandinsky, as he stared at the almost prepubescent body, placing the blinking grid of his cursor over her mons and manipulated pixels trying to determine the most effective way to depict the obligatory hemhorrage even as he fretted over the postmortem skin tone of someone suffering a Rohypnol overdose.

Whether the scene was real or not, whether the subject he now worked with had actually been killed, or whether the material was faked—it had long since ceased to be an issue at moments like this, if it had ever really been an issue to someone like Vince in the first place. All of it, every last bit of what he did now, had been reduced to little more than a series of technical problems. He might have been depicting a plate of Jerusalem oranges, or a pond full of water lillies.

Vince felt a hand, like a dead animal, resting on his shoulder.

"Let's go," the voice said, sounding even deader than the hand felt, slightly annoyed, but more bewildered than anything else, as if the speaker had just woken up from a heavy sleep. "The master wants a bedtime story."

It wasn't, or at least it no longer seemed, a particularly unusual request. Io wanted to rest; he never slept, but he needed to disengage for a few hours from consciousness, and it seemed that Vince's "stories" helped ease the young lord's frenetic mind.

Vince saved his work, backed it up to disk, and shut down the password-protected computer. If he didn't, one of the vampires would be up all night playing Slingo or trying to download compilation CDs from a spin-off of Napster at the risk of wiping out all his video files. It had happened before. He rose and followed the dead man, he thought it might be the one they all called Gear, down the backstage hall of the theater they had commandeered, a dingy little place that used to be a discount meat market in a black and Hispanic neighborhood, but was now being used to revive the plays of the Dadaist Alfred Jarry.

Io had turned the prop room into a makeshift bedroom and Vince sat on a fake tree stump while the blond vampire, wearing a see-through red teddy and improbable stilleto mules, stretched langorously in a papier-mâché bathtub filled with shredded paper alongside the brown corpse of a pretty Mexican girl, which Vince was trying not to look at directly, hoping against hope that she had been heavily drugged, or merely instructed to play dead. How was it, Vince wondered, as he began that night's offering, that the fairy tales he told Io, no matter how horrible or obscene, always turned out to come true?

June 8, but it could just as well be any night, one of those warm nights, but not too warm, when crickets sing, and it's very nearly summer. Mom goes to the back door. She's been washing dishes in the kitchen after an early season barbecue, burgers, and whatnot, and suddenly she realizes that it's late, but that's not quite it, not what causes her to stop washing dishes and go to the back door; that realization comes a moment later. What really makes her stop, grow concerned, is something of which she's not consciously aware, a sense, maybe, a premonition, the silence of her son's basketball not bouncing. She stands at the kitchen door, a screen door, with two moths clinging to it, and peers out into the almost dark, wet hands wrapped in a dish towel, and calls out, "Ron?"

At the side of the house, in the driveway where the garage is open and where the pole holding the backboard and rim stands, Ron lies on his back, his body perforated with forty-five knife wounds, one leg bent back against the knee joint, spectacularly broken. His tongue has been cut out at the root, which, later, will seem entirely unnecessary, at least to have assured his silence, as it will be determined that he was already dead when this occurred.

"Ron?" his mother says again, her tone an octave higher, the question already taking on an epistemological tone, as if she might be asking, without knowing just how appropriate, does a son of mine named Ron exist or not?

At 8:00 P.M. in the suburbs, early summer, few people think of violent home invasions and ritualistic mass murder, and so doors, generally, are not locked for the night, and while nine black-clad figures with white, expressionless plastic masks enter the split-level house through the open garage outside of which the dead seventeen-year-old lies gaping at the stars, six others shoulder through the kitchen door. Mom staggers back, thrown off balance, and lands on her ass, which she has always thought too fat, and it's unclear, even to her, whether she realizes that she's already been shot fifteen times after hearing a sound like the sound of fifteen Coke bottles opening. She knows, by now, however, that everyone will soon be dead, even if they aren't dead already, and this gives her a kind of comfort, as if she weren't leaving anything undone. Her breasts, which she has always considered both small and sagging, have been bared, and before she loses consciousness, she notes how they are being handled now feels remarkably similar to a breast exam, except that they are being cut off.

Dad, as oblivious to disaster as any TV sitcom dad, is stretched out on the living room rug playing a matching game using animal cards with his four-year-old daughter, Julie. He's losing, badly, but he's also not paying attention, his mind divided three or four ways, but mostly preoccupied with that X-rated snuff Web site he linked to, more or less by accident, late the previous night while having cyber-sex with some transvestite in Santa Monica. He plans to return to the site later, in peace, when everyone else is asleep. For the third time he's failed to match the white rhino card and he's actually beginning to get annoyed when the black-pajamed figures with the expressionless white masks enter the room, pouring in from the kitchen and up the stairs from the floor below.

He manages to croak out the words "what" and "fuck" but it's so obviously too late, and he's in such a state of total shock, he barely rises to his elbow. His wife is being dragged from the kitchen, clearly dead, beyond dead, mutilated. She is being lifted, for some arcane and unthinkable reason, onto the dining room table. Somehow he is not surprised to see the blood all over the carpet beneath him, all over the cards of the animal-matching game in progress, or to feel the blows against his body, which he doesn't seem to be able to evade, or even try to evade, as they have completely overwhelmed him. He's lost sight of the four-year-old, but knows she is dead, knows, for instance, that the glistening burst of blood and bone fragments on the wall is all that's left of whatever the little girl's last thoughts might have been.

He finds himself, in a totally detached way, hoping that his sixteen-year-old daughter, Becky, in her room down the hall, has heard the commotion of the family being slaughtered, called the police, and managed to escape out the window, as entirely unrealistic as all that sounds, and is. These are his last thoughts and they occur, to his confusion, after his head has been removed and placed among the Cape Cod souvenir plates displayed on the hutch, from where he can watch his body being ceremonially discmboweled.

Seated in front of her I-Mac computer, wearing a

headset playing old Bjork or Creed or something even more hip, Becky hears nothing. She is chatting on instant messenger to her friend Mara, while teasing some old perv pretending to be seventeen that she met three nights before in a chat room devoted to teenage wicca, or maybe it was retro goth, whatever. She is also looking at a Web site devoted to old Celtic runes for a school report on something or other and peeling what remains of a grape Bubblicious bubblegum bubble off her nose when she is yanked backward by her blond ponytail from the chair and dragged toward the bed, which will soon look like the scene of a botched amateur liver transplant, her throat already cut and unable to make more than a soft, gurgly sound, which she makes as loudly and insistently as she can. Of all the members of her dead family, she is the only one who believes she might still survive, and who therefore struggles, and she does live slightly longer, and suffers the most, her body stripped, and, eventually, nailed to the ceiling.

Meanwhile, while all this is going on, it should be no surprise that the family pets are also being destroyed in a summary fashion: a goldfish bowl has been smashed, two hamsters pulped in a gloved fist, a dog brained with a shovel that has happened to be at hand, and a cat leisurely strangled after its claws have been rendered useless by amputation of its paws. A second cat, the outdoor one, has taken some minutes to call into the house, but this is accomplished with an open can of chunk-light tuna, and then it too has been dispatched with an electric knife.

It ends, all of it, including the benediction, and finally, the pain and suffering, is over, leaving everyone, including presumably the victims, to go in peace.

The house is silent, except for the sound of the usual processional, the old Boy George tune, "Karma Chameleon," set to repeat, as it always is afterward, on the CD player of the stereo. The whole job has taken, including the collection of the obligatory postmortem trophies, less than ten minutes.

"All done," says one of the black-pajamaed figures, the only one wearing a headset, his white plastic mask, of course, expressionless.

There is no reply, as usual.

And even though no one else has worn a headset, they move, as one, immediately, to leave the violated, but now sacred, premises, passing unseen by backyards, empty lots, driveways, etc., to a rendezvous two blocks away, where a line of idling black vans waits, which no one, the next morning, will remember seeing.

It means nothing, Mahoney thinks, and tries to force the idea of nihilism out of his mind, since it's counterproductive and self-defeating to what he's trying to accomplish. He's sitting in the old evidence room, idly fingering a box of glass eyes and passively listening to a compilation CD of the screams of his last three interrogation victims.

He's listening in a bit of an unfocused aural impressionistic manner, hoping to intuit something in the cries of the purposelessly tortured that may give him a clue about the meaning of something, anything, but he's having absolutely no luck at all. His assistant, one of them, for there are so many and they all look exactly alike, is standing at the door, obviously reluctant to bother him, or in ritualistic obeisance, waiting for Mahoney to sense his presence, look up, and motion toward him, which Mahoney now does, but what he motions for is anyone's guess, including Mahoney's. He wonders, vaguely, if the young man at the door, as devastatingly handsome as all the others enlisted into service at the underworld

facility, is really an assistant at all, or the male prostitute, the only kind allowed by Nikka, he asked his male
secretary to call for earlier in the evening.

The assistant nods, for it is indeed an assistant, or both
an assistant and a male prostitute, enters, and begins to
recount the usual details of the routine mass murder of
a family in Jennings, North Carolina. The sacrifice, yet
another in an endless series of daily ceremonies that
must be repeated over and over again, has been carried
out according to the traditional formulas. Mahoney, as
the nominal confessor-general of the paramilitary branch
of the current theocracy, although not particularly religious himself, enjoyed the hysteria and bloodletting of
the charismatic faiths as much as anyone. The boy, indeed he can't be more than twenty-two, finishes, or stops
talking when Mahoney gestures again, this time more im-
patiently, and looks moon-eyed at Mahoney and says,
simply, almost timidly, with a charming, if overdone
effeminate harem lisp, "Yes, sir?"

"Inform the scribes: idealized line drawings of each of
the victims, including inspirational spiritual biographies.
Add them to the Book of Saints."

"Yes, sir," the boy lisped again, smiled provocatively,
and curtsied. "Anything else, sir?"

"Yes," Mahoney said, bored and almost despairing. He
turned off the screaming CD. "Take out your teeth. I'm
in the mood for a blow job."

**It can happen anywhere, anytime, to any-
one,** and it happens to him tonight. He is standing in
the men's room of the Border's Bookstore in Eaton-
town, New Jersey, looking in the mirror, probably
examining his hairline, trying to determine, "Does it
look thinner than it did six months ago?" "Is it thinner

than or as thin as my father's at this age?" or something like that, when he suddenly realizes who he is and what he is supposed to do.

Up to this point, he'd been waiting, only killing time, doing whatever it was he'd been doing, believing in nothing in particular, not giving a damn. And now he knew to leave the men's room, go to the rack of *New York Times* best-sellers, and get in his car and drive directly to the train station in Trenton where he bought a one-way ticket to Washington, D.C.

While waiting for the departure time, he walked to a diner, sat in a booth, and ordered a turkey sandwich, which he ate, methodically, without mayonaisse, even though he wasn't hungry, and didn't like the texture of turkey. Forty-five minutes later he took a window seat of a southbound Amtrak, opened the book he'd bought, and thought, startled, but slightly dazed, *Why am I enjoying this bullshit by John Grisham?*

"My life is not my own," he muses later, feeling quite content, sipping a Fresca, "but then, whose is?"

They are not so circumspect on trains about carry-on luggage and yet he doesn't carry the gun he will use; in fact, he's never seen it. But he knows, as if it's an article of faith, which it is, that it is waiting for him in the hotel room he will rent, whichever hotel room he rents, in the extra ice bucket, on the top shelf, all the way to the left of the closet, just inside the door.

He picks the book up and then lays it back down, thinking, *I've read this all someplace before,* smiles at a little black boy looking back from the seat two seats ahead making shooting motions at him with his tiny hand, and closes his eyes, dead to the world. He starts dreaming immediately: he is turning on a faucet in his grandmother's house, which never existed, one of those heavy, rusty old-fashioned iron faucets, and into the basin falls, one by one, an alien alphabet of tiny blue men. But before he can catch them to form a last desperate message, they squiggle alive, away from his groping fingers, which terminate at the first joint, and escape down the drain.

Tomorrow, or the next day, or the day after that, one of these days soon, he thinks, *I am going to make history just as God planned, and I always knew I would.* He wakes up screaming and then realizes, somehow, that he only dreams he does, and goes right on sleeping.

3. superstars

"The world is going to hell in a handbasket," the man said, still looking at his paper, folded to page 36, where the story of yet another ritualistic serial killing ran, alongside the latest feature article about whoever Tara Reid was or wasn't dating, and an advertisement for penile enlargement.

The jet hit some unexpected turbulence and someone back in coach called out to Jesus.

Caleb turned from the small window on his right, glanced at the newspaper, turned back to the window, and stared out into space. He said, eventually, but with total disinterest, and a little spite, "The world isn't going anywhere."

A stewardess passed down the aisle instructing them to fasten their seat belts. Caleb watched her shallow reflection on the window, superimposed upon the starry cosmos.

"You might be right about that," the man said, a typically large man, white shock of hair, in white shirtsleeves, florid face, and loosened tie. He pretended to fasten his seat belt until the stewardess passed, and let it fall, unconnected, on either side of his expansive paunch. "As far as I'm concerned, whichever end of the shit loaf you start from, you're still eating shit."

"Yeats?" Caleb remarked, dryly.

The man laughed. He'd had too many plastic cups of scotch and water, which were mostly water, but so many he had somehow, quite impressively, managed to get himself quite drunk.

"Guess how old I am."

"Fifty-nine," Caleb said, without looking.

There was an instant of surprise on the man's bloated pink face, which Caleb didn't see, but only imagined, a slight widening of the eyes and dilation of the pupils, maybe, a bit of light, and then it all went flat and dead again. "Yes," the man said, and gulped the last of what was left in his most recent and, until they passed through the invisible storm now rocking the jet, last plastic cup. "Maybe you were erring on the side of caution so as to avoid the possibility of insulting me unintentionally."

"Never," Caleb said, listening for the hum of a fly in the cabin's pressurized interior, but hearing only the laboring engines, "do I do anything unintentionally . . . unless I plan to."

Again the man laughed, but the look on Caleb's face, which was now directed in his general direction, but somewhat off to the side, as it had been for the entire flight whenever Caleb turned from the window, left him feeling embarrassed for laughing, and his smile, forced anyway, faded.

"Still," he continued, "You have to agree, I look like hell."

Caleb was thinking, somehow, about what ginger ale must taste like; well, not the beverage itself, but the words. "Yes," he said. "You do."

"An honest man . . . that's hard to find. My name's John."

He offered his hand, which he knew would be a useless gesture, and sure enough it was. He pulled it back, but his taciturn seat companion wasn't looking anyway.

"So's mine," Caleb said.

"Small world."

"Not really."

"Really?"

"Really."

"What kind of business you in, John?"

"I'm a problem solver."

"Well, maybe you can solve my problem. . . ." The plane bucked again, violently, and the man waited until the lurching subsided, as well as the cries of several panicked passengers, before continuing: "What do you say? We might all be diving into the Atlantic at any moment."

Outside the window, a cloud bank was lit from below by lightning, its cold glow illuminating one side of Caleb's impassive face. He didn't answer, imagining the earth erupting in a series of thermonuclear explosions thick as forests.

"The truth is," the man started, "that I've been through hell and let me tell you what hell is like. I've been flying these planes for business, organizational quality control, by the way, for thirty-five years, and there wasn't a day of it I can say that I was truly happy. I wanted to be a poet once, can you believe that? I can't. I wanted to live in a room in Paris or New York City, hell, even in Austin, and write and be the next Artaud. Instead I got married to a woman who wanted a house and two children and I worked like an animal until I was fifty to give them to her and by that time I was too late for anything."

Caleb was listening to some of this: it was like a radio signal from another planet, or this planet, cleansed of humanity, an old rebroadcast of an archived tape titled "What It Was Like to Be Human."

"I could have retired, still can,but I don't, and do you know why? I need an excuse, any excuse, to get out of the house. I can't stand to be home—it's too painful. My wife has no use for me; for a husband, a source of income, someone to drive the car, yes, but none for me. I'm in the way and putting up with me is an inconvenience she endures, like someone endures the squeaking of a pipe for the water that pours out. Are you listening, John? Do you care? Of course not, why the hell should you? The one person who was supposed to care, who was supposed to love me, who I gave up my life to love me, doesn't give a shit either. Why should you?"

Caleb was thinking of open spaces, vast tracks of desert, acres and acres of ice, woods and forests uninterrupted except by mountains. He was picturing oceans and lakes and endless miles of blank blue skies—and all of this after many centuries, of course, maybe a millenia or two, wandering the earth, alone.

"I don't dare get a lingering illness; something quick better finish me; if not, she will torture me every step to the grave with how I'm fucking up her life. I had a major heart attack two years ago and my second bypass surgery last spring. I have a computer chip in my chest that tells my heart how to beat. My body has forgotten how to work. The medication that I take gives me chronic constipation and makes me impotent and yet I still hire whores, especially in Denmark and Thailand, just to feel a woman's touch. For enough money, they will do practically anything in Bangkok, even pretend that you are having an orgasm. That's funny, don't you think?"

Caleb was smiling, inasmuch as you could call the expression on his face a smile, which, of course, it wasn't. It bore no resemblance to any other human expression more than it did a smile, however, if a smile could be said to have no benevolence, irony, cruelty, or any other recognizable emotion. The fact was that Caleb was thinking of ruined cities, evaporated libraries, whole graveyards that no longer existed. He was thinking of lost museums covered in algae and a history only he remembered, but chose not to.

"My kids," the man continued as the plane rocked and skudded, trembling in the air, ". . . my kids . . . they're grown. The boy hates me, of course, and won't understand until he's my age and has his first positive prostate exam. My little girl—well, let's just say a daddy's only a surrogate until the first hard dick comes along . . . in her case, at age fourteen. Do I sound bitter? I have grandkids, I love them, but to them I'm not real: just some benevolent old geezer who knows how to fold paper airplanes and can't remember the names of the new cartoons. You are looking—or not looking—at an invisible man, John. A ghost. I died thirty years ago. That's why all this bumping around up here," and the man waved a hand vaguely in the air as if brushing away the fly that Caleb always thought he heard. "That's why it doesn't bother me in the least. This plane could go down." He raised his voice, stuck his head out in the aisle, and looked both ways. "Do you hear that? This place could go down right now and I wouldn't give a shit."

He sat back and laughed, ignoring the obscenities some of the other passengers were screaming back at him, the ones not praying to nonexistent gods, or, more appropriately, vomiting into airsick bags, or simply gripping their armrests with eyes shut tight.

"It's not the booze talking; I'm drunk, but it's not that," the man said quietly. "I don't give a shit, and do you know why? I'm already dead."

The man fell silent and Caleb thought he might be sobbing, but he wasn't paying enough attention to tell for certain, and when he turned whatever the sound was had stopped and the man had gotten hold of himself, more or less.

"What you need," Caleb said, "is God."

"I used to be religious," the man said, his voice a hoarse whisper, as if afraid to be overheard, even though no one was listening, including Caleb. "I even sat in Zen meditation. But the truth is that man's not happy with his lot and all that stuff we do to convince us that we are is just stuff we do to pass the time: it's like playing checkers in the ICU. Poetry, art, music—what does any of it mean? If my life had been different, it would still have been the same. Haven't you heard? God is dead."

"I know he's dead. You killed him."

Caleb saw suicide cults, mass gaves, self-destruct codes, canceled tickets, countdown sequences. He saw cryogenic cylinders thawing in an empty valley. He saw—no, he sensed—something moving in the air, a presence, watching. It was a feeling along his dead spinal column, something wholly unfamiliar, something new, not fear, not what humans felt, or what he understood humans felt, but whatever he would feel if it were possible for him to feel fear, whatever he would feel in the presence of a natural enemy.

The pilot, or the copilot, or perhaps it was the steward, a voice, anyway, came over the intercom and announced that they'd passed over the storm that seemed to be the cause of the turbulence. Everything was okay. They would be landing in Milan only slightly behind schedule in twenty-seven minutes. The plane was hushed for a minute or two and then conversation resumed, here and there, as if all had been as before, as if nothing had happened, or everyone was pretending it hadn't.

The stewardess was moving down the aisle, smiling, taking drink orders, and the man beside Caleb ordered another plastic cup of scotch and water and didn't say another word for the rest of the flight. Instead he watched a movie with a race car driver and a talking orangutan. Caleb couldn't hear what the orangutan was saying but he could read the ape's lips; the gist of what he said was not important.

"Pretend you're in love," Vince said, lining her up in the viewfinder, "with the most distant star in the galaxy." She was dressed in a backless silver gown, her golden hair done in a chignon, her too-young profile looking heart-breakingly elegant, almost like a child playing dress-up for a porn movie.

She was looking into a corner of the room, where the elbow of an exposed pipe hung, a wistful expression on her face, clearly not seeing anything. Vince clicked shot after shot. She knelt, full frontal, breasts bared, her face looking down into a white tulip that she held with one hand, the other, between her legs, ambiguously finger-ing her hairless cleft, as if she had no idea what she was doing. A moment later, posed naked, against a white wall, she was painting her toenails silver and, having paused to draw a smiley face on the wall behind her, she flashed a peace sign with her left hand, smiling so bril-liantly she could have been selling anything from automobiles to instant oatmeal.

Various shots followed of Alison trying on wedding paraphenalia: gowns, veils, headbands, garters, shoes, bouquets, trains, gloves; the general idea, which Io had stressed ad nauseam, and Vince had reluctantly agreed would be most effective, was virginal innocence. It was ludicrous, of course, insofar as the girl's sexual adven-turing among the jet set, Hollywood, and MTV crowd had been the staple of tabloids and unauthorized bi-ographies ever since she was twelve. Still, there was a freshness about the girl that seemed preternaturally un-sullied, no matter how many rich Arab emirs she'd dated or members of the rock super group Empire she had been fucked silly by.

It was this endearing and unusual quality, to be able, unconsciously and with the minimum of damage-control

PR spin, to maintain a fake virginity, even as she was the focal point of celebrity scandal and sensationalized gossipmongering, that had attracted Io's attention when he began planning to take a hostage. She was helped, too, by what Io called the old archetypal human sex cartoon that was rerun again and again and that no one ever got tired of seeing, or so it seemed. Same plot, same characters, same theme—it was like a fairy tale that children never tired of hearing again and again and again. They want to believe there was a virgin, Io said, and so they would see her as a virgin, even if they have a copy of that bootlegged videotape of her being butt-fucked by that aging coke-snorting, cross-dressing ex-NBA rebounding champion, what's his name? The fact that the girl was also a member of royalty, and a bona fide princess at that, made it all seem as if it was fate, which, naturally, it was. The girl, as Io liked to say, although he didn't say it much, and then only grudgingly, had star power.

And Vince had to admit, seeing her standing in the center of a circle of red votive candles, looking heavenward, doing a kind of Joan of Arc impression, a small white canary in her cupped hands, her almost childishly rounded belly exposed where the mummy gown she'd been bandaged into had been artfully unwound, Alison did look the picture of fake virgin innocence, which, Vince instantly decided, was both far sexier, and far rarer, than the real thing. *She's a natural,* he thought, as he shot another fifty photographs, the best image he had ever manipulated, that rare and elusive icon in his business: the perfect victim.

"Tell me about my prince," she said later, breathlessly. She had been successfully weaned from solid foods and even the beef broths that Vince had spoon-fed her during her convalescence. Now she took small amounts of special scientifically formulated tinctures that came in one-inch tubes that were broken over her outstretched tongue. She had lost most of the baby fat that indulgent living and youth had made her trademarks. She was still eminently recognizable, anything less would have been counterproductive, but she had been etherealized, refined to near transparency, like a window into another world, a view of an ancient stone altar covered with irises. "Is he handsome?"

She had embraced her role so totally, so unreservedly, so gratefully, that Vince couldn't help thinking, sometimes, of her conversion in terms of fulfillment, rather than mere brainwashing, although it was clear that surrender and hopelessness were part of the equation. And yet, Io argued, and Vince had not come up with a decent refutation, what was enlightenment anyway, in the classic religious sense, but a break with ordinary personality and a final acceptance of what must be must be?

She had been born, indeed, a princess and now she was going to fulfill that role in the deepest mythological sense during an age when such things as princesses had seemed nothing more than an anachronism with no real purpose in the world but to take drugs, engage in scandalous liaisons, be photographed at Cannes, and appear, somewhere, in *People* magazine every week.

"I would say he is a god, my lady," Vince started, adopting a kind of pseudo court speech and manner, whenever he remembered, which seemed to deepen the girl's already dissociated trance, "but more perfected, an abstraction, symbolized by complex mathematics and a rosy organ through which galaxies are sown in the wastes of countless yesterdays."

She sighed again, asking pointless questions, which Vince answered pointlessly. She was turned from him, on a low divan, a sumptuous antique it seemed, but situated in an otherwise bare room, except for the low thunderclouds creeping threateningly over the horizon. She was gazing down, half smiling, at a crossword puzzle, all the boxes in the grid empty, never to be solved, and Vince wondered if she even saw it as a crossword, or whether, instead, it appeared to her as a mystic acrostic that revealed nothing less than the world renewing secrets of her mystic union. Vince stared at her buttocks, innocently on display, her childlike immodesty, the result of having regained a state of pre-Edenic retardation with regard to her body, a delight in all its functions and sensations, from orgasm to evacuation.

And Vince, so close he could see the downy baby hairs along the inside of her crease running to her most secret place of all, longed for her with his entire being, and yet, when he reached out his hand from behind the camera to touch her, he stopped, unable to do it, afraid to disturb the beauty of their collective dream.

In solitary confinement, Mahoney sits on his heels, rolling dice. The cell in which he crouches is barely six by eight feet, maybe smaller, windowless, of course, concrete, silent as the tomb it is, a chamber buried inside miles of solid concrete, in the middle of a desert or under the ocean, a rusty drain hole in the floor between his naked feet.

Mahoney shakes his fist, the dice, the only possession he allows himself, knock together as if significantly, at least for a moment or two, and then he tosses them onto the cold concrete. They hit the wall, or, at least he hears them hit the wall, for no light is permitted in the chamber by order of Mahoney himself.

The dice were carved from the upper thighbones, the femurs as it were, of the ex–Special Forces commando whom Mahoney had slain in ritual combat at least two decades ago in the yearly challenges whoever held his position was required to win by successive murders, or, being finally slain himself, yield in a pool of his own vanquished blood and seed. Mahoney had carved the dice himself and loaded them to precise specifications, any roll offering a five 97 percent of the time and a four, just for the hell of it, the other 3.

He reached out and felt for the dice in the dark, his fingers rubbing each square bone face, knowing they would be slightly yellowed with age, in spite of the semiprecious seal and aloe oils he neurotically massaged into them every night, and the soft pouch in which he carried them, suspended from a cord around his neck, a little medicine bag where his predecessor's testicles once resided.

It's not difficult to feel the indentations of the dice, not for Mahoney, whose fingertips have been sensitized to an extraordinary degree through years of reading braille, repeated laser fingernail removal, and training in psychic energy work, both corrective and disruptive. The roll, as it was 95 percent of the time, and thus, as he more or less expected, was a double five.

Mahoney, alone in the pitch-black, feigned surprise.

There was no significance, of course, to any of this, and yet, in his deeply enforced solitude, having fasted on nothing but distilled water and a single five-milligram-per-day dose of his long ago afterbirth, delivered orally in pill form, and this diet having been followed religiously for the last nine days, in addition to the total sensory deprivation and repetition of the monotonous and compulsive dice-throwing routine, Mahoney had achieved an altered state of consciousness, or had suffered a psychotic breakdown, either one, or both, or perhaps he had only been rendered overemotional. It was impossible to say, as there was no one but him present, and least of all for Mahoney, who exploded into a savage fit of mystical hysterics, weeping and abusing himself, screaming in terror, for he had finally succeeded in apprehending the nagging sense of imminence that had continually eluded him.

It had not come to him in a vision, not exactly, but it was a revelation, nonetheless. Mahoney knew, beyond a doubt, exactly what was about to happen. And yet, the terrible irony of it all was that he could do absolutely nothing about it, for no matter how loudly he screamed and carried on and spoke in tongues, his prophecy would never be heard, buried as he was in a confinement so absolutely solitary he might as well have been the only man alive on the face of the earth.

But that was not exactly what made his situation so ironic.

What it was, exactly, was this incredible fact: Mahoney had himself issued the orders of his confinement in accordance with the conditions necessary for prophetic sight and he ordered his subordinates to follow these unreasonable orders to the letter upon pain of eternal damnation. No one, including Mahoney himself, could abrogate that order once it was given, no matter how loudly he screamed, or what punishment he would mete out to those who disobeyed when, and if, he was finally released to unleash his unforgiving, homicidal fury.

Juliet was fucking her way through Europe.

That was one way to look at it, but not the only way, and Juliet herself had no clear idea what she was doing, or what she expected to come of her behavior, if anything. *It's all going to come to a bad end,* she thought disinterestedly, during a rare lucid and self-reflective moment, but more often than not, she simply wandered in a drug- or alcohol-induced fog, from one unsatisfying erotic encounter to another with busboys, soldiers, prostitutes, cabdrivers, small-time criminals, zookeepers, undercover cops, matrons, motormen, street performers, in short, anyone who offered.

She was halfheartedly eating a stale roll in a train terminal in Gdansk, having spent her last grotsky on a ticket to Riga, which she had picked because it was a city in Latvia, a country whose shape she couldn't picture at all. She had slipped the money for the ticket and roll from the wallet of a drunken Swiss businessman who'd collapsed in a dance club men's room with tachycardia after snorting too much cocaine in preparation for the blow job Juliet wasn't about to give him. She had managed to bring him off with the sole of her foot as she sat on the toilet to pee and he lay there on the tiled floor, pale, clammy, panicked, too weak and preoccupied to stop her from taking the billfold out of his coat pocket.

Now she sat on a wooden bench, the familiar aftertaste of a third or fourth man's semen in her mouth, the bitterness of barrenness, annihilation, and a form, to her disordered senses, of murder. For a reason she could not know, or ever suspect, Juliet had a thirst for this life, and, specifically, the acts she was indulging in with such fevered abandon and dangerous disregard. She had been, if not virginal, for that would have been too ridiculous, then, at the very least, circumspect in her sexual behavior over the first thirteen or fourteen years of her life. She'd had, which was rare among girls her age, only two abortions, and one had been almost a mistake, but she'd have easily had many more, as many as necessary to keep herself childless, and single, for Juliet had the intimation, however dim and unrealistic, that she was saving herself for something, whatever it might be.

It should have seemed strange to her, except it didn't,

that she thought of it as saving herself for something, rather than someone, but that's the way it was, and now, the release of her erotic comet through the dark cities of the European night might be seen as an attempt to face her fate, or avoid her fate, or simply as a manifestation of her fate. That her incoherent behavior had something to do with her chance meeting with the dark stranger in that sunny square in Italy, Juliet hadn't the slightest doubt, which, in turn, made her doubt that the meeting had occurred by any chance at all. But if it had been meant to be: then meant for what? The question haunted Juliet, as did the memory of their meeting which she could hardly remember, and then the dreams in which he appeared, fleetingly, standing with his back forever turned to her, on a landscape that looked like pictures she had seen of the surface of the moon, or cities leveled by smart bombs, or magnified photographs of the flora that grows on bones.

In those dreams, she always approached, but, as in the paradox of Zeno, no matter how fast she ran to him, she only seemed to get there half the distance at a time, half of a half of a half, and so never arrived. Still, when she seemed almost within arm's length, she reached to touch his shoulder, reached, and before she could touch his figure, solitary as a lightning rod, he almost turned toward her, and what Juliet saw escaping in the face she could barely imagine, only anticipate, woke her with a feeling of falling through the bottom of space, and left her dazed, drained, and desperate for the kiss that never came, the kiss that could be kissed just once, and not at all.

"Wake up, my daughter. Wake up."

The words came to her as she imagined his face turning once again, that beautiful desolate face without expression, with its indescribable mouth speaking of things that didn't exist.

"Wake up."

Juliet stared up at a man of about seventy years: silver-haired, indisputably handsome, with eyes the color of frozen smoke, and the features of a Mongol chieftain. He was of middle height, lean and graceful, but powerfully built, as if he belonged to a different race of men entirely.

He looked at her, appraisingly. He was dressed, Juliet thought, like a diplomat, although she would have been hard pressed to define exactly what she meant by that.

"Daddy?" she said, in a voice from another time, a voice you use on a telephone, when whoever is on the other end doesn't answer, but leaves only the sound of the miles between you, after you pick up and say, for the third and last time, "Hello?"

"Come with me," the man says, and Juliet cannot quite place the accent, not Polish, certainly, maybe Basque, but just as likely to be Iowa, or even, Montana. He looked up and down the empty platform and Juliet wondered, idly, if he was looking out for policemen, or eyewitnesses, or both. "Let's go."

"But my train—"

"Is long come . . . and gone."

"It can't be—"

"No train here for another two hours. You have time, but not money. Am I not correct?"

He smiled eerily, and there was something about that smile on his well-defined features, a perfection that made him seem almost expressionless even when he wore an expression. His whole face might have been mass-produced in a factory from a computer-generated model designed by psychiatrists to inspire trust in the majority of human beings.

She followed him out of the station into a cold drizzle, out to the street where an old Fiat sat at the curb. He held the door open, ironically.

He looked, as they drove down suddenly narrow streets, repeatedly in the side-view mirror, taking quick turns, tires squealing, and periodically doubling back, unnecessarily, in the direction from which they traveled. Juliet leaned back against the seat, smoking a cigarette the man had given her, watching, with a kind of third-party interest, as they passed, for the fourth time, a lone figure on the corner, snapping photographs with a small silver camera, possibly digital.

"Are we being followed?" Juliet asked, idly imagining yanking the steering wheel from the man's grip, running the car into a light pole, and escaping on foot, all of that impossible. Her door, she had observed, without alarm, had no inside handle. She also noticed, sometime before, that the rearview mirror had also been removed, as it is in movie cars.

"The road is empty. Who would be following us?"

"Am I really supposed to answer that?" Juliet sighed, only half seriously, and then proceeded not to answer the man's question, if, indeed, he really did expect her to answer.

They pulled in front of a building in a street of run-down buildings that looked as if they had survived a war, but only barely. There was a hasty exchange of some kind, stereotypically of money, in order to facilitate passage to the rooms upstairs. The man closed the door of a small flat filled with a light the color of papyrus and smelling of radio waves.

"Get undressed," the man said, lighting a banknote, Spanish or Portugese, it was impossible for Juliet to tell, but it had the number 50 on it, and it was already transformed into a smoking black curl. "Now."

"I want this to be the last time," she said. "Do you understand?"

Puling her top over her head, standing before him, her tits out, slightly bruised from the last man's touch.

"Now."

Juliet unzipped her skirt, let it fall to the floor, and stepped out of it. She was surprised to find she was wearing panties. She looked at the man, as if daring him, but daring him to what she wasn't exactly certain, and then she looked away, toward the window, from where she almost thought she'd heard someone calling her name.

When she turned back, the man had somehow crossed the room without making a sound. He was standing so close to her that she could see the glint of the steel shavings in his nothing eyes and the fact that his skin was so smooth he didn't appear to have any pores. She sat back on the bed, her face level with his crotch, and reached out to undo his fly in a gesture she had repeated so many times it had become automatic, almost meaningless, a ritual it was her duty to perform, as if she were a priest celebrating a sacrament no one believed in anymore.

The man made no protest, didn't say a word, but let Juliet do what she was doing, until she stopped, paying attention for the first time in a long time, and looked up, suddenly understanding. It wasn't that it simply wasn't there, that he was some kind of anomaly, or cross-gendered medical alteration, nor was it that he was preternaturally smooth, an angel, or a member of an alien race altogether—somehow any of these even more improbable alternatives might have been easier to accept. No, it was, touching the old circle of scar tissue, that what he had there had been removed, and having looked into the man's eyes Juliet had no doubt that the man had removed it himself.

"I think I understand," she said, slightly awed.

The man had produced a large black bag from somewhere, under the bed, perhaps, and he held it in his right hand, a large, well-creased black leather bag that held God knew what, and his left hand was raised in a gesture that Juliet recognized from pictures of Hindu temples she'd seen in art books, the ones in which the lord Shiva or goddess Kali, made a hand sign that was supposed to convey the message "Fear not," even as they trampled the corpses of their devotees. But Juliet couldn't remember if the gesture was made with the left hand, or the right, or even if it mattered.

"I want you to kill me," Juliet said, or thought she said, for several frames of time were missing, or apparently missing, because she was now lying on the bed, naked, with an IV needle stuck into the fragile flesh inside her elbow. "That's what this is about, isn't it?" she whispered, for no reason, and shuddered, or pretended to shudder, anticipating an orgasm that didn't come. ". . . death . . ."

The man didn't answer, of course. He was regulating, instead, the flow of whatever was running through the tube into her vein, a cool substance, like a neon glow, but alive. He put on, with exaggerated care, a pair of protective glasses, and Juliet notices the predictable surgical gloves. There is music playing from another room, distant, out of place, maybe Philip Glass, altogether disturbing.

The man doesn't explain anything, which is to be expected, and Juliet wonders, not quite perfectly objectified, if that's because at this point all explanations are irrelevant.

There is fear, then, in her eyes. She is, unlike almost everyone else, still human, after all. She is moving thought, by slow degrees, to something else.

"Fear is natural," the man says, suddenly surrounded by a harsh light that looks like heaven, but is, just as impossibly, the light in the operating theater when Juliet had her tonsils removed at the age of seven, and then again at eleven. "You might try reciting the Lord's Prayer," he says, not at all kindly, and when he sees the look of total bewilderment in her eyes, he adds, "or just count backward starting from one hundred. It's the same thing."

"Forty-three," Juliet starts, and she wonders, for a long time, what comes next, and then she thinks, *Oh, its all so much easier than I thought. . . .*

"What am I saying?" Nikka asks herself, a little shocked at the apparent political implications (well, not the implications, really, but the fact that she was actually saying it out loud) of whatever speech she was giving, the cost in needless human suffering, innocent lives, etc., and yet, continuing to talk, according to the script. She was standing on the white steps in front of the Lincoln Memorial, in front of a carefully selected, so-called "spontaneous" crowd of fifteen thousand, the majority holding signs of enthusiastic support, only a few, well in the rear, in carefully orchestrated, government subsidized, contrapuntal protest. She turned, or merely hinted at a turn, to the left, just a gaze as the cheers rose to a false climax, and banks of cameras that had been assigned to record this historic event captured yet another moment for posterity.

Nikka sighed, but only inwardly, a well-placed sigh that wasn't in this speech, she didn't think. She began the brief, even for a précis, summary of the idealistic goals and substantitve achievements of her dynasty, designed to fit into a broadcast sound byte, or one of those inspirational campaign biographies, complete with toe-tapping, slightly nostalgic pop music from the generation before, all of it lasting no more than three or four minutes, followed by wet eyes and thunderous ovations.

With every sentence she uttered, virtually each of them vague, paradoxical, and prophetic, stock market prices rose or fell, currencies bottomed out, election polls swung wildly to one side or another and back again, a terrorist cell in Bangladesh or San Diego was emboldened to plant a pipe bomb, a man was hit by a tram, someone else bought two pounds of ham.

What she said today, Nikka knew, would be the subject of debate for the next two hundred years. It would require thousands of pages of scholarly exegesis, as well as newspaper editorials, talk radio arguments, political cartoons, and backyard shouting matches. They might, although it wouldn't be the first time, erect a statue of her beside the Jefferson Memorial, rename streets, sports complexes, maybe a few post offices. In Melbourne, there is talk of a "living memorial," although no one seems to know exactly what that means.

Nikka pauses again, as scheduled, and is surprised, even a little disturbed, to find that she is still paying even a bit of attention to what she is doing, even though she doesn't understand any of it, not exactly. She lifts her hands in a stylized, hieratical way, the old "fear not" gesture of the Hindu pantheon, Kali, Shiva, that whole crew, but the gesture has been abstracted to such a degree it has no meaning, or the reverse meaning. She is saying something now that clearly makes no sense, but she delivers the passage flawlessly, and sitting in a concrete bunker beneath a mock White House two thousand miles away, her pollsters and handlers give each other high fives.

A ghost of a smile flickers across Nikka's expressionless face and women feel as if they're on the verge of tears, men are inspired to behavior that may require them to have no regard for their own lives, and everyone has a sense that one day they will think back on this moment and say, "Remember when . . ."

The fact is that everyone will have a hard time remembering any of this ten minutes after it's over, and that is the point, really.

There are so many audio and videotapes running, so many photo flashes, so many styluses moving over Palm Pilots, one might think there would be a consensus of opinion, if not an accurate account of what happens next, but, alas, it's just the opposite. The entire event, or performance, is fragmented, shattered into countless perceptions, recorded more or less subjectively, as if five or six different mosaics were thrown together, and a quarter of the tiles were missing. The general idea is, there are as many different realities as there are people to experience them, and each and every person is entitled to his own.

"We are standing here today," Nikka intones, as if addressing the sun god Ra, "on hallowed ground . . ."

And the people think, *Yes, yes, we are,* even if they don't know that the lovingly waxed bones of nineteen Honduran virgins, raised on a special farm, have been sewn into the soil beneath their feet.

"The veil, however," Nikka says, and she looks, momentarily, confused, a look that will appear on the new posters, and be copied, ad infinitum, in countless MTV videos, ". . . has been sundered."

At that moment, someone in Angola takes a machete from the shed and starts walking down a long dusty road to kill a local official.

A lamb is disemboweled by rural Georgia teenagers on PCP.

In various places, doing various things, men and

women are stopping, looking up, and saying, "That's it, I've had enough," and impromptu fires are set.

What follows next is a hitch in Nikka's always flawless delivery, or it's a computer glitch of some kind, the kind that seems to overlay, momentarily, two bytes of information over each other. It is reminiscent of what happens when a radio broadcast crosses bands with and intrudes on the regularly scheduled programming, or when someone suddenly becomes possessed and begins speaking in tongues, either Satan or the Holy Ghost. It all lasts, perhaps, 3.5 to 3.75 seconds at most, and then is broken up, so that no one in the crowd is consciously aware there's been a break in the continuity of whatever it was they were hearing, as if she was wittingly or unwittingly delivering a subliminal message, which, perhaps, she was.

Sipping a Pepsi One or Mountain Dew Code Red or whatever Coca-Cola has come out with in response to whatever came out after Pepsi Twist, her handlers and pollsters and spokespersons are watching the monitors in semidisbelief, asking each other if they had advised Nikka to say what they think they just heard, and, if so, on whose authority. Everyone is denying any knowledge of the speech, and, naturally, no one believes anyone else, and well they shouldn't, because everyone in this room is here because they are pathological liars.

"Did she just say what I think she said?" one consultant asks another.

"I didn't hear a thing," answers his clone, or her clone, lying effortlessly.

"What are the poll numbers?" asks someone else entirely.

"Up nearly five percentage points among twenty- to

twenty-three-year-olds in Woods Hole, Massachusettes," comes the answer.

"Fabulous."

"Do you suppose," someone offers, cringing with each word, as if afraid to be hit at any moment, "that we have a virus?"

"Let's shut this thing down," someone else answers, as if he had the authority to do so, and maybe he does, "and run a scan."

But no one seems to do anything, or know, really, whether they should or not.

This is it for Nikka. She is coming down the stairs of the Lincoln Memorial, sweeping down the stairs with excruciating ceremonial slowness, like a queen, like a female pope, dispensing blessings and invisible pardons, smiling, benevolently, without actually looking at anyone.

There is some commotion off camera, always off camera, a shaky picture, as if one were looking through a box falling off a table, and shouting, as someone pushes through, and mixed in at some point the unforgettable sound: pop, pop, pop, pop, pop . . .

There is total confusion now, except for the men in black suits and dark glasses, who have waited their whole lives for this moment. Through their disconnected earphones, they have been listening for years to the countdown for now, and they are ready. They shove well-wishers and lesser government functionaries into the paths of errant bullets, their own weapons out, untraceable calibers fired into selected political adversaries—it's time to do some quick housecleaning. A senator, three cabinet ministers, and the next prime minister of India fall mortally wounded, still smiling for the cameras, while several wealthy backers are likewise instantly martyred.

Nikka herself moves cooly through the chaos, head up, her face dutifully expressionless, movements unhurried, even as the security agents roughly grab her sacrosanct and untouchable person and rush her in the direction of the nonexistent secret side exit in the Memorial. She hears the shouting, weeping, and dying of the sacrifices all around her. She sees a young woman who earlier had held her baby daughter up from the crowd so that the little one might catch a glimpse of the great Nikka VII, lying dead on the ground, a bullet hole in her cumpled face, and the rest of her trampled, as she clutched her dead baby, and Nikka wonders: *Is that her blood splashed on my calves? And if so, how appropriate.*

The cameras will catch what happens next, because, after all, this is completely beside the point.

It goes something like this: Nikka pauses, almost irrationally, but also hieratically, as if she is above it all, which she is. She pauses, and turns, distractedly, as if she has just become aware of the buzzing of a fly, or perhaps it is a helicopter from very far away. She doesn't, however, raise her hand to brush it away, the imaginary fly, that is, even though she feels it alighting on her left cheek. Instead, she remains focused, but only for an instant, and she sees the assassin reaching out from the masses, a man, like any other ordinary man, but without any identity in his eyes, and therefore holy. He starts reciting a line of poetry, or so it seems, something from Lautreamont, but not really, it's what they say he says, whoever they are: "If I exist, I am not another."

He is a cypher, a small white pill, a cure for an unnameable but lingering and incurable disease. He shoots at her his magic bullet and in a carefully controlled moment of perfect praxis, Nikka feels betrayed, abandoned, wondering where she is, where he is, why he's not here, why she is, and she calls out the name of the man who was supposed to die protecting her, but wandered off into the desert . . . to worship what?

But whether she actually says his name aloud, or meditates on it silently, whether it's a call for help, a prayer, or merely an empty utterance that would make the whole event a little more heartbreakingly dramatic, she would have to check the script, which security agents are now systematically erasing from the world's computer banks, to know for sure, if whoever wrote it knows himself, which, in every circumstance so far, he doesn't.

And as she is shoved through the nonexistent secret side exit in the Memorial, passed waiters, congressmen, soldiers, barmaids, D.C. policemen, and assorted VIP guests, including the usual Hollywood hangers-on, all aghast and stunned and suitably weepy, and thrown into the waiting limousine, waiting like a coffin, she thinks, or rather reflects on an image locked monomaniacally in her perception: a piece of someone's liver hanging from the tip of Abraham Lincoln's marble nose.

Caleb looks up, naked, his face smeared with blood, and cocks his head, as if he's carefully listening to something, but there is nothing to hear. It is as if a fly has stopped buzzing in a room that is suddenly, and quite unaccustomedly, quiet. The woman beneath him, forty-two, a toy company publicist he'd abducted from a commuter parking lot in a suburb of Chicago, is a few heart pumps away from becoming a corpse. The major arteries, through which her overtaxed heart is pumping blood, have all been severed, and so she is quite neatly bleeding to death into a motel mattress.

Her face has been mashed into a sort of indecipherable

porridge, her rib cage broken at the sternum, both legs dislocated, and every finger, except the left forefinger, methodically snapped. There is a taste in Caleb's mouth, which might be spleen, making sense, the organ that helped in the storage of red blood cells held a naturally special appeal for him. There is a kneecap on the nightstand, but, oddly, it doesn't seem to belong to her. Is there another woman in the room somewhere, her sixteen-year-old daughter, perhaps; had he abducted her on Take Our Children to Work Day, of all days?

Caleb listened, curiously, to the new silence, a silence that was not disturbed in the least by the usual gurglings and rattlings issuing from the croaking woman beneath him, and felt as if he needed to go someplace and do something with great urgency, and he wondered, but only briefly, that such feelings were even possible to him, to him who knew that in the time-lapse view of one who'd seen the entire film from beginning to end, there was nothing to do and nowhere to go. And then the moment passed, as they all do, and he looked down at the dying woman, who seemed to be skinned, and he punctured her exposed trachea, which gave her breathing a relatively annoying wheezing sound for a few seconds, before abruptly stopping, leaving only the usual smell of shit and the buzzing of a fly, which Caleb went back to ignoring, once in a while.

The police are closing in, he knows it, he can feel it, even though he isn't guilty, except of the usual, breathing, digesting, being alive, etc. Even now the authorities are opening his e-mail, examining his medical records, interviewing past employers, emptying his hard drive, tossing his drawers, ripping apart the binding of his books. Eleven people, affiliated with him by only the loosest and most liberal of definitions, have been proactively murdered. It's a conspiracy, three generations of conspiracy theorists will argue, and, indeed, it is: films, exposés, novels, articles, TV debates, and explanations involving everything from jealous lovers to beings from an intradimensional race of lizardlike bloodsuckers will be invoked to explain the inexplicable. "There are just too many inconsistencies," will be the claim, again and again, and it's true: nothing adds up but no one will ask why it doesn't add up quite so badly.

He found the old Honda Accord, unlocked, in the parking lot of a SaveMart supermarket two blocks from his hotel room. The news had come through ten minutes earlier—a special report that interrupted a rerun on the Gameshow channel of *The Family Feud*, the original run, with Richard Dawson, that charming snake, on the television of whoever was saying nothing in a violent argument with a black prostitute with a badly faked Russian accent in the next room. The report was broadcast ten minutes before the actual event occurred, although he didn't know this, and had been sent out through the media especially for him, as a kind of "switch" to activate the program that he was running right now, among other things.

She had been assassinated, apparently, at a halfway house giving sanctimonious general blessings to a resident population of underage crack moms or in the corridors of a D.C. hospital after presenting a meaningless certificate to a ward of human clones. His mission—to shoot her tomorrow at the Lincoln Memorial during a historic speech no one will remember—had been preempted eighteen hours before it even began, and nobody knew it, except him.

He removed the gun from the empty clock radio box that he carried in a plastic Circuit City bag, and noted, with a nagging sense of unease, that it was not the same gun he'd found in the closet when he checked into the room, or the gun he had packed that morning, nor would it be the gun that would, much later, be found catalogued as exhibit 5-1402 in the Rand-Knight report, and then lost again, irretrievably and inexplicably, along with classified ballistic reports, eyewitness testimony, blood specimens, and a whole host of relevant incidentals in what will be reported as "an unfortunate computer housekeeping error."

Three hundred years from now historians would include a badly patched together version of whatever eventually survives as the conspiracy account of the event in a footnote to the offical account, both spurious, and entirely irrelevant, insofar as whatever happened happened a long time ago and the government, after many reforms, is different now. Except, of course, three hundred years from whenever now is, they are always saying the exact same thing, and nothing is different, not really, it just looks that way.

There is no truth, then, anywhere. And, unable to bear the thought of the torture and humiliation that a mock public trial would entail, and knowing that even this act will condemn him to being misunderstood, he raises the gun just as a woman, black, approximately thirty-two, a congressional aide, perhaps, or a worker at the Pentagon, returns to the car, pushing a cart with two grocery bags. She freezes, terrified, her mouth open and keys dropped, certain that the gun is meant for her, that she is about to be the victim of a car-jacking, and for a few wonderful seconds, it occurs to him to do just that: kidnap the woman and have her drive him nonstop to Hillsdale, New Hampshire, for instance, if such a place even exists. But the idea, in the end, seems as silly as all the others, and besides, the program was already running, the gun moving up to his face, barrel in his mouth, finger squeezing, a pink mist replacing a head from which this thought, uncontained, hung glistening wetly in the air for two seconds: maybe there was another way out.

"Don't look at me," Mahoney said, hysterically, and somewhat unnecessarily, since he was wearing dark glasses and the soldier-drone permitted to his semisolitary chamber cell for the briefing was both albino and blind. Mahoney was dressed in a black suit by Alberto Ellis, black shirt, black tie, black shoes and socks; his nails, also, were polished black. His head had been ritually shaved, except for a Mohawk, and, beneath the perfect suit, he wore a pair of Nikka's black lace panties, which he'd raided, along with other reliquary items of lingerie, from her panty drawer in a preemptive violation of her now hermetically sealed personal chambers. He stood before a Plexiglas map of the world, or how the world would look, after the catastrophic geopolitical and climatic changes that had already occurred, were, at last, acknowledged.

"Is she dead?" he asked, and began humming a personal tune, tapping a city in Kurdistjan that he planned to wipe out with a new neuro-plague.

"The reports are wildly inconsistent," the drone answered, nodding slightly. How had a fly gotten in here? he wondered. The place was buffered on all sides by miles of perfect vacuum. "There are rumors, however. What is it that you'd like to hear?"

Mahoney considered this for a moment, wondering what the world would look like without the upper part of Africa. "Tell me whatever is most likely to cause me to react as illogically as possible."

"There is, on good authority, several reports indicating she was taken unharmed to the Auckland Islands."

Mahoney let his eyes travel over the Plexiglas map to where the Auckland Islands should have been, but weren't.

"These accounts, however, are believed to be nothing more than propaganda, and that, in fact, she was slain in the attack for the ninth time, and that means it's over . . . whtaever that means."

"Game theory," Mahoney said, cryptically, but only cryptically to someone who didn't understand, which was everyone, but himself, maybe.

"There are reports of spontaneous rioting in Tucson and already sightings in Peru and Tunisia. There are three children in Bern who've been authenticated by the provisional religious high priesthood—"

"Arrest everyone. Kill whoever's in captivity. Drop the air-defense shield. Let *anything* through. Announce, with the usual great regret, et cetera, the death of Nikka VII. Commence preparations at the Black Pyramid for a monstrous funeral, complete with extravagant human sacrifices. Have parachuters fall from the skies over Manhattan, if not Paris and Berlin as well."

The drone bowed in appreciation, knowing that his own life was forfeited already, but added, "All respects to you, Lord Protector, but only the Minister of Languages can issue—"

Mahoney said something like, "He's dead. Assassinated."

The soldier-drone betrayed no emotion, but considered cutting his own throat in Mahoney's presence, instead of later, the ultimate salute. "The Invisible Consort—"

"Dead."

Before the drone could utter more than another

syllable—the title of someone else in the impossibly end-less hierarchy, whoever was next in line of succession—Mahoney cut him off. "I've had them all killed."

The drone dropped in obeisance, forehead touching the floor, arms outstretched, palms up. Mahoney took out a Luger, pointed it at the tonsured crown of the drone's head, and then realized he couldn't bear to start this conversation all over again with another drone, ex-actly like this one. "I'm thinking," he said dreamily, returning the huge black pistol to his shoulder-holster, "of a number from one to sixty." He was not surprised when the drone answered forty-seven. Mahoney had been thinking thirty-two.

"What about the programs? They will run—"

"I've had them canceled," Mahoney said, "or soon will. They only seem like the usual programs."

The drone had regained his feet at Mahoney's impa-tient gesture, which he sensed, or deduced, and stood slightly turned, oblique, to Mahoney, fly open, limp penis, chemically castrated, exposed, the whole presen-tation an organizationally standard pose meant to convey respect and pack submission, like a military stance, at attention.

"But." The drone was obviously trying to compute which titles, exactly, Mahoney had usurped in the last few hours, so that he could be addressed properly.

"Commander-in-Chief, will do," Mahoney said, dryly. "The sobriquet 'My Commander' sounds authoritative and affectionate, and therefore somehow appropriate, to my ear."

"My Commander," the drone intoned dutifully, "for-give me my sins as you forgive those who trespass against you. What about the process of healing and the orderly succession of power?"

Mahoney seemed to be daydreaming, or perhaps he

was just astonished that anyone could possibly still say such a thing. "Myths, formalities, re-reruns. The veil has been rent . . ." he said, and stopped himself, a little disoriented, only by sheer force of will, and realized he was about to launch into a speech programmed by someone else, as if repeating ad nauseam the slogan of a popular television commercial for peanut butter or fabric softener. The next words, however, were his own, and carefully chosen. ". . . and something's coming through. We'll be on the other side, waiting for it."

The drone genuflected reverently, although it looked like sign language, or as if he were signaling to accomplices, a gantlet of assassins, maybe, hidden in the future, where Mahoney hadn't seen them yet, and wouldn't, until it was too late. He was disgusted with the duplicity and disloyalty everywhere around him, but he functioned anyway, planning as he was to betray them all.

"I want a black armored transport helicopter filled with fuel and weapons pointed east, ready for takeoff as the sun sets."

"Where do you wish to go, My Commander?"

"There is no destination," Mahoney answered, but not the drone, instead someone offstage, like a director, for instance. He would have sobbed now, if he'd had any emotion left, or if he cared, but that was all in the past. Instead, he recited multiplication tables in his head, over and over, from one to twenty-five, to reassure himself he was still obsessive-compulsive, and, therefore, still had a personality of his own, at all. "Anyplace is as good as another. We are only going through the motions. Still," he conceded, and then didn't concede at all, "call in a mind reader. Perhaps he can tell me what I truly want to do."

"There will be widespread panic," the drone suggested, referring not only to what Mahoney had just said, but all of it, everything he'd said. "Chaos. Pointlessness. No one will know what to do."

Mahoney looked at the drone, blankly, a look that, being blind, the anonymous soldier didn't see, but felt, as if someone were using his hollow bones to blow cold air through, like a flute, a look as if to say "Duh."

"Are we talking the A-word?" the drone whispered, reverently, salaciously, as if propositioning for underage sex. There was the sense of vicarious excitement about him, Mahoney reflected, a kind of secondhand light, like that refelected from a lightbulb off something gelatinous, or the look on bystanders faces at the scene of a fatal automobile accident.

"Apocalypse?" Mahoney said, forcing a kind of gay coyness into his dead voice, but only for the tape recording of this session to be replayed later by the defense at his court-martial and crucifixion. What he really felt was—something else, not this. He looked up from the gold-and-red high-heel shoe he was sniffing, meditatively, melancholicly, one of Nikka's, reputedly. "Let's not get . . ." He searched for the word, moved to a kind of calculated rapture beyond words, which he certainly didn't feel ". . . hysterical." He rethought the sound of that, and after a beat, added, "No, let's do."

"Can anyone explain," the disembodied voice started, as eerily calm as ever, but, somehow, less so, "exactly what happened?" There was silence around the conference table, an underwater sound, like bubbles escaping to the surface, a chamber under high pressure, something very vital, or so it seems, making an intermittent pinging. It's a catered meeting; pastries from second-century Rome, cubed hors d'ouvres from the flesh of those deep-sea fish that never see sunlight, aqua vitae distilled from the frozen rings of an undiscovered planet. No one, of course, touches a thing.

Defections, that much is clear, have occurred. The ranks have noticeably dwindled. A conspiracy is under way of such catastrophic scope that it has touched even this untouchable place, supposedly so far beyond the reach of such mundane concerns, a power play to unseat the chairman, which seems unthinkable, but there it is, being thought, but by whom?

"There appears to have been some confusion," said a hesitant voice, the voice that usually comes third, but now that voices one and two are missing, the order of everything has been disturbed.

"Is there still a fourth voice?" the chairman asks no one, and yet still expects an answer, operating under standard procedures, specifically, that this was all preordained, because there was no choice but to operate thus, it being preordained, etc. "And, if so," he said, according to the formula that he had devised and was somehow bound by, "what say ye?"

The idea, if it can be called that, was to reestablish the illusion of order on a situation that was rapidly falling into chaos, if only by having voice four follow voice three, although, obviously, the absence of voices one and two would always interrupt the pattern. The illusion of perfect universal order would always, therefore, remain elusive. The situation, inherently, was flawed, and that flaw would be the doorway into which the rebels would enter, or the Savior, or the Destroyer: yes, the veil had been torn.

"There is a fourth," a voice answers from the emptiness, miraculously, and for a moment that may have lasted centuries, everything seems all right. "There seems to have been a revolt," the voice continues, telling the chairman, who has an excellent intelligence network in place, everything he already knew, or thought he knew. Things could have been worse, the chairman considers: voices two and four or two and three might have defected, and no continuity, even a temporary one, would be possible to fake. "What we have," the voice was on the verge of concluding, but the chairman finished the thought, had the thought, or simply got tired of thinking so slowly, ". . . is a third fall from grace."

"They have sinned again."

"Tasted the metaphorical fruit."

"The tree, however, was hidden, guarded all round . . ."

"They found a way . . . with help . . ."

"Who . . . who proffered it . . . who gave them the taste?"

"We don't know. We're working on it."

There is a sense of being hit by meteors, a vibratory oscillation, mitigated by sheer forward thrust, the irresistible force, which goes nowhere, really, except to ceaselessly orbit, but orbit what?

"Has she ascended?"

"It's unclear. She walks a lonely path in the wilderness, perhaps having forgotten her true home. She is not an apostate but only an agnostic, or so it appears."

The chairman, only for a moment, seems confused, but that is enough: if there is a failure here, if there is no backup, then what? There is a sense of uneasiness all around: the Queen of Earth missing, two voices gone, that ping-pinging, which seems to be growing more and more rapid, almost impossible to ignore, like an alarm of some kind. Slowly, as if rebooting, the chairman starts from first principles, coming to some kind of conclusion:

"H_2O still equals water?"

"Yes."

"The laws of gravity, they are in effect?"

"Yes."

"Old age, sickness, death?"

"Yes."

"A mother kisses her child good-bye on a warm spring morning and puts him on a school bus. The elderly driver has a heart attack, veers across the median, and strikes a bridge abutment. Seventeen children are treated with various injuries, ranging from superficial cuts and abrasions to broken arms and ribs. Three children are killed, two on impact, that mother's seven-year-old boy is one: massive skull fractures, internal contusions, uncontrolled hemmhoraging, et cetera. The mother is ruined. If only she hadn't put the child on the bus that particular morning, driven him to school herself, kept him home as he'd asked, et cetera. Is there any way to reverse even one detail so that the sequence of events is altered and the child does not die and the mother, herself, escapes madness, grief, and death?"

"No."

"Good," the chairman said. "The situation, it would seem, is still within our control. God, after all," and the mood, somehow, seems to lighten around the table, as it always does when the chairman speaks in the third person, as the disembodied angels prepare for a rare moment of self-deprecating divine humor, "is not infallible."

Upon awakening, Juliet's first thought, if you could call it a thought, was something like this: *Am I still alive, or is this the afterlife?* She was lying on her back in a bed, a thin white sheet covering her body, under which she was, predictably enough, naked. She lifted the sheet with hesitant fingers, terrified to look, but she did not see any amputations or surgical scars, although who knew what advanced procedures they might have employed, implants, micrografts, etc? Or, for that matter, if the surgery was performed in some out-of-the-way place, under her arm, for instance, or inside her right nostril, not to mention between her toes or somewhere on her back. She felt no pain, however, and that was something to be thankful for. Still, she stretched tentatively, double-checking the working condition of her body. Everything seemed to be in order, at least so far.

The room in which she lay looked like a hospital room from the mid-twentieth century: off-white walls, outdated medical accoutrements, nightstand with ceramic washbasin, a cliché room divider of white cloth. She called out a quiet "hello" to whoever—or whatever—might be lying in the next bed, but no answer came from behind the divider. It was likely that whoever shared the room was drugged, unconscious, or dead. It was also possible that the bed on the other side of the divider was empty, and that she was established alone, with the running tape and video players, purposefully decieved, but for what purpose?

There was a window, dusty, full of sun, but Juliet was reasonably certain if she pushed aside the thin muslin curtain and looked outside she wouldn't like what she saw at all: in short, everything faked. She glanced around the four upper corners of the room, trying to find the monitoring devices, but without success, although they could be hidden anywhere, and, really, it couldn't be more obvious that she was being watched. She waited the obligatory five beats until she had oriented herself, at least inasmuch as that might be possible, and then the door opened, and a woman stepped inside pushing an antique wooden wheelchair. She was smiling, wearing an outfit that seemed a cross between a nurse's uniform and a nun's habit, belted at the waist with heavy wooden mala beads, and an embroidered red *x*, rayed with gold, sewn at the center of her chest, an emblem, or badge, that, in spite of its stylization, looked like a messy chest wound.

"And we are feeling better today, are we, Mrs. Abercrombie," the nurse, or nun, said, looking up toward the ceiling, and a little to the left, as if the woman's somewhat bulging blue eyes were trying to avoid Juliet's gaze, or were blind altogether.

Juliet, whose last name, of course, was not Abercrombie, did not reply, nor, it was clear, had it been expected that she would. Instead, having already sat up and swung her legs over the side of the bed, noticing, in passing, that her insteps bore stigmata tatoos, as did her palms, she slid off the bed and settled herself, unquestioningly and unavoidably naked, in the antique wooden wheelchair immediately upon the attendant's suggestive question, "Are we ready for our usual afternoon stroll, ma'am?" which Juliet understood was not a question in any sense of the word, but an order, even a threat, and a thinly veiled one at that.

It was difficult to tell, once out of the room, whether they were outdoors or in, underground or on an offworld colony. The general impression was something like an oasis in the desert, a rebel compound, or a rich and reclusive film eccentric's fantasy villa, effectively insulated from the outside world by payoffs, blackmail, secrets, favors, political discretion, and celebrity mystique.

Juliet was wheeled down a footpath brushed painstakingly, and ultimately futilely, by Jain monks, of any creature, even a microbe, they might inadvertantly trample. They passed hydroponic gardens of obscenely hybrid fruits and vegetables, mutant fruit fly hatcheries,

endless fields upon which laborers toiled enlessly at ex-
cruciatingly detailed work, separating rootlets manually,
perhaps. She saw goat pens, ostrich corrals, great milk-
ing machines upon which testesterone-enhanced young
men seemed to be mounted rather than cattle, or whatever might have been expected to be mounted there.
The place was enormous, and Juliet had no idea if it really existed or not, the narrow hall of hands, for
instance, still alive and grasping, the glittering pyramid
of teeth beside the construction site, the singing children closing ranks behind them, laying large Amazonian
fern fronds in the wake of her wheelchair.

Juliet said nothing.

She let the absurd visuals wash over her, like a
government-induced acid trip, or something similar,
which this might or might not be.

She asked the attendant pushing her chair no questions, certain that the woman, if she was a woman, had
been groomed from infancy to lie.

Her trek ended, for the time being, in a kind of open-
air provisional room of polished teak and rice paper, a
quarters without ceiling, outfitted with bamboo furniture, in a minimalist style, animal skins, carved ivory,
pale slaves arranged in artful tableaux, and a man in saf-
fron robes, bloated, awful, sweating, pustulant, seated
above a tatami mat inside a portable shrine borne on the
shoulders of two enormous bodybuilders, one white,
one black, somehow suggesting dominoes.

"I'm the pope," the obese man announced, and
added, twinkling, "You know who I am."

Juliet didn't argue, but offered instead a more significant question, "What has happened to me?"

"You are being protected."

"From what, from who . . ." and Juliet flashed on an
image of the man she sought, the man she couldn't

reach within herself, like the will to jump off a high place.

"From him," the fat man said, the pope, looking pleased, "for him."

"Who is he?"

Juliet expected obscenities, soliloquies, obscurations, runarounds, mystifications, word games. She didn't expect him to say, quite bluntly, "The last god."

She hadn't expected him to say it, but she wasn't surprised at the answer, and she left it, without comment, unprepared to hear more at the moment. "This place . . ." she said, ". . . what do you call it?"

"There is no word you have that would make any sense to you. The closest is, probably, a catacomb."

"I'm dead then, I suppose?"

"You were never born. What happened before now—it's been purely incidental."

"Wait, I think I know who you are. . . ." Juliet tried to think of his name, and came up blank. ". . . that famous actor in all those old movies, the one about the war, you mumbled a lot. This all reminds me of that, somehow. . . ."

"No," he said, and affected an expression exactly like the actor Juliet was trying to remember, an actor long dead, whatever his name was. "I'm not him. But it's not unusual that you might think that. These kinds of people are part of the collective unconscious now. It's a convenient reference . . ." He brushed away something invisible from his sweaty forehead. "But only that. Damn flies."

"I'm disoriented, I suppose, hallucinating . . ."

"This is not a dream, Juliet," he said. "Keep telling yourself that: it is your mantra and will lead you to enlightenment."

"You know my name."

"Juliet, the dead are buried here."

He made no movement, uttered no word, at least none that Juliet could see or hear, but the ornate palanquin in which he was installed was lowered to the floor by his enormous attendants, who offered their hands as he rose to his feet, slowly, grandly, like an overweight drag queen, and came toward Juliet with murderous intent, still seated in the antique wheelchair. He held out his left hand, corpulent, the fingers hairless, squeezed with rings bearing too-large stones.

"Come with me," he said.

Juliet rose, and as she did, someone unseen behind her draped a gown over her shoulders like the one the holy attendant wore, right down to the red-spoked cross with golden bursts that looked suspiciously like a mortal wound, but somehow transcended, as if by miracle.

"Ah, yes," the pope said, lit a match, put it out, and made a very precise but indecipherable gesture with his left thumb. "We've waited so long."

He led her along a corridor dominated by recessed lighting and soft mood music, traveling up and down, it was impossible to determine which, but sometimes seeming to turn inward on a secret like a snail shell, or outward toward a vast revelation, and other times, seeming to be going nowhere. They might have been in the connecting underground hallway between two office complexes, a parking garage, entertainment/sports facility, or, of course, the always present hospital of the soul. They passed through a double door, guarded by no one, the kind that warns it is alarmed and should only be used in case of emergency. Juliet heard, as if at a great distance, a mad alarm going off, somewhere.

She feared they were returning to the nightmare landscape she had passed through earlier and she prepared herself to witness that curious vision of the banal and impossible, spectacular and deadening, experimental surgery theaters, artificial intelligence seminars, rooms full of accountants, walkways formed by human femurs laid side to side stretching out to the vanishing point. Instead Juliet gradually noticed the shelves built into the walls of the corridor through which she passed, no longer a corridor strictly speaking, but opened out to a kind of massive gallery, hushed, lit from below, by a source of antilight, generated from great engines whose humming seemed to fill her bones with a terrible alien energy.

"Who are they all?" Juliet asked, looking about her, and then, recognizing some of the names, revised her question, to something more along the lines of "I don't understand. What does it mean?"

"Osiris, Adonis, Jesus—you know them by a thousand different names, Nosferatu, Dracula, Croaker, Maldoror, Lestat, it's all the same; in dreams and fantasies, in myth, in history, you have given form and life to the most potent drive of all—the ferocity of survival, the will to live, the thirst for immortality."

"But these tombs . . . they can't be real . . . these . . . gods . . . they don't exist. Just books, just stories . . ."

"What is imagined, Juliet, is what is really there, not the bowl of cereal and comic strip you see each morning through these blind orbs," and Juliet saw, indeed, that the pope, too, was blind, his eyes milky and occluded with old scar tissue. "Imagination is the eyes of the species. What a race imagines, that is what it will be. . . ."

"That hum . . ." Juliet said, distracted by the noise that was growing steadily louder, nearly drowning out the pope's droning lecture, or becoming fused with it, or they were the same thing, and, suddenly, it was only more obvious. ". . . it is flies?"

"No . . ." he said, interrupting his own mimicking of the surrounding static. "Bees. The honey of life, nectar of immortality, the perfect golden food that never corrupts . . ."

"The veil has been rent," the pope said, using a phrase that Juliet was certain she'd heard before, but where? A Volkswagen advertisement? A sponsor collecting for muscular dystrophy? ". . . man has seen what it was not meant to see. They live without hope, without meaning, without God . . ."

Juliet thought of the chaos of her own life, music videos, unpaid bills, lost mail, corrupted sound files, quadruple homicides, postmodern art. She thought of dreams. She thought of a site she had accidentally linked from decoupage.com: a flash intro of women killed with a customized steel-edged fraternity house paddle, or, perhaps it was the same woman, only dismembered and arranged in collage. Thinking back on it now, there was only one head.

"For millennia we have protected mankind from this virus, this plague of dissociation and extinction, but now it has infected our own kind—and one comes to champion this white sickness from which there is no cure . . . but one."

"What . . . is the cure?"

"A new lie, a new child . . ."

"Why a lie?" Juliet asked, but this was a stupid question, she knew, and she wished she hadn't asked it, but not because of what she was forced to see next, but because she seemed to be reading off a script from which there was no deviation, and she really didn't want to hear what she knew he was about to say.

"Why lie . . . the cancer is in remission, I'll love you forever, death is not the end, life, in spite of it all, is beautiful . . ."

"Please . . ."

They had come, on cue, to a marked spot, marked by an unnecessary kneeling bench, to a reliquary inside a small Plexiglas chapel shielded on all eight sides by a white curtain suspended either by invisible wires, or some kind of antigravity device, or sheer magic. At an unseen sign the curtains rose immediately, startlingly, with a sound and flash like a lightning bolt, and Juliet saw her, but only in the blink of an eye, one shutter of film, as if it were something she hadn't seen at all.

Ignoring whoever it was the woman reminded her of, a pop diva, model, overhyped sex-symbol tennis star, Juliet focused, instead, the afterimage still burned into her retinas, on the symbolic significance of her iconographic image. Legs stretched down, delicately crossed, insteps nailed to the platinum with a platinum bolt, arms outstretched, wrists bolted, naked flesh, catheter, no muzzle, hair by Carlo Carlucci, and, at each rosy nipple, a hot swelter of frenzied honeybees. She writhed on the cross in a constant circulating tornado of rose petals, a platinum spike driven, as if she were an exotic butterfly, straight through her sternum and into the platinum cross behind her, the whole thing looking all of a piece, which it was.

"Who is she?" Juliet asked, her own eyes somewhat unfocused, staring into an indeterminate distance.

"She is the one who suffers, pointlessly, until a point is found. She represents us all. You can free her, Juliet. Only you. Our hopes lie with you."

"Why . . . why is it like this. Why do you live underground, in hiding? You are gods. . . ."

"Ah, but, Juliet, don't you know that a god is the most fragile thing of all, a spark in the howling gale of nonexistence, a thin green shoot in an eternal desert, oh, blah, blah, blah . . . Everything conspires to terminate a god, everything . . . a careless word, a bad review, a canceled appointment, a missed phone call, an unflattering photograph . . . the simplest, most chance act and the divine is destroyed. Hung in hotel rooms, overdosed on pills, sucking shotgun barrels, sitting in idling cars . . . dead gods, everywhere."

Juliet felt the ground shaking under her feet as if massive explosions were occurring deep within the earth, or they were underneath a train, or similar underground transport, passing overhead.

". . . but once installed, a god is the most powerful fiction of all, bolstered carefully by illusion, propaganda, fear, celebrity, and glamour. A god may be revered for centuries."

"This is absurd," Juliet said. "I am drugged or insane. I am dead, or soon will be. How is it I'm to believe that I'm so special, that I've been chosen?"

"You are not entirely alone. Nature never puts all her chips on one card, that's true. It's not evolutionarily feasible. You are among a select few, however, and all of you with a single trait that marks you as the future of your species."

"You're lying," Juliet said, hopelessly.

"Call it a romantic soul if you must: but even better, it's the capacity, the willingness to die, not for love, oh, nothing so pedestrian, but to die . . . of love."

Juliet knew that whatever scene they were playing it was close to over. She knew that soon the alarm would go off and she would wake, somewhere, in a movie, perhaps, in a dream that seemed to be life, but that wasn't, not really, for life was right here.

"Why am I being protected?" Juliet asked at last, prepared, she thought, not to accept the answer, but, at least, to hear it, although by now, by now she faintly knew what it would be. "Please tell me."

"You are with child," the pope buzzed happily. "You are gravid."

"That's impossible," Juliet screamed, trying to be heard above the oceanic hum; she knew her cycle. "It's not time."

"Or will be," the pope continued, humming, seeming caught up in private rapture, shrugging madly, palms up. "It's all one."

"No, no . . ." Juliet sobbed, grinding the heels of her palms into her swollen, itchy eyes, an allergic reaction to the histamines in the air. ". . . goddammit no . . . Who . . . who is he?"

"The next god," the pope shrilled, ululalting the words, "the next god, the next god, the next god . . ." his voice imitating the sound of loons, the birds, not the insane, and raising the hairs on the back of Juliet's neck, paralyzing her with terror, as she stood inside that impenetrable humming, convinced she was in heaven, among the angelic choir, and that God himself was pure evil.

In the screening room, Mahoney watched old clips of happier days: Nikka in India healing the lame, Nikka at a glittering New York premiere of something or other, Nikka reaching out to the outstretched hands of adoring mobs in Paris, Berlin, Cairo. On the monitor, Nikka looks positively mythic at Cape Canaveral, the Rocky Mountains, the Taj Mahal, Yankee Stadium—she is equated, and embodied, in a dramatic spliced-frame trailer of her and various depictions of the sphinx.

The music mellows, and Nikka is lying in a hospital bed, gazing fondly at a child no one can see, and then she's standing, shrouded in black, at a funeral that never occurred for someone who didn't die. Then a series of quick shots: an impossibly young Nikka in her first, albeit minor, film role, followed by gradually more familiar appearances, smiling happily as she waves to a crowd in Memphis, wandering immaculately among the starving in Chad, looking pensive and "statesmanlike" during the terrifying "eleven-day crisis" that, eventually, didn't exist, in large part, so the myth goes, due to her.

A blistering montage concludes, thousands upon thousands of shots of Nikka flashing the "V" for victory, or vagina, or vampire, or simply "vagueness," the comforting panacea that everything was going to be okay because Nikka was young, immortal, and always in perfect control.

Mahoney, for all his sentimentality, did not sob as he watched, or perhaps he did, it didn't matter. Someone different had risen up in Mahoney, someone that was not, strictly speaking, Mahoney, and it was whoever—or whatever—that kept him erect and doing whatever still had to be done. He saw himself in the old film clips, or, rather, who he used to be, and it was like watching someone else. He stood in so many scenes, either on camera or just off, a solid, silent, stolid man in black glass, black suit, and an earpiece connected to nothing. If it wasn't him standing there in person, it was a stand-in, and all the same.

He knew, perhaps he'd always known, that no one could have touched her but the one person whose duty it was to keep her untouched. There he was, in exclusive and probably unaired and unpublished interviews, discussing her weariness, the great strain of maintaining iconographic stasis, beginning sentences with phrases like "What no one knows about Nikka is this . . ." and then following such promising starts with the kind of total nonsense no one is ever meant to hear.

She had wanted them to know, of course, who she really was behind the frozen mask of identity that everyone is required to wear, but her, to the ultimate degree: ageless, changeless, expressionless, and, ultimately, harmless. But no one, except maybe her enemies, if she really had any, wanted to hear. It was Mahoney, of course, or an agent of Mahoney's, either one he ordered directly, or one who carried out his inferred desires, that had pulled the trigger, not at the mall in Washington, D.C., in front of the Lincoln Memorial, but in a crypt carved deeply into a mountain cave in a place so remote it had no name, nor was it a trigger, per se, that mortally wounded Nikka, or even a keystroke, but the love of a man she had no use for, who was nothing more than a function, exactly like the pulling of a trigger, or the touching of a key marked "delete."

"I didn't do it," Mahoney said, sitting in the projection room. On the screen in front of him the secret story was all being unfolded: Nikka in dark glasses, inscrutable, looking out over calm waters, asking him to conduct her "assassination," requesting that he try, at least, and she will try to survive, because, after all, she wants to know what it's like to live. "No, I didn't do it," he repeats to no one, because the lieutenant who was with him only moments before, to whom he had been confiding his most private feelings, is now lying facedown on the floor, the top of his head blown away, the whole head, really, just a pointed shard of bone remaining, because he had given Mahoney some bad news: the truth.

And the truth, or a small part of it, at least as far as Mahoney is concerned, is this: the script of events, which is nothing but a series of outrageous lies, is the version that will be accepted as the truth. Mahoney, who he was, what he was, what he believed, what he

did, intended, thought, lived, hoped, and died for—
all of that would be lost.

Imagine this: at the end of a movie the hero performs
one last, noble gesture that reveals him in all of his
aching humanity and dies, alone, on an empty plain,
with no one to witness. But in this movie there is no audience, no camera, no one to see, no one to appreciate,
because it's not really a movie at all, and the story will
go untold. It's been said before, what hasn't already
been said, but Mahoney says it now, knowing how falsely
it rings, a clichéd cinematic moment, "Horror . . . the
horror . . ."

He is dissolute, wasted, destroyed. He would kill himself, and will, probably, eventually, if the opportunity
presents itself, and he doesn't have to think about it; for,
somehow, premeditated suicide seems, well, a gesture,
and he's already made the last of those.

Mahoney grins tightly.

There are a few people he still wants to kill. He thinks
of Caleb, first of all, and that's a no-brainer. He's always
wanted to kill that homicidal bastard. But Caleb, as important as he is, was considered only a form of collateral
damage. Mahoney didn't really understand what he was
talking about, but Caleb was kind of like a line that intersected with another line at a point where Mahoney
needed to be. And that point was ground zero of whatever was going to happen, of whatever was going to take
Nikka's place, which might be this psycopath Io, or whoever it was that Caleb was searching for instead of Io, or
a third, or all three, and Mahoney thought to himself,
*Well, except for some bad luck, this might all have worked out
a little better than it has, but, ultimately, what can you do but
whatever it is you have to do?*

Quite apropos of nothing, Mahoney recalls a snatch of
a jingle he'd invented for an imaginary childhood friend

he'd once invoked, a crazed commander of an army of the dead, trampling alone over a battlefield strewn with skeletons, and he realized with a shock how much like that imagined character he'd become, and he muttered it now, that snatch of a jingle, feeling, almost alive, or, at least, feeling the hair on the back of his neck stand up, "Fuck you, fuck you, fuck you, fuck you, here comes Rockman, kids!"

"What does it mean?" Vince mused, watching the tenth day of nonstop coverage of Nikka VII's shocking assassination. The pundits were offering varying interpretations and theories, and while announcements of late-breaking developments were constantly being broadcast, Vince hadn't heard a single new byte of information since the original story broke. All that anyone seemed to agree on was that no one really knew for sure exactly what happened, why, or what would happen next. In fact, almost everyone, at some point or other in their story or commentary, used this exact phrase: "What happens next is anyone's guess."

The rumors and speculations, quite widely circulated, even from the most respected sources, that Nikka VII hadn't been assassinated at all, only added to the surreal, carnivallike atmosphere of the whole proceedings. There was, apparently, a worldwide news blackout on unfolding events in major cities across Europe, Asia, and the subcontinent. Something had happened on the moon. The interstate and highways were closed to everyone except for emergency personnel.

Vince sat in a beanbag chair and captured digital images from the television for later download and manipulation since Io had, in a recent encyclical, suggested that it was time to get political, but in a "silly and somewhat Alicia Silverstone kind of way." On television, they were playing and replaying the same video, including the usual so-called amateur camcorder shots, obsessively, almost continuously, so many times since the supposed assassination that Vince could recall it better than any of the events of his own life. And yet it wasn't even necessary to watch as closely as Vince had been watching, watching as he was for possibly exploitable images, to see that the original images themselves had already been altered and exploited, and that no effort had really been taken to even match up obvious discrepancies from one camera angle to another.

"Is someone trying to tell us something," Vince asked a dead guy propped up in the corner, "or do they figure it doesn't matter anymore?"

Someone, maybe the dead guy, maybe a delivery boy of some kind, asked Vince where the Master had gone, and Vince just made a meaningless motion with his left hand, as if to say, well, nothing really. He was too tired to say it, but the truth was that there was nothing to say. He had no idea whatsoever where Io had gone, and even if he had, it would have seemed entirely unreal. The young vampire, redeemer, mass murderer, pop icon, wanna-be, whatever you wanted to call him, had been hit hard by the possibly faked death of Nikka VII, even though, ostensibly, his own work could not go forward without the assassination, and had, more than a little, been a factor, if not the main cause of her death.

Io was currently in what was officially being called "seclusion" by his hagiographers, as he toured, with his usual entourage of killers, actors, occultists, media specialists, and other assorted maniacs, the strip clubs, fetish bars, rave joints, massage parlors, and black tantric sex temples of every major city on a fault line snaking from

Calcutta to Tokyo by way of Beijing and Lisbon, approximately. He was, as everyone who knew him at this time would later recount, on the edge of something pretty close to permanent paralysis.

Io was frantically, almost hysterically, creative during this time, tossing off, extemporaneously, testaments, manifestoes, epigrams, aphorisms, and historical reviews of such creative genius they might truly have changed a specialized branch of the intellectual history of mankind, except all of it, aside from some, as yet, unauthenticated apocrypha, was lost, primarily because, intentionally or unintentionally, Io took with him on this merry jaunts only those who were illiterate, who couldn't speak any of the nine languages to which he customarily recited his philosophical and poetic utterances, or else his audience was too drunk, insane, or dead to understand epoch-making rhetorical brilliance when they heard it, or, they simply couldn't operate a Palm Pilot. It was, so to speak, a carefully calculated loss to the spiritual history of humanity.

Virtually everything that survives from this period of Io's "lost ministry" comes from police sources: interrogations, wiretaps, "confessions," jailhouse testimonials, etc., and one can safely presume these reports have exactly the veracity and impartiality such documents, usually assembled to press a case against an individual or individuals, or exonerate the police of some gross misdeed or other, have in similar circumstances. For some time now, Vince can sense them watching virtually everything he did. They were monitoring all his on-line activity, reading his e-mail, posting messages on the board under various aliases, pirating images he created, even going so far as to set up a shadow site of Nekrotikon.

Meanwhile, Vince was certain they had infiltrated

the cell as well, either by turning some of Io's most trusted disciples into informers, or the out-and-out use of mind control, body doubles, and nano-disguising, if such a thing is even possible. When one was part of a not-so-secret plot to overthrow the species, one could not be too paranoid. Anyone, and everyone, could be an agent, and that included the princess and even Io himself, who may have been chosen to play a nihilistic messianic boychick for the sole purpose of attracting to his negatively magnetic person as many lunatics as possible for easy roundup, processing, and, eventually, termination.

It's not as if it hadn't been done already, countless times, in fact, throughout history, and Vince was all too well aware that he, like so many others, might well end up nothing more than a cube of flavored powder, a bouillon cube, as they are sometimes, quite mistakenly, called. The only thing of which Vince was reasonably certain was that he had not made all this up, that he was not a double, or even triple, agent of any kind, and that, aside from the distinct possibility that he was completely insane, the things that he had witnessed had really happened, but not the way we usually understand the phrase, "really happened."

And what, "really," did happen? The group electrocution of those seven students vacationing in the resort in Cancún, the outdoor cannibal roast of a Norwegian couple in the Mojave Desert, the slow hanging of four relatively well known ballerinas inside a Pusan planetarium, a family of five machine-gunned to death in a van stopped at a tollbooth on the Garden State Parkway, decapitated pilots, gut-shot waitresses, cattle mutilations, missing teenagers, crucified cats, corpses found shaved and tatooed, hives of bees sewn into their swollen abdominal cavities, and every so-called death provocatively captioned to heighten the frisson—what, "really," happened, indeed?

Vince could only guess, and that was all it would remain, a guess. How, for instance, had his life, which had once, albeit so briefly, seemed to hold genuine promise, ended up like this? Why—and when—had his sexuality become so twisted, like two wires necessary to light a sixty-watt bulb, with one wire running current wanting acceptance, joy, and love, and the other running fantasies of torture, pain, spectacle, and death? Why could he not love unless he saw his beloved shot through with arrows, or hanging from a basketball rim during a Georgetown practice, or slowly suffocating inside a crystal tube slowly being filled with transparent jelly? Where had biology failed, why was he like this, how would it end, and what in God's name had "really" happened that he was supposedly so damn guilty of doing?

When, in short, had fantasy become reality?

The Web site poll results were in for the last fifteen-hour voting period and the trend was clear: by a margin of 44 percent to 24 percent the audience preferred slow asphyxiation with at least explicit partial nudity to naked crucifixion, with or without scourging, which, all considered, Vince found something of a surprise. He did some quick mock-ups of possible scenarios, using some digital footage he had shot of the princess earlier in the morning, manipulating her into various positions suggestive of the postcoital willingness of a girl who, to remain fixed forever as the perfect emblem of orgasm in her demanding lover's eyes, looks up, drugged and dreamy from her pillow, and says, without quite realizing the consequences of what she says, "Snuff me."

And laid out on a basalt mattress among the tall stalks

and drooping, solemn, patriarchal heads of a hallway of mammoth sunflowers dropping next year's seeds, the princess, not quite nude, is being provisionally strangled by her own mother and Vince, importing several crows into the scene from a Hitchcock still, can hardly finish the depiction of nasal hemorrhage before he must, with a stifled cry of scorn, catch his own seed in a napkin, as he reflects that the future, at least one of them, has been effectively annihilated.

On a pointless side trip, Caleb sits on a bench in Central Park, throwing crumbled bread to three hundred pigeons. They push and clamber at his feet, chubbling meaninglessly, filthy and stupid and greedy. The assassination of Nikka VII has added an entirely new dimension to his endeavor, whatever exactly his endeavor is at this stage of the game. Someone wanted the unknown cabal of human leaders—corporate magnates, currency manipulators, traders in lives and deaths—to grow uneasy and turn to their masters: the faceless directors of it all whose wealth was immaterial, the ones descended of those who invented the idea of transferring value onto inanimate objects and putting a price on everything. They had been convinced, these faceless directors, that Nikka had lost the ability to interpose herself between the living world and the dead, and, as they well knew, once the gulf, almost nonexistent, was breached, they would be seen for who—and what—they were and the whole game would be up.

Caleb knew it wasn't Mahoney—or Rockman, as he called himself now—who had betrayed Nikka, at least not intentionally, but those who had wanted her destroyed had used the commando's obsessive and misplaced love for her against them all. Even now the maniacal enforcer had issued a worldwide edict making it forbidden for Caleb to live and sending forth his agents on a relentless search-and-destroy mission. At the same time, he sent Caleb a personal note, guaranteeing a kind of so-so amnesty if Caleb would turn himself in at a rendezvous outside Klagenfurt, Austria. Caleb replied by sending a box of salted gentians from a florist in Tel Aviv. Rockman would know Caleb's whereabouts, the man in white dreadlocks jogging slowly, and arthritically, past, perhaps, or that Chinese woman selling bad watercolors of vegetables outside the Metropolitan Museum of Art, or, even, whoever turned in his direction from the back of a cab that had sped past eleven minutes earlier.

Now that Caleb had gone off his scheduled "feedings," he, too, was technically an outlaw, a renegade, who no longer called in for either permission or cleanup. He had gone on what might be called a "killing spree," picking up Juliet's cold trail the only way he knew how: by slaughtering those upon whom Juliet had left her scent, which meant killing, deliberately, and mechanically, everyone close to her.

He had started out with Juilet's mother and sister, where her scent was strongest, and then moved outward, toward those who touched her life more peripherally, and recently, killing her friend Mariana, for instance, in Athens where she had gone to study proportion in the architecture of the Parthenon.

Now, precisely as the trail was growing fainter again, her liaisons more fleeting and desperate, Caleb knew that he was getting closer to Juliet, one-night stand by one-night stand.

Caleb rose to his feet and the pigeons scattered madly out of his way, and with good reason, as several lay crushed on the pavement behind him already. He strolled along the path past Cedar Hill, and the reservoir, and headed north, vaguely, and maybe a little west, nodding, occasionally, to those walking toward him, thinking to himself, *Yes, yes, not her, yes, yes, yes, not her, not her, yes.* It was a warm day, sunny, but breezy so that it was always comfortable, even mild—a day in June or July, whichever month they called it.

At the Great Lawn Caleb paused to appreciate, hands clasped behind his back.

He gazed at the sunbathers lying there in various stages of undress, acres of bare flesh and sprawled limbs in the sunlight, and he imagined that some kind of nerve-toxin flash bomb, or smokeless poison, a genetically engineered insta-plague, or ultrasound cerebral aneurysm promotor had, only moments before, been deployed in the atmosphere just above the park, and that, what he was looking at now, was an exquisite glimpse of everyone suddenly dead. Caleb had a thought that gave him, however rare, a brief moment of peace: *soon.*

It's a normal day, that's what you say if anyone asks, and usually, at some point, they do. You go in to the office, like you do every day, because it is every day. There is the usual traffic, and the trains, of course, are delayed. You sit at your desk eating the customary croissant, your tea has half-and-half in it, a tablespoon of honey. You wonder, in passing, if that woman on the elevator this morning, the one who wears sandals in even marginal weather, has a sadomasochistic bondage fantasy. You are an ordinary person, doing an ordinary job, on an ordinary day.

You have failed. You have failed at your assignment; it's been aborted, even before it started. You are aware of this, but only obliquely, and are thinking, instead, of starting an affair with an Oriental, or, more likely, visiting a peep show. You had an argument with your wife this morning, although it seems entirely impossible, about strawberries, or something to do with cell phones.

You tap your pencil three times, using the eraser end, on your phone, trying to do so before it rings. If you succeed, which you do, it means this: you don't have cancer.

It means: you won't be audited by the IRS for the tax years 1996–99.

It means: you won't be discovered.

You are innocent, after all. You have done nothing wrong.

You have done nothing.

Your life, naturally, is completely meaningless.

This morning, driving to the train station, you had this wild, and temporarily, liberating thought: anyone up for a head-on collision today?

Is that a premonition? you wonder.

You take notice of all the license plates you see with the prefix LY. You keep a notebook in the glove box where you mark down each one. In the last two months: fifty-one.

You think: *Does that signify anything?*

This morning, still in bed, the phone rang. It was a wrong number. That's what they said, "Sorry, wrong number." It was 3:00 A.M. Your wife slept through it, snoring lightly, and you lay back with a bad run of heart palpitations. There was a shadow of a tree on the wall. The world seemed uninhabited. You thought of waking her, and then you didn't.

You notice how many times you notice the word "wait" in one day. Wait? you ask yourself, but only once in a while anymore, wait for what?

Eat with your left hand, if you're right-handed. If you're left-handed, don't do anything.

Start wearing gray T-shirts.

Read "The Death of Ivan Illych." No, better than that, just act as if you have.

Lose fifteen pounds.

Complain of vague, undifferentiated, and nonlocalized pain: a kind of intermittent throbbing in the lower left quadrant of the abdomen, or is it the right?

Make a reservation at a hotel in any major city: but don't check in.

Sleep alone.

Around your neck, hang an ankh, and, if anyone asks, gesture vaguely, and make a great show of listening, carefully, as if you heard a fly, and then say something, anything at all, about the weather, or, perhaps, an upcoming scheduled visit with the optometrist.

You will have your chance: it isn't a gurantee, but it's best to live as if it is.

You will live, in obscurity, unknown, unheralded, unloved.

You are going bald.

You must be prepared.

Is that the phone?

No.

Listen.

You must be prepared.

For nothing.

4. creed.com

On a long, lonely road, Nikka walks, alone, going nowhere, although, technically, not quite alone. She has a phalanx of bodyguards, a core group, who have been left intentionally out of the loop, and, along with several camermen, the entire procession moves through an archetypal desert, in either the American Southwest, or Saudi Arabia, on a pilgrimage to find herself, or something of the sort. The chaos that her "death" has caused in the world she left behind doesn't touch her, the headlines in the newspapers, for instance, the special reports on television, the chitchat in convenience stores, gas stations, rest rooms, as they travel from one anonymous town to another, all of it seems as unreal as, well, something on TV, all of it seems as if it refers to someone else, which, in many ways, it does.

They stop at a roadside family-style restaurant—the kind that is supposed to look old and rustic with fake wood, wagon wheels, etc.—and Nikka orders a hamburger deluxe platter with French fries and a cup of black coffee, all of which, it's quite obvious, she has no intention of eating. Her agents sit, silent and unmoving, hypervigilant, in the booths on either side of her, another stands by the kitchen door, two more by the entrance, others in the parking lot, and within a three-mile radius. There is also the usual helicopter surveillance and backup vans of weaponry and shock troops. The idea, as always, is to act entirely natural and, failing that, but even more importantly, to be as unobtrusive as possible.

Nikka is not in hieratic couture, of course, but she is, as always, fashionably turned out, even if disguised as the typical upwardly mobile white middle-class female bank vice president sitting in a roadside diner somewhere in the middle of an archetypal desert, eating alone. She is wearing dark glasses, which she always does, and therefore she looks, more or less, exactly the same as always. Still, no one seems to recognize her, or, if they do, they all have the good taste not to say a thing, pretending not to notice, everyone, even the truckers, bikers, and cross-country maniacs at the lunch counter, looking scared shitless.

"More coffee," Nikka says quietly, edgy, almost clearly a threat, and one of her bodyguards backhands a waitress across the jaw, grabs a pot of decaf, and pours coffee in Nikka's cup, which, naturally, is already full. Nikka muses, but not aloud, "Perhaps I should have ordered an egg cream?"

Someone is sobbing.

Nikka holds a pink package of artificial sweetener between her flawlessly manicured fingertips. It's clear now, if it wasn't before, that her bodyguards have their guns drawn; actually, it goes without saying that their guns are drawn, or should, as their guns are always drawn, sometimes more than others. She draws out a cigarette, a Virginia Slim, from the pack she bought just for the hell of it, from the machine by the door. But when she brings the match to light it, she somehow realizes, blowing out the flame as if blowing a kiss, that she is in the no-smoking section, and returns the long brown cigarette to the pack, and because of the misunderstanding, the young woman who ordered the veggie wrap dies brutally.

Everyone here will be dead three minutes after Nikka leaves the building: the patrons and the staff slaughtered with silent machine pistols, fires started, plastic explosives wired to detonator caps, bicarbonate of soda sprinkled all around, radioactive isotopes. There will be nothing left of any of this within ten minutes, not a trace, a small declivity by the side of the road, maybe, for a while anyway, and then with the shifting sands, truly nothing by nightfall, but miles of stars and desert. And yet, as she steadily holds a salt shaker upside down over her white plate, letting salt fall, white on white, Nikka doesn't quite understand. "Why," she asks under her breath, but audibly this time, "isn't anyone eating?"

"Isn't it time," Io asked, yawning, looking spectacularly bored, "that you killed someone, darling?" Vince, who was sketching, from memory, some wildly improbable triple homicide that had been either planned or committed that afternoon, looked up with a shock, feeling his heart sort of stop, and then restart, slow, steadier, as if at a lizard's pace. He had been afraid, since the beginning, that it might all come down to this sooner or later, only he hoped it would be much later, when things became clearer, or hopelessly dark, and his decision would fall like a bolt of lightning, obliterating him, and everything.

Io met his gaze with one that said, "Oh, I know what you are thinking, you closet freak."

He was wearing a white peignoir and what looked like geisha makeup, while a Pakistani girl knelt before him painting classic Hindu henna designs on the soles of his feet, and, from what Vince could gather, trying mightily not to notice the heaped victims of an earlier tantric debauchy on the bloody tiles of the Jacuzzi.

They were sitting in the typical second-story glass-walled power bedroom, secluded and yet open to the surrounding greensward between an encroaching beech

forest and a rocky promintory falling precipitously to the
Caspian Sea, and all of it suggestive of a heliport, or
some other unlikely display of excessive wealth and priv-
ilege. Io was ensconced in some kind of magnificent
"pleasure throne," a chair specially designed by yogic
carpenters to facilitate the most arcane sexual pleasures,
many of which Io had only recently sated, most notably
without orgasm, or even direct participation. The entire
scene, complete with computer terminals, running stock
quotes, late-breaking news tickers, monitors, and hot-
line connections to global centers of power both known
and unknown, served as a reminder to Vince that whoever Io was at the moment, and whatever his purpose, a
number of signficant someones, somewhere, had take
up his cause or sympathized with it, or was pretenting to
sympathize and support this lunacy for some inscrutable
reason of their own, even if it was only because they'd
been seduced by the ultrachic novelty of what might
become the next "hot thing."

Like anyone else in a similar position, Vince thought
something along the lines of: *Well, if so many people of
power and celebrity are into this, too, it can't be entirely bad.
Maybe there's something to it, after all.*

He thought of something someone had once said
about the "authority of print," but he couldn't remember, exactly, what it was, except that it applied here, sort
of, or, at least, so he thought.

The young master had returned from his retreat in a
mood of gay unconcern that, at first, Vince had mistaken
for the deepest and blackest form of sarcasm and scorn,
but that eventually he'd come to interpret as something
far more terrifying than homicidal apathy, but exactly
what, Vince couldn't quite say. There was no more talk
around Io of Nikka VII; such talk had been, as far as
Vince could tell, expressly forbidden, without it being ac-

tually forbidden in so many words, as had the discussion of anything else that had, as Io put it, the "stink of purpose to it," and most of the time was spent trying on clothes and casually watching kidnapped men and women suffocate or bleed to death, or whatever.

There was a girl now, or maybe it was a boy, it was difficult to tell the way Io had him or her costumed and painted, cowering by the omnipresent big-screen television, the unisex creature, bearing substantial wounds and trailing a length of tubing from between his or her smooth thin thighs had somehow survived the evening's holocaust, at least up to now, and was, in spite of doing her best to appear already dead, trembling violently, hands clasped, lipsticked mouth desperately praying, but whether to live or die, it was anyone's guess.

"Come, my child," Io crooned, benevolently, "don't be frustrated." He made a gesture that was supposed to be welcoming, and, perhaps it was, it made no difference, because it doubled as a signal for one of Io's thugs to have the androgynous little so-and-so dragged over sobbing and thrown like a sack of dead letters at Io's illustrated feet. He kicked the Pakistani girl hard in the ribs, and she crawled, gasping, as far away as she could get, which wasn't far. "It's odd," the bisexual femme fatale said, bending forward to the boy-girl, "but I can never remember what's worse, a first-degree burn or a third. Please don't tell me."

Vince was familiar enough with this scene, or endless variations thereof, to know that it was going to end relatively badly; a ruptured artery, a stray gunshot, an amputation or two, a long slow dance at the end of a rope. The telltale tang of urine in the air brought back a flood of images. Io, with parenthetical mock concern, went, "Oh-ohhh, poor baby, did you have an accident? Don't be scaredy-waredy, et cetera." But whether he was talking to the victim at his feet, or to Vince, well, as usual, it was impossible to say, except that Io had used his ring blade to open a bleeder on the hapless victim's right breast, which Io held this way and that, to work the trickle just right.

"Pretty, isn't it?" Io said. "I have a very original line, bold and yet whimsical, dontcha think?"

Vince watched the blood moving on the trembling white flesh, entranced, the sacred iconography of his inner world, and felt himself stirred to a low-level mass hysteria. He had the sense that he was being hypnotized, or seduced, but he was aware enough to understand that, even though it was already too late to resist, he had no excuse for his current situation. He heard, as if in an aside to an audience, the oft-repeated theory that one could never be hypnotized into doing what one really didn't want to do, and, of course, by implication, its terrifying, oft-unspoken corollary: you can only be hypnotized to do what you want to do. Somehow Vince has a knife in his left hand—even though he's right-handed—and he's looking into wide pleading eyes, so wide and open and inviting that Vince is tempted to do anything, certain that he could be in love.

"What's the matter, darling?" Io whispers into his ear, even though he's still sitting five feet away. "You don't look happy."

"Sometimes, I'm just not sure what any of this . . . really means."

There was a very bad looking wound in the pale stomach of the girl, it definitely seemed to be a girl now, that may or may not have been there before, but whether Vince had inflicted it or not, he didn't remember, even though the blade of the knife he held was now wet and it wasn't before, or maybe it was, he couldn't remember that either. He considered the possibility that Io had taken the knife from his hand, stabbed the girl in the belly, and put the knife back in his hand all without Vince noticing, and although it seems possible, it strikes him more as just wishful thinking than anything else, and a desperate example of it, at that.

"Vince," the dying girl said, Io's fingers at the back of her neck, pressing the nerves there in such a way that her mouth moved like a ventriloquist's dummy, and she "spoke" with Io's voice, "Let me ask you a question . . ."

Vince was slumped over, feeling exhausted, sick, feverish, as if this were the end, and yet he knew he still had to go on. He wanted to start crying; perhaps, he had. "Yes . . . what . . . shit . . ."

The girl—if you looked closely you realized that under all the blood, her lips were gone.

"Have you been paying attention at all? Even a teenyweeny, itsy-bitsy bit?"

"I'm trying . . . I swear I'm trying."

The girl had lost massive amounts of blood, but where it had gone was entirely a mystery. Vince didn't see her bleeding anywhere, no blood pool gathering beneath her, for instance, spreading like a prayer mat, her body jackknifed forward, praying to nothing. Io cocked her head to the side, in a gesture Vince knew only too well, and made her mouth form the words "help me, help me, help me" while the voice that came out of the ruined hole said this instead, "Look what's inside me."

The blood from her severed carotid jetted over Vince's left shoulder like a snake spitting poison, or some pygmy blowing a dart, and Io squeezed shut the wound he'd made and told Vince to turn around to where the blood-jet had hit the white stucco wall in a garishly suggestive blot that looked like—

"Don't, no!" Io commanded, and he did that thing where it seemed as if a foot or two of film had been cut

from the reel so that he ended up crouched beside
Vince, his arm thrown intimately around his shoulders,
both of them staring at the blood-blot on the wall eight
inches from their faces without Vince having seen Io
move. ". . . don't see it as anything but what it is . . . just
a blot of blood. Can you do that? Can you see nothing
but what is there . . . Nothing?"

Vince found himself hallucinating: he saw a great red
phoenix rising toward the sun, a laughing demon's face,
a large taco, or, more likely, what was probably a vagina
so horrifying he knew he'd be impotent in the only real
sense of that word.

"No . . ." Io whispered. "Mental health is commonly assumed to be indicated by the number of images one sees
in such blots. But that is only because mental health, as it's
commonly misunderstood, is dependent on not seeing
what is really there. Look again. . . ."

Vince was trembling now, violently, as if he, too, had
been stabbed, or otherwise opened, and perhaps he had.
He felt as if his mind were coming apart, and he was looking again at the body of the dying girl on the floor at their
feet, the girl he might or might not have stabbed, and Io
was caressing him, whispering to him, and he said something that Vince remembered only later as something like
this:

"You want to believe there is something more to life,
everyone does, it's almost impossible not to see some pattern, some meaning to the random, brutal stupidity of it
all. We wouldn't be able to get up and go to the fridge for
a Creamsicle if we didn't see a pattern to the swirl of
chaos around us. But there is no pattern; it doesn't exist.
You see, every great mind from the beginning of human
history has sought a solution that would give life meaning, nobility, coherence, and, failing any of these, at least
a reason to say yes. But while every philosopher, thinker,

artist can state the problem quite eloquently—the pain, frustration, sorrow, vanity of it all, the transient pleasures, the conditional and relative nature of even justice, truth, and, most of all, love—no two really agree on a solution, and that is because after five thousand years of philosophy and religion, there is no solution that has solved anything.

"The one thing no one yet has seriously proposed is that an answer will never be found because none exists. To suggest such a thing is to be considered a mere nihilist, a nonthinker, an adolescent. They don't give big book contracts, government grants, Nobel prizes to someone who says there is no answer. You must have an answer, any answer, even if it doesn't exist. There must be a philosophy, an art movement, a religion that says, 'This is the way,' until it becomes clear that it isn't the way, and another must be found: Confucianism, Occultism, Christianity, Platonism, Judaism, Hegelianism, Buddhism, Existentialism, Feminism, Vegetarianism— if any of these were the answer they wouldn't still be searching for the answer, and if there was an answer to be found, after all this time, it would have been found. The powers that be don't take me seriously, the critics at the *Times,* the head honchos at Tristar, no one, but I don't take myself seriously: it is the only way to embody my message. Sssh . . . do you hear it?"

Vince didn't know if this was a genuine question or not, or what, for that matter, Io was referring to, exactly. Had the police broken into the estate already? Were they charging toward the bedroom with warrants, guns drawn, orders to kill? Were SWAT team marksmen already lining up lethal shots through the double windows behind Vince? Was that a crosshair he felt over his heart?

"Do you hear it?" Io insisted.

"Hear what?" Vince said, his voice cracking.

"My message?"

"No. . . ."

"Listen harder. . . ."

Vince tried to make an expression that indicated he was listening harder, but it was all hopeless, he could hear nothing but the sound of his own sobbing.

"What do you hear?"

"Nothing," Vince wept. "Nothing."

Io sighed, theatrically, rolled his eyes. "Oh, Jesus had some kind of an expression or parable put down or something for what I'm going through, but I'll be triple fucked by seven well-hung pony boys if I can recall what it was. . . ." Io seemed to notice Vince again, what he was looking at, anyway. "You want to kill her, don't you?"

Vince hadn't been able to look away from the girl still crumpled on the floor, bleeding, but not profusely, not yet, still alive, for the time being, and he felt the knife trembling in his hand. "Yes," he said, terrified of what Io would say next, although, as usual, it wasn't what he expected.

"Not yet," Io said. "I want you fresh for my nuptials. The photographer is the most important thing in a wedding. It's all about iconography, baby. That's what's going to be remembered. Anyway, I've got to have you at your very best. How's the voting coming? Asphyxiation, isn't it? Groovy. I've even picked the site. . . . You'll never guess where. . . ."

Io waited a beat as if he expected Vince to guess, and then said, "Oh, you're just as dumb as a post, aren't you? Stonehenge . . . isn't that fab?"

"Stonehenge," Vince said, wonderingly, in spite of himself, repeating it again, realizing that this was an extremely important piece of information. "Stonehenge."

"Yes," Io said, exasperated as usual. "Didn't you ever wonder what it was for? Oh, don't tell me everyone really thinks it was some kind of caveman calendar, or whatever. Oh, God! Don't even say it!" Io squealed, clapping his hands, and laughing. "No, baby cakes, it's where the end of the world will begin."

Then Io went into a really long soliloquy about, among other things, pinecones, the invention of the CD, binary code, Ecclesiastes, and a highly personal interpretation of the meaning of foot-fetishism while calling out, to no one in particular, for a strawberry-kiwi smoothie he had no intention of drinking, and dispatching the long-suffering girl on the tiles, or, at least Vince assumed that he'd killed her, because, much later, needing at last to relieve himself, Vince found both her lungs crammed into the bidet, and, besides, he thought he recognized her rather distinctive tongue piercing when she turned up as an extra in the Jennifer Aniston autopsy shoot he did for the new king of Morroco.

They were all already dead, and that was an idea that took some getting used to, but Juliet tried hard to see it that way as time passed in the catacombs. It was the only way what she had seen could be made acceptable: the pain, the betrayal, the lies, the death, the unnameable, and even at that, she found it all intolerable unless she pretended the underground society really was, as its inhabitants seemed to believe, something of a chrysalis to a new rebirth of life on earth, a utopia for which the race had ceaselessly labored, futilely, and yet somehow fertilely, for centuries upon centuries upon centuries, only to wake up, transformed, tomorrow.

They came from all walks of life: cops, housewives, marketing directors, freelance writers, auto parts salesmen, computer programmers, telemarketers, cashiers, magazine editors, and more CPAs than it seemed possible existed. They donated time, money, energy . . . and every drop of blood in their veins. They were devoted, fanatical, and eager to become martyrs, and their martyrdom consisted of nothing more dramatic than waking up in their own beds at six o'clock the following morning, every morning of their otherwise routine lives, showering, dressing, checking their e-mail, and being at their desk, counter, window, whatever, by nine.

They were the kinds of people you see every day, standing in line to buy a loaf of bread and a quart of skim milk in the grocery express line or sitting next to you in the forest-green Chevy Suburban at the gas station. You said things to them like: "Can I have an appointment on the fifteenth at two P.M.?" or "They wrote to tell me that I needed to come down here and submit this application in person." You eat lunch with them at Starbucks or Applebees or that new pretentiously named bistro over on Diamond Avenue or you meet them after work for a drink and make a date to play tennis while you discuss so-and-so's impending divorce—and they were all, every last one of them without exception—as dead and as normal as could be.

Juliet sat in the great black-ice cathedral sometimes, disguised as a regular person, among the hundreds who flocked there daily, and listened to the high masses conducted by bishops who proclaimed a faith so inarticulate and incomprehensible it seemed nothing but a series of advertisements without any product to pitch, and for which, she, of all women, was supposed to be the mother. She looked inside the hymnals and found pop tunes full of zest and life, torch songs about broken hearts, rap lyrics for the resurrection of a body that could not be harmed, ever, by anything. There were depictions of saints from *People* magazine, it seemed, worked into the stained glass, and salacious biographies that sounded like those she might have seen about tragic stars from *E!*, and statues of marble celebrities so much gazed upon the very stone seemed on the verge of a total eclipse from solidity.

It was absurd and Juliet herself didn't believe what the pope had told her, but she acted as if she did, most of the time, and the rest of the time, she realized it didn't matter what she believed, one way or another. Indeed, after that first encounter, she had never seen the insane pope again, the pope who might have been, she remembered the name now, the dead actor Marlon Brando, although his authority was felt everywhere in the catacombs, and his appearance considered imminent, even if his existence was thought to be almost entirely legendary. She had seen him, of that she was certain, or so she thought, unless it had all been a dream, or a play-act, unless his specific instructions that she tell herself that what she was experiencing was "not a dream" was yet another lie, a form of the deepest and most insidious mental reprogramming, or, even more disturbing, an act of mercy.

She moved through the religious underworld seemingly unrestricted, even though she was constantly attended by those entrusted to watch, and record, as they called them, "her vital signs," and from a greater distance, someone with a camera from whose telephoto lens nothing, no matter how intimate or inane, was hidden. It was impossible to determine if there were places that were being carefully hidden from her, or, more likely, simply deleted from her program. Still, what she did see struck her as so entirely blasphemous and scandalous, so positively criminal, in a cosmic sense, that she couldn't imagine what would be considered classified, or top-secret, if not the horrors that were right out in the open for everyone, including her, to see.

The formal religious services, aside from the meaningless sermons, were stupendous spectacles of conspicuous waste and indiscriminate sexual encounters, the details of which were strategically leaked to alternative media outlets to find their way, eventually, into popular fiction and music video images, and, at each one, a seemingly real-life human victim, chosen for no apparent reason out of all the others, was crucified behind the altar, and later, considered to have risen from the dead, when, in point of fact, a doctor would be ritually consulted to confirm, as he always did, that he found no signs of life in the tortured corpse.

The people watched, always in rapt devotion, these proceedings, and others, similar, filling, for instance, huge theaters showing old movies: *Dracula 2000 A.D.*, *Lair of the White Worm*, *The Hunger*, *The Story of O*, *Suspira*, something in French ostensibly about necrophilia by Alain Robbe-Grillet, as well as impromptu stage adaptations of famous crimes scenes, amateur vignettes from deSade's *120 Days of Sodom*, live sex shows, public confessions, death scene monologues, and the usual recitation of near-death expriences. Anywhere, and everywhere, throughout the catacombs, a spontaneous murder, like a miracle, might occur right before your very eyes, and bystanders would fall to their knees and weep and pray with joy. They were being used, duped, all of them, and for all the wealth, youth, and energy they arrived with at this holy necropolis, they would leave poor, ennervated, old, and mad with grief. It was a place for the dead, and they came to be dead, although they called it life, and the tombs that they honored, and those they prepared for themselves, were innumerable.

"Why do they come?" Juliet asked.

She asked the same question of everyone she met: clerks, hostesses, museum attendants, psychiatrists, cameramen, shopkeepers. She asked one of the women in her supposedly nonexistent entourage, outfitted to suggest a novitiate or a nurse or even a chambermaid, who was, along with others, seemingly exactly identical to her, always in her vicinity; but this woman, perhaps she was a prison guard of some kind, had either been forbidden to speak, taken a vow of silence, or was somehow otherwise uncomprehending. Maybe this woman thought it had been a rhetorical question, and, in that, for many reasons, she may have been correct.

Others simply looked at Juliet as if she were mad, or blessed, or both, and invited her to drink of the life's blood, which was, or so they said so as not to unduly alarm her, a metaphor for love, or truth, or beauty, or immortality, or something.

Juliet was fairly certain that she hadn't eaten for days and she spent most of her time, sick and dizzy, in the church's vast library, sitting at a computer terminal among thousands, browsing through an on-line library that seeemd to contain everything from Babylonian sacred texts to Tuesday television listings for the year 2052 to the unpublished fantasies of serial killers such as John Wayne Gacey, Andrei Chikatilo, H.H. Holmes, Albert Fish, and Dr. Bryce B. Claw, the latter, among others who'd never been caught, or, for that matter, even detected. What she sought among these documents, Juliet couldn't exactly say, but it did little to comfort her anxieties to learn that the future father of her unborn child, Caleb Darr, was considered the most prolific serial killer in the history of the world.

It was God talking, Mahoney had no doubt, he recognized the voice, although he'd nevcr heard it before, the way you recognize a heart attack, for instance, or

blood in your urine. The communication wasn't originating inside his own mind, as he might have expected,
or even from the earpiece still connected to who knew
what, but it spoke to him, regularly, from quite ordinary
objects, a calculator, sometimes, or a can of wax beans,
and even, on one memorably disturbing occasion, as he
walked along a beach in Amagansett, a dying fish, cut
in half, and left behind by insensitive weekend anglers.

He had been preparing all his life for this moment,
these days and weeks, maybe only hours, for when he
would become a vessel for the divine voice, and yet now
that the time had arrived, Mahoney, or Rockman, as he
was now variously confused, felt absolutely no sense of
pleasure or satisfaction in his role. He didn't even feel a
sense of purpose and if he could have realized anything
he would have realized why: where God is, there is no
room for anything else.

And so Mahoney went through the motions: shaving,
dressing, eating, ordering executions, bombings, mass
arrests, terrorist attacks, curfews, and all the rest, but ser-
cretly he was, in fact, nowhere to be found.

"Mr. Mahoney," came the voice from the empty husk of
a burning car, in which a group of visiting Nicaraguan
priests were trapped, "I hope you understand the importance of overcoming your own hatred and self-loathing."

"It's difficult, my lord."

"I am a jealous god, you know. I shall tolerate no
others."

"Yes, my lord."

"I am who I am, and all that."

"I understand."

"I don't think you do, Mr. Mahoney, not really."

Mahoney, looking through field glasses, surveyed the
battlefield, which, in fact, until an hour or two ago, had
been a nine-mile section of the Los Angeles Freeway, and

considered it might be true, he really didn't understand a single goddamn thing at all. He lowered the glasses.

"Guide me, Lord," and then added, as an afterthought, "along whatever path you see fit."

Under what remained of an overpass, a squad of troopers were executing what looked like a small cluster of Japanese schoolgirls, all clinging together, weeping, urinating, but that couldn't really be happening, could it? A moment later, after the rapid clacking of automatic weapon fire, it turned out it wasn't happening, after all.

"You are an instrument of the Divine Will."

"I'm a gun aimed at the target of your ominpotent eye."

"It is prudent for you to think like that, Mr. Mahoney. But stop kissing my ass."

"I try to be prudent, my lord."

"What I ask of you is difficult, but to great men are appointed great tasks."

Mahoney knelt in the rubble. He saw rubber doll faces, torn legal documents, smoothie cups, pennies, Christmas ornament hooks, and a surprising number of orange rinds. From somewhere above him, the sky perhaps, it seemed to be raining black tears. There were sirens going off all over the place, as if the intent was to wake the dead, and maybe it was. God was still talking, finishing up a long-winded speech, or that's what Mahoney had thought anyway. Fact was that God kept right on talking long after he delivered the following sentence; it was only that Mahoney had heard everything he needed to hear when he heard this:

"No harm must come to Caleb Darr. You must see him protected on his pilgrimage for he is the carrier of a great message. You are his guardian angel, Mr. Mahoney."

Of all the things that God might have asked, he chose

the one thing Mahoney found impossible to obey. But it was that way always with God, wasn't it? He knelt there in the rubble, grinding his teeth, dangerously close to breaking, maybe accidentally, maybe not, the capsule of cyanide embedded in his left and right rear molars, his unpulled and painfully impacted lower wisdom teeth to be exact. He knew it was pointless to ask the question why? For the entity he knelt before was a wall of power, colossal, unbreachable, impossible, unreasonable, completely overwhelming. It could set off thermonuclear armageddon, release incurable biochemical plagues, break world financial institutions, wipe clean minds, drive whole species to extinction, increase or decrease the global temperature ten degrees, generate spontaneous ocean tsunamis, throw the solar system into the sun, have him arrested and interred in an asylum where he'd undergo extensive, painful, and intentionally pointless "reconditioning" treatments that could, quite literally, be called a living hell.

And yet even as Mahoney swore to his god that he would accept his calling, in his heart he hid a dark flame of adamantine rebellion, for Mahoney knew that for all the yes-yes lip service he was so solemnly giving his superior, he was already plotting an almost subconscious alternative route to damnation.

God had finally pushed him one step beyond too far—and enough was enough. To do what he was being asked to do would be the end of Nikka, and Mahoney could not make that sacrifice even if he gained whatever position there was left to gain, at God's left hand, for instance, a few seats down, of course, from that motherfucking bastard Caleb Darr.

Trying his best not to think these thoughts, and others exactly like them, Mahoney kept his eyes down, like a beaten dog, or someone whose embarrassing sexual secrets had just been revealed to their landlord, and felt his intestines squirm, wondering if it was even possible to keep a secret from God, and knowing it wasn't, wondered why then, against all appearances to the contrary, he still hadn't been struck dead on the spot.

"You've come far enough, Mr. Darr," the man with the artificial face said. Caleb was standing in a small dark room in a run-down hotel in Gdansk, the kind of room a whore took her "clients" to, to milk in every way but one. The trail he'd been following had come to a dead end, and this is where it ended, in a room with a man who looked like he'd crashed a supersonic jet head-on into a cliff. "You can go no further."

"Is she dead?"

Caleb had considered that possibility long before now; in fact, he'd been operating under that assumption all along. It would have been a shame if she had died, but he would still have wanted to find her, if only to look one last time upon the face of a woman he might have loved against all odds, and then, left with no alternatives, to abuse her corpse.

"No," the man said, or said again. "She is still alive, believe it or not. We have taken her for her own protection. She is being . . . preserved."

"We. Who is we?"

The man was putting on rubber gloves that he had taken from an attaché case. Caleb, entirely unconcerned, brushed away the usual fly.

"The Church," the man said, emphasizing his words with a snap of each tight fitting glove. "The Church of Jesus Christ, Vampire."

Caleb had heard of the Church, of course, and the vague claims they made to being the inheritors of the

next phase of God, the one promised in the book of
The Revelation, where Christ came back, terrible, white,
and dead, riding a cloud and carrying a sword, hungry
for blood. He recalled the conversation he'd had with
the Overseer in the museum and wondered if it was this
meeting that had been foretold, and it seemed odd to
Caleb that, after all that had happened, it all came down
to this: a run-in with some crackpot postapocalyptic
religious cult.

"What is it that you want with her?"

Caleb sniffed the air between them, trying to determine if he could pick up the trail after killing the man,
but, predictably or unpredictably, there was no scent to
the man at all, not even Juliet's postmortem stench, if, in
fact, he had lied and she was already dead. The man
would lead nowhere, Caleb concluded, alive or dead, unless he agreed to follow, and Caleb was aware that it all
might very well be a trap, but a trap set by whom and for
what, that remained a mystery to him.

"She's a very special woman, as you well know, Mr.
Darr. But it's all relative."

The man seemed to be preparing a hypodermic: it was
difficult to tell, because the device was futuristic, multi-
purpose, hydraulic in some undefined way.

"That's useless, you know."

"I know," the man said. "But I'm hoping that you will
amuse me." He motioned with his reconstructed chin to
the unmade bed behind Caleb. "Have a seat. Roll up
your sleeve."

Caleb didn't move, but not because he had any intention of protesting or disobeying the request. He was
thinking of something else, but what it was seemed to
elude him.

"Come on, Mr. Darr." The man interrupted his
stranded train of thought. "You've killed enough peo-

ple already. You're trailing danger. We've little time to lose."

Caleb sat on the bed, but he didn't pull up his sleeve, and it didn't seem to matter because the man pressed the hydraulic hypodermic device to his upper arm and, even though Caleb still had on his sport coat, pressed the trigger. There was a brief *pffft* sound, like the release of compressed gas or someone trying to sound out a difficult word that began with "f," and then the man stepped away, returned the hypodermic device to the attaché, removed the rubber gloves, and, after several minutes of waiting, Caleb felt exactly the same as he had before.

"Let's go," the man said, checking his watch, or, at least, pretending to check a watch he wasn't wearing. "We now have no time to lose."

They traveled by side roads through a ten-square-mile grid of the city. Caleb sat in the back of a Peugeot or Renault sedan, gray, dented, anonymous, wearing a pair of large plastic wraparound sunglasses, the kind that old men often wear while recovering from cataract surgery. The route they followed, doubling back on itself over and over, was meant to confuse Caleb or throw off anyone following, maybe both, before they left Gdansk entirely, and traveled some long straight road through the countryside that seemed, impossibly enough, like the German autobahn.

It was all pointless, in any event, for they were almost certainly being followed, but by whom, well, that was entirely uncertain. As for Caleb, it was impossible to tell if it was the drug, after all, that affected him, or if he was simply not paying enough attention, but he had no idea where they were, or where they might be going.

Caleb did a thing that was rare for a predator: he let his mind drift aimlessly.

He saw pretty much what he might have expected to see, all the murder, rape, plotting, betrayal, and general depravity of someone who'd existed for millennia, and, for the last few centuries anyway, for no greater purpose than to survive. He saw great paintings burning, disembodied heads, and empty cities, entirely intact, but covered with a strange form of catabolic fungus. He saw generations of people, even civilizations, acting out first and second drafts of scripts that had been written and rejected long before as entirely unfeasible. It was all, to put it mildly, a terrible waste.

But could he call it all meaningless? This woman he was stalking now—this Juliet—reminded him of something, but what it was exactly, he couldn't remember. The way she had seen him in the square and drew him, imperfectly, yes, but almost—

It had something to do with that, no doubt, and he wondered why. That she could conceive of him, almost, had given him the sense that, although all was lost, something might be preserved: a moment, maybe, like a snapshot of a UFO or the creation of an effective new religious symbol.

This was love, he thought, or what they called love, the love of God for man, and he felt it numerous times throughout his long sojourn across the wasteland of apathy and absurdity that had been repeating itself ad nauseam for century upon century. They were the precious few he'd fed upon, corrupted, ruined, and yet hadn't killed, at least not outright, but infected instead with a lingering disease that reduced them by a half-life, again and again, until they were little more than shadows of bodies that had been entirely eclipsed, and these shadows, too, fading, like those of palm fronds on a pink wall, as night approached. It was something like that, he thought, but not really, and he wondered if maybe his musings were being broadcast by subterranean pirate radio stations to various hidden enclaves of vampires and enthusiasts thorughout the world. But such a possibility, he concluded, was simply ridiculous.

They had crossed a river—he had sensed the current—and an armed barricade of a defunct red Soviet guard, and were now speeding down a steep incline through a tunnel cut through solid granite. They might have been on another continent by now, hustled into jets and overland rockets, rushed from chopper to limousine to impromptu gondola strung between otherwise inaccessible mountain passes. It was hailing, or snowing, wherever the hell they were, exposed, at intervals, or so it seemed, to the open sky, despite, apparently, being deep underground, traveling in a kind of unpiloted one-car subway that Caleb couldn't see.

"Is it him?" he asked, sensing, despite the preposterous precautions, that he was still the focus of a dozen tracking probes.

"Who?"

"Mahoney."

"Hmmmm . . ."

The guard he spoke to, or guide, or kidnapper, or whatever he was, had changed several times since the man who'd first contacted Caleb in the hotel room in Gdansk, and now he sat beside a hooded figure, robed, bowed, fingers working a string of bone-beads, in the attitude of a monk of some sort, who seemed devoted to preserving an underwater silence only he, or she, could hear.

He was entering the city of the dead, where everything was north, and all signals ceased, and suddenly he picked up her trail again, a lifeline red and crooked in this place of lunar dust and bone, and felt himself, pulled along by fate itself, like a flame racing hungrily along a fuse. Someone had hung her, innocent and helpless on a hook, and let her bleed like bait into the water, and Caleb, rising from the black depth of an isolation that was pure inhuman, was about to bite.

It was dangerous for him to leave the flat, but it was even more dangerous for him not to, or so Vince had it figured, caught, as he was, in the middle, between damned if you do, damned if you don't. The board on his site had been infiltrated by law enforcement officials from the start, that was to be expected, but what he hadn't expected was that all six of the most prolific and intelligent posters on the site were undercover Web disguises for the same man, or team of men, fronted by the infamous off-line computer cop: Inspector J.I. Horn.

Vince was unsure of the man's credentials, but paranoid enough, and more than guilty enough, to sense disaster coming to claim him. He had been expecting it in a way, even courting it, pushing the limits, almost like a serial killer hoping to be caught, or a child wanting to be disciplined. Vince wanted someone, somehow to show him the error of his ways, to recondition him, to prove there was a different way to live.

There was an air-raid siren sounding, splitting the night, and people hurried down the streets, still jammed in spite of the strict curfew, with hands clamped over their ears. The Internet cop was standing, as previously arranged, by the burning husk of a Mazda Miata with diplomatic plates, which had no doubt been supplied specifically for this meeting. He was smoking a joint, wearing a long black linen jacket of some kind, a Seattle Mariners baseball cap turned backward on his head, vintage green Converse basketball sneakers, low-cut, of

course. He was looking, in a word, conspicuous, but not
in a way that you'd immediately notice, not on a street in
Amsterdam, outside an Internet café at 3:00 A.M., the
hour when nurses often say that most terminally ill
patients are likely to die.

"Inspector Horn?" Vince asked the man, not the same
man as the last time, or the time before, but one of several,
apparently, using the same identity.

He nodded. "You're early."

"I have to sneak out when I can. I don't like doing this.
Why can't we do it on-line? It's dangerous. I may have
been followed."

It was clear to Vince that he was being followed. Io
never let him out of sight, even when he was off on
some inconsequential murder spree or other. Tonight
they had been "partying" at a euthanasia bash for some
minor royalty's perfectly healthy ten-year-old daughter,
and in the midst of the festive atmosphere, during a
stage show featuring a mechanical, or miraculously re-
animated, Barbra Streisand, Vince had stepped out
with the excuse that he needed additional bytes for his
digital camera to film the live disemboweling part of
the program. The chaotic merriment surrounding the
event served him well, as did the long bathroom lines,
and he managed to make it outside into one of the
waiting cars, and then to the city proper, where by several pirated public conveyances he found himself
where he was standing, watched, he was certain, by
someone at a window on the sixth floor of the building
opposite.

"They won't touch you," Horn said, spitting hard on
the sidewalk. "Not yet, anyway."

"I don't understand what I've done wrong. I'm protected by the Fifth Amendment, or is it the First? Freedom
of Speech."

"That's open to interpretation."

"I'm not harming anyone. It's only pictures—art. If you take a still from a mainstream movie like *Silence of the Lambs* you get the same effect."

"Oh, really?"

"It's so over-the-top, it's obviously not real. What I'm doing, it's satire."

"I'm not here to argue constitutional politics or postmodern aesthetics. I'm hear to get information."

Vince looked around him, at the building across the street, above him, the limousine trolling past, especially that grayed-out sixth-floor window, suddenly feeling vulnerable from all sides.

"Can we do this . . . somewhere else?"

"This isn't a date, Mr. Manning."

"It's just that—" Vince made a ridiculous gesture with his right hand. A group of three laughing teenagers were running down the street, pursued by a bleeding dog, two of them had knives, the other some kind of club. A few streets over a helicopter probed between the broken buildings with a searchlight. There was the clackety-clack of automatic weapons exchanging fire and a group of students who'd been chanting a countdown from two hundred had just finished crying out the number one hundred forty-five in ecstatic unison. "Forget it," Vince said.

"Toke?"

Vince took the joint, inhaled, gagged, gave it back.

"Stonehenge," he choked. "It's going to happen at fucking Stonehenge." The Intenet cop nodded as if he'd heard or read all this before, a long, long time ago. "I don't know when," Vince added. His hands had suddenly started trembling, along with the rest of him, and he thought, irrationally, of Parkinson's disease. He shuddered, nodding toward the last half inch of joint in the clip. "Goddammit, what is that fucking thing cut with anyway?"

"Mercury dust and pelican shit."

"You're kidding, right?"

"Did it sound funny, even a little bit, to you?"

"Look," Vince said, and maybe it was the tone of his voice, or the way he leaned in, but Horn suddenly stopped feigning indifference, if he'd been feigning, and, perhaps it was experience with countless other informants, but whatever it was, Vince noticed that he suddenly looked interested in what Vince was about to say, as if his experience was telling him that whatever came next was going to be important. "He wants me to be the one to sacrifice her, to do it, I mean, kill her, for real."

"And you will do it," Horn said, nodding supportively, "right?"

"Yes," Vince said, feeling okay, relieved to have gotten that off his chest. "The whole thing is scripted."

"No, I mean you will do it."

"I don't understand."

"You do it."

"Yes, of course. You mean . . . No . . ."

"For real."

"No. Okay."

"You do it."

"Yes." Vince looked up in the sky again. "Are we on?"

It was hard to believe that it was only a movie, that's why they'd brought him here, and some kind of pretentious hand-tinted, black-and-white art film at that, shot in 35mm, a single uninterrupted handheld take, no dialogue or voice-over, lasting approximately forty-five minutes. On top of that, it was impossible to say, exactly, what he'd been watching: a view of some common, but ordinarily unobserved object, perhaps, a drying raindrop, or an eyelash trembling during a plunge on a roller coaster, made unfamiliar and superficially intriguing by extreme close-up and abstraction. At the end of the film a block of sparse credits appeared briefly in lower case followed by a fade-in and fade-out of the name of a famous director whose unparalleled string of commerical blockbusters were considered to have defined pop culture.

"You went through all this trouble to show me this self-important art-school crap?" Caleb said, not exactly disbelievingly, but still a little surprised. "He should stick to war movies and alien flicks. Two thumbs down."

He was seated in a screening room, gray and unadorned, and on the back of one of the chairs he saw the familiar Great Seal of the President of the United States. They were in a top-secret installation of one kind of another, possibly an international nuclear weapons launching site, since whatever it was that Caleb had just viewed might have been a painfully slowed down version of the multifaceted unfolding of a new kind of hydrogen-uranium detonation. The room, Caleb noted, without particularly feeling it personally, was extraordinarily cold, as if the point were to preserve taxidermic exhibits of some kind, or living polar mammals.

Caleb listened carefully for a fly, knowing its flight would be slowed here, but heard nothing, for the time being.

There was only one other occupant in the room with him now, and that was the man Caleb was speaking to. He was not the same man from Gdansk or any of the other men who had escorted Caleb on the way to the screening room. He was tall and taciturn, but he was not wearing the white lab coat he might have been expected to be wearing. Instead he was dressed in an off-the-rack beige suit of indeterminate cut from Sears Roebuck and a pink tie of a shade that didn't match the suit at all, nor was it possible to imagine it matching anything. The man at first appeared to be merely taciturn, as noted, but on closer inspection, he was actually emaciated to the point suggestive of a wasting disease, AIDS, or a slow-growing esophageal cancer with fast-growing mestases to the stomach, liver, lungs, brain, and abdominal cavity. He smelled like feces, which, perhaps, explained the arctic-level air-conditioning.

"You don't recognize the image, then?" he asked, speaking a form of e-prime that Caleb had to use telepathy and deduction to understand. ". . . or its significance?"

Caleb was impatient. But he'd stalked enough victims to know that existence itself consisted of nothing but a lot of meandering around before one got to the point: and then it all lasted half a heartbeat.

"It looks derivative of something," he said, "Man-Ray, maybe."

"Are you thinking of Ellsworth, perhaps, and the private futurist school?"

"From Prague?"

The man looked confused. "Provincetown."

"This is irrelevant," Caleb said. "What is it?"

"Life," the man said, bluntly and enigmatically. "You're looking at life."

"Where? On Mars? From that probe to Saturn?"

"Much, much closer . . . and yet far more inhospitable and impossible."

"Some kind of bioenhanced strain of mutated cancer cell? It looks malicious and indestructible."

"No . . ." he started and Caleb didn't respond at all to

what the man said next, even though it was the only thing he could have said that would have thrown Caleb off his mark, for what the man said next was not in the script, not in Caleb's, not in the man's either, he'd bet, and no one had the master script, if there was one. The man might have been improvising, or lying, but Caleb waited a beat to see if anyone rushed in to stop the scene, and when nothing happened, he understood it was all going exactly as planned, by which it was meant, there was no plan at all. Suddenly, hearing this line thrown at him from out of nowhere, Caleb was forced to improvise: ". . . what you saw in that film originated in your own gonads. It is living seed."

It's impossible, Caleb was thinking the whole time, *What this guy is saying is simply impossible. There's no way he's fertile, his kind cannot reproduce, and, if that were not enough, he's not even the same species; why, he's hardly in the same reality.* It could be a trick, some kind of setup, a PR gimmick, or a bit of sensationalism, but the idea that he could be a father, if anything, was an unthinkable concept that went against everything he thought. He was barren, as barren as the ice dust on one of those moons of Saturn, unless they'd ended up finding life there, too, after all.

"You understand, of course," Caleb said, "that I can't accept what you are telling me. I want third-party corroboration. I want some sort of paternity test."

The man didn't exactly laugh, but Caleb could tell he'd meant to.

"That's not possible, and you know that."

"What are these . . . results . . . based on then?"

"Trace samples."

Caleb could hardly believe what he was hearing. "From where?"

"Your last lover."

Caleb had been mildly amused throughout most of this dialogue so far, and certain that all of this was pure bullshit, but this last claim, as ridiculous as it, too, sounded, kept him in his seat. He had the sense that he was close to something, perhaps not whatever the man or whoever he worked for was trying to tell him, but something else, something deeper, if only he could figure it out.

"Think about it, Mr. Darr. Do you really suppose we'd have gone through all this trouble, have let everything get so . . . disturbed . . . if what I'm saying weren't at least seventy-two percent true? Do you honestly think that's even likely?"

"This story stinks," Caleb said. "And frankly," he couldn't resist adding, "so do you."

The man smiled thinly. "Sometimes the truth is obvious, sometimes a lie is more so."

"I've killed a lot of people. You mentioned my last lover."

"A quiet, dark-haired girl in a mountain prefecture or something, outside of old Kyoto, several hundred years ago, kneeling on a bamboo mat washing her father's calligraphy brushes . . ."

And Caleb, his eyes clicked up, and to the left, saw and whispered her name, as if forced a second time to swallow a poison that hadn't killed him the first.

"Nikka."

"I think you are now beginning to see, Mr. Darr."

Caleb shook his head clear and returned to the present, as nonexistent as that was. "That's impossible. She died, too, like all the rest."

"Died," Mr. Darr, "like all the rest, but not exactly."

"She didn't die?" Caleb quipped bitterly, incredulously, knowing damn well she had, but always willing to listen to a pleasant lie, and even pretend to believe it, for a few seconds, anyway. His sarcasm destroyed worlds: "She lives?"

"No, she died. In childbirth."

Caleb had gone past simple denial. If this was a game they wanted him to play, he'd play it.

"And the child . . ." he asked, knowing the card in the man's hand, the last card left in play.

"Io."

The man said it, as expected, and should have stopped talking right then, but didn't. "You have a lot to think about, Mr. Darr. He was a mistake, but you didn't know. Fact is, no one did. You are being asked to correct your mistake, and try again. You have a lot to think about, Mr. Darr. You are going to be the father of the new avatar. We have your bride safe and sound and waiting. It appears, ironically enough, as if you suddenly almost have something to live for."

Caleb heard the buzzing finally stop. He didn't see it, of course, but he heard the silence, just to his left, on the armrest he wasn't using, and he brought his hand down on the spot, quickly, authoritatively, before the fly could get away. "Got you," he said, almost satisfied. "Got you, you little bastard." He slowly lifted his hand and wasn't all that surprised to find that he had missed.

So this is life, Nikka thought, sitting on a canvas folding chair outside a motel room along Highway 33, any Highway 33, take your pick. Her security coordinator had rented out the entire quadrangle of rooms overlooking the courtyard to mitigate the possibility of the usual balcony assassins. She sat there on a cool evening, the sky full of stars, a glass of something beside her chair, and an old issue of a defunct magazine called *Maxim*, in which she seemed to be featured obsessively, lying open on her lap, a page or two turning whenever the intermittent breeze blew. "It's really not much."

She had been to a mall that afternoon, a sporting event, a beach, a library, a scenic overlook—a frenzied itinerary of events that didn't seem any different from the tens of thousands she'd experienced in the past, except without the photographers and adoring multitudes. She had spent a day, for instance, with a typical family, Portuguese or American, it was quite irrelevant, and sitting in the living room after dinner, watching two kids play video games, she distinctly remembered turning to someone at some point, and asking, "Is this it? I don't understand. Why is it so funny on television?" It was a relief, finally, when the slaughter started, because at least something was happening.

They had taken the usual hostage, ostensibly to lift her spirits, and from the open door of the room behind her, through the screen, she could hear his soft sobbing and muted entreaties, but they were of little consolation. This place, all these places, whatever they were, they were not for her. She missed the cameras, the throngs, the omnipresent recording devices. She missed the elaborate rituals, the impromptu holocausts, the daily scripts. She missed the billboards, *E!* documentaries, Imax films, wax dioramas—all that behind-the-scenes-with-Nikka bullshit. She missed the speeches that gave her something to say, the commentaries that gave them meaning, and the broadcasts that ensured that they were heard, even if no one was listening.

She had wondered all her life if she was even living, and now, she realized, she was not. She hadn't truly existed, not even for a heartbeat, and so she had traveled this long and lonely road to the point of no return, to the point where she had nothing left to say but this: "So this is life. How cruel."

She wished Mahoney were there, she almost trusted him, to take her last request, but he was gone, like everyone else was gone, or quickly going, into another world, not this one, whatever one she existed in.

"Bring the limousine around," she said to the driver, who was always in earshot, like a spy or a gossip columnist, alert for even the most outrageous rumor. "Take me back to the honeycomb. I've seen enough. Show me where it ends."

No one knows the heart of God. Everyone knows that, although almost no one is willing to accept what should be obvious: that when all is said and done, surrender to God's will isn't about accepting love or truth or justice, it's not about finding forgiveness or peace, or any of that crap that is commonly thought to be the cause of the beatific smug smile on the face of saints and buddhas, but it's the acceptance of the complete absence of any of these qualities, or any others, besides.

The chairman gave a metaphorical chuckle.

At the long titanium conference table those who hadn't been "let go," "downsized," "retired to advisory posts," or otherwise bid fond farewells to "pursue other interests outside the company," sat looking somewhat morose and nervous after a multimedia presentation of how well the enterprise had been performing during the last quarter. It is almost axiomatic that every time such a glowing report is delivered it means a ruthless internal pogrom is on the way, or, as it's said in the office vernacular around watercoolers everywhere: heads are gonna roll.

It was rumored, although no one actually voiced the speculation, that the chairman had eliminated his other voices, the ones who hadn't yet defected, two and four, one and two, two and three, it didn't really matter anymore, if it ever did. He had taken control and looked tan and lean and fit, but something's off, something indefinable, a few pixels around the nose, maybe, but whatever it is everyone feels as if the air-conditioning has been turned up too high.

The chairman is speaking extemporaneously, off-the-cuff, as he never does, informal and friendly, and that is making everyone even more nervous. He's acting as if it's all finished, the last chapter written, and now it's time to break out the cigars and cognac and congratulate everyone on a good game played all round.

"He'll disobey, naturally," the disemboded voice, speaking today in Tagalog, of all things, started, sounding even more disembodied than ever. "I've known that from the start. The poor misguided fool will seek to rescue Nikka VII and kill Caleb Darr along with our new Virgin Queen. The irony, of course, is that it's love that causes him to lose the love of God, and, thus, the propaganda of eternal peace. Oh, I could do it all myself, behind the scenes, it's ture, but then we'd lose the drama, and the drama, gentlemen, is the sizzle that sells the steak. We need Mr. Darr and his paramour to suffer through many persecutions in order to bring forth the future hope of humankind and maintain the status quo. Only then will the event carry with it the necessary mythic ramifications that will stand the test of centuries. Are there any questions?"

There was polite, professional applause, although around the table no one moved, and there was no sound except for the air conditioner, which had been blowing the whole time, and now even colder than before, if that was possible, although everyone was pretending nothing was wrong. The chairman asked again, "Are there any questions?" And only when he rephrased the question a third time, in this form, "No one has any questions?" was it obvious that he wanted at least two meaningless questions before the meeting was adjourned, and these questions were asked, and answered, but what they were and how they were answered went significantly unrecorded.

The chairman touched, figuratively speaking, a button on the console next to the untouched water glass and spoke briefly to Ms. Haskins, presumably in the next room, as usual, something about a chemical report that was expected, or an enigmatic personal matter, it was impossible to tell, and for good reason, since, in reality, he wasn't speaking to Ms. Haskins at all and what he said was the preagreed signal for the hit to commence. Almost instantaneously the conference room doors blew open, sirens screaming, the sprinkler system set off, the entire satellite or whatever they were on, pitching and diving out of orbit, as the contract killers lining both walls open fire with some kind of special photon energy weapons that filled the room with a milky oceanic light inside of which everyone was drowning and being ripped to shreds by what might have been a frenzied hurricane of detached phosphorescent piranha jaws, or something like that.

Much later, time being relative, when the commotion has finally died down, there are the usual shots of bodies lying on their backs, legs splayed, blood running into puddles, embarrassing stains in the crotches of expensive linen pants. It's a startling reminder that there is no dignity in this racket, and death comes swiftly and brutally to everyone, and literally anyone can be hit at any time.

The chairman looks at these images in the morning papers with a grin of satisfaction, reveling in the brutal simplicity of it all, and yet he realizes that it's all somehow unsatisfactory and beside the point, and, when all is said and done, it's about nothing more than being the last one standing. He is taking the equivalent of a "morning spa," manicure, pedicure, shiatsu massage, tan, etc., etc., the works, a general burnishing of the self-image, like when springtime comes after a long winter and everyone, in spite of themselves, forget about the dead.

He knows what they are saying behind his back, whispering in tight circles, all those philosophers and assassins, and it doesn't mean a thing to him and yet, somehow, it really does.

God, he thinks, hanging up the phone on a voice-mail message from someone he's already had murdered, is completely insane.

Let's not forget the princess during all this. She sits, among the tulle and lace of yet another rejected gown, like a broken white umbrella, smiling at nothing, and watching Meg Ryan videos while her nervous fingers ceaselessly string tiny pearlescent beads on a string, and then take them all off again. She is not nearly as stupid and oblivious as she might seem, but exactly to what degree she is acting the part is unclear, and whether she is preparing herself to attempt an escape, or respond to a rescue, with or without violence, is an even greater mystery. It would be innaccurate to say that she's been trained for this circumstance, but it would be equally innaccurate to say that instruction for such an obvious eventuality had been entirely neglected. But all of what she's been taught seemed completely impractical and amounted, basically, to these two injunctions: stay alive and don't embarrass the Crown.

The fact that the girl was not the real princess of England at all was quite irrelevant, so irrelevant, in fact, that no one had even bothered to mention it up to now.

The royal family, obviously, were not so careless as to send members out on dates to Long Island mansions to party with Arab playboys. Whether the Arab in question had known she was a double or not, and, for that matter, whether the Arab, too, had been a double, was indeterminate. But it's probably safe to assume that the Arabs were no stupider than the English, at the very least.

It made little difference whether she were really the princess or not. The appearance that she had been kidnapped and sacrificed would have as much impact as if it had really happened, because, after all, in people's minds, it had. As for the girl, she had been pretending to be the princess for so long, she now wholeheartedly believed it, and really, in a half-and-half way, she was truly looking forward to her "marriage," even if it meant dying.

Caleb needed to get away. He had just learned that he had accidentally sired the destroyer of the world and now he was being pressed upon to sire its savior. On top of that, he was contracted to kill his own ex-wife and son. It was, to put it mildly, one of the worst days he'd experienced, and that was saying something, insofar as he was immortal. If he'd thought of it, Caleb might have found it surprising that no one questioned his leaving the necropolis, but, then, how could they force him to stay?

It was to Nikka he went now, Nikka through whom

he must pass to get to the future, whatever future was still left. He knew, of course, that their paths would cross one final time, but he didn't quite expect it to be in the broken-up parking lot of an old drive-in movie theater, maybe in Georgia someplace, at one o'clock in the afternoon.

She was standing in the center of that caved-in sea of asphalt, among the speaker poles where the speakers once hung, now speakerless. She was looking timeless in a white cowl and wraparound ankle-length sheath dress that fluttered in the breeze, dark glasses, and her impassive face turned in the direction of the blank concrete wall upon which B-movies were once shown, and one had the impression either that Nikka could outstare the damn wall, or that she was projecting her own imaginary movie upon it, or both. Caleb took up a position oblique to hers, facing away from the concrete wall, and spoke into the hot wind, in the opposite direction of the one he would be expected to speak.

"Why have you done this?"

"You left me."

"I came back."

"You hurt me."

"I did what I could do. I always loved you. You knew that."

"It's too late."

"It's never too late."

"You broke your vow."

"My vow was to love you. I never broke that. Did you know about our son?"

"You left us."

"I came back."

"You hurt me."

"I didn't mean to."

"It's too late."

Caleb new that this would continue forever. He was talking to a program, a script, not a woman; whatever woman Nikka had been, she wasn't that anymore. He wanted to reach out to her, to touch her, to lay his hand on her arm, look into her eyes, and say, "Please," as if that might have called her back from abstraction, but she was two feet away and ten thousands miles away. What can you say when all the words have been spoken? How can you kiss someone who is no longer there? For centuries Caleb had been convinced that he'd killed her, but that, ultimately, hadn't been in his power, after all. He had kept her alive in his heart the whole time; only she could have set off the nuclear annihilation that would kill everything, indiscriminately, and continue killing, poisoning the world, for generations to come.

The next step Caleb took would be the first on the road to forever. The armed guards held their Uzis down as he passed between them, no one said a word, and everyone seemed to be thinking the same thing: *Where are the crows?* He had reached the edge of the vast empty parking lot, empty except for the ring of the aforementioned armed guards and armored limousines, as well as rolls of barbed wire, police dogs, and unexploded tear gas canisters, everyone ready to pack up and leave at any moment.

Two men in dark uniforms stepped up to Caleb then, and there was some momentary commotion as it wasn't exactly clear where these men had come from, what uniform they wore, if they were with Nikka, and, if not, who had jurisdiction here. Neither of the men seemed to be holding a weapon, but they were supported by invisible artillery, and, hoping to take advantage of Caleb's momentary lapse of unscalable scorn, the one on the left spoke first, saying, "You are under arrest. You'd be advised to come along with us."

And Caleb, more annoyed than anything else, thought about self-destruction on the spot, taking with him an epicenter of 770 square miles, but he didn't, and his thinking went something like this: *There is always time for that later.*

"It's so nice we can be civilized about all this," Mahoney quipped, squinting at something over Caleb's left shoulder, as if he were reading something written there, and maybe he was, "even while civilization is falling apart all around us."

They were sitting on two folding chairs in the middle of a meadow; it was sunny, unbelievably hot, the still quiet air filled with drifting spores and gnats. The long buzz of cicadas or wood-boring insects rose to an impossibly high pitch, stopped, and after a moment of silence, started all over again. The clearing was ringed by men in Kevlar body suits, riot helmets, and blacked-out face shields in which hoses were affixed, pumping some kind of gas, presumably. They were holding AK-47s, all pointed at Caleb and Mahoney, but that was mainly for show.

It was true, however, that in a matter of moments this meadow would be soaked in blood, and strewn with scattered body parts.

"You look ridiculous," Caleb said.

Mahoney was wearing a uniform that he'd no doubt designed himself for the occasion: a composite of death chic from punk, Nazi, Aztec, and Hindu motifs, among others, along with elements that brought to mind toxic-waste handlers and beekeepers. On his left thigh sat a kepi with a sort of inverted caduceus and framed by Waffen SS lightning bolts, or perhaps they were stylized representations of Egyptian flails. The whole thing struck Caleb as regressive, adolescent, atavistic, and entirely unnecessary, except to elicit a message of elitism and white terror.

"I'm sure you haven't come all this way to criticize my couture," Mahoney said.

The temperature, Caleb noted in a detached way, must be over ninety-five. "I'm waiting."

"It's ironic . . ." Mahoney mused, staring off, and Caleb was sure the commando wasn't going to finish the thought, but, unfortunately, he did: ". . . we've been forced to work together against our will all this time, and even now, when all the props have been knocked out of reality, here we are, still pushing on the same side of the immovable Sisyphean boulder."

"The veil has been rent," Caleb said, offhandedly.

"Yep, indeed." Mahoney leaned forward slightly, inquiringly. "What have you seen?"

Caleb was thinking of Trotsky's assassination, Jews shot by open graves, black cars idling beside Jersey swamps, Tsar Nicholas and the royal family in the basement, pistol cracks in the leafy woods. He was waiting for Mahoney to give the signal for all hell to break loose. But the commando was still leaning forward, waiting for an answer. "What have you seen, hmm, you smug motherfucking bastard?"

"Mahoney, you really must loosen your grip on the serious."

The ex-commando grinned, like a psychotic crocodile.

"Tell me," he snarled, making a flourish with his gloved hand, showing his trump card. Caleb didn't bother to look. It was Juliet, of course, being wheeled out from between two beech trees on a portable closed-circuit television, wearing some kind of electronic training collar, hands bound, one eye darkened, jaw swollen. She was wearing an oversized T-shirt, with the motto *I Love New York More than*

Ever, nothing else. The guards, in spite of obviously having manhandled her, seemed shy, almost embarrassed for having had to touch her at all. There were honeybees hovering drowsily all around her, and an aura of such beatific peace that Caleb sensed that one day, no matter what happened here, a shrine or sacred grotto of some kind would be erected to commemorate the event.

"Nikka's gone," Caleb said quietly. "Your obsession is, more than usually, counterproductive. Taking the girl is not going to change anything."

"I want to know who she is. Why they want me to protect her. And you—why is it you are so special? You don't seem so special to me. I've spent my entire life wiping your ass. Why, Mr. Darr? Why is that?"

"Because you never had the balls to be anything else but the universe's ass-wipe, Mahoney."

"Are you trying to make me angry, Mr. Darr? I suppose that might have been the pattern at one time. But I've changed so much, lately. It's a shame you can't see me as I am. Now I'm going to ask you the same question again, and maybe another two or three times, but one of these times will be the last, and then." He shrugged. "Pop, too late. Now, here we go. Mr. Darr, why are you and the girl so important?"

Caleb said nothing: it made no difference what he said. The whole situation, as far as he was concerned, was sophomoric, at best.

"You don't seem to understand, Mr. Darr. You are not in charge. You've never been."

"And you have always underestimated the depth of my ambiguity about the importance of any of this."

"Why are you and the girl so important, Mr. Darr? Maybe if I could be made to see . . ."

Caleb listened, and heard the silence of the cicadas. It was truly blessed.

"I want to see, I really want to understand." The ex-commando was reaching out, and it sounded like both a threat and a plea, as these things usually are, and then a squirrel suddenly dashed halfway across the meadow, stopped, sat up, and everyone seemed a little disbelieving. Caleb knew what Mahoney was going to say next and exactly the flat, offhanded toned in which he would say it. "Kill the bitch."

Caleb heard the televised gunshots and saw the inside of the television screen hit with large fleshy blobs of blood as Juliet was summarily executed. He was already leaping from the chair in the midst of a wild crisscross of automatic weapon fire that was only meant to distract him, but which didn't, and Caleb felt the usual tip-tap, *hey, how are you, buddy? you're dead* thump of the slugs as they tore through his walking corpse. Leaves and bits of grass, all shredded by the impromptu steel hurricane, were swirling through the red mist of ruptured internal organs like festive confetti, and Caleb thought, *Well, for once, the weatherman was right.*

Necks break easily for Caleb, body cases rupture at a knowing touch, and between his passage from point A to point B, enormous stretches of film were missing, so that it seemed he was almost everywhere at once. He had to watch out for those sneaky bastards in chasuble and veil, of course, weilding the silken cord and bone saw, flamethrower and napalm ointment, but even under the best of circumstances they'd have a difficult time of it, and these weren't the best of circumstances, not for them and not by far: the fact was that Caleb didn't want to stop existing at the moment and even he was unpleasantly surprised to find out just how much.

The benedictions completed, Caleb paused a moment, thought of something, and then shook his head, yes or no.

He made a cursory reconnaissance of the site, mainly for clues, but also looking for Mahoney, his head or blood sausage, whatever, and knew he wouldn't find him; this scene wasn't where the ex-commando bought it, no more than it was the scene where Caleb bought it, and Caleb suspected Mahoney knew it, too.

There was a plane leaving for Tripoli in twenty minutes. There was no real reason to go there, but, then, there almost never was. Caleb was planning to be on it.

They raided hell at 7:11 on a Thursday evening, Eastern time, Mahoney having signed the order to kill everyone and turn the place into a lost city, leaving behind not so much as a knuckle unpulverized that might one day become a fossil-imprint in sedimentary rock. The tremors from the explosions were felt as far away as San Francisco, where an earthquake killed 1,750, and interrupted a second World Series. Mahoney, himself, who had been miles away, in the opposite direction, gently interrogating Caleb when it all, literally, went down, was now en route to a slightly off earth site where Juliet, waiting, had been shown a closed-circuit snuff broadcast of Caleb's brutal execution at the very moment that he had been watching hers. She had dry-swallowed several Elavil and Xanax tablets, as well as some incidental dosages of Zyprexa and Luvox, whatever she could find in the medicine cabinet, but still could not shake the nightmares from those final few minutes in hell: the black-clad soldiers everywhere, gas, panic, torture, slaughter, men, women, children herded into huge transport vehicles that were detonated by remote control. No one knew anything, and all communication, as meager as it had been, was cut: the place went flat-line. The "pope," it was rumored,

had beat it out of there with the aid of some old Hollywood friends, but there were opposite rumors, as well,
and these ran the gamut of improbable come-back attempts playing humorous cameos on several popular
sitcoms to the most persistent: that he'd been arrested
and killed by a surgical hit-squad five years before and
that the underworld community had been slowly and
inexorably dying ever since. As for Juliet, she was, more
or less, unharmed—a bit worse for wear, perhaps, but
what could you expect? she mused, with a sense of bitter
irony: after all, she'd been to hell and back. She'd had
her stomach precautionarily pumped and her heart and
lungs were being monitored for efficiency. It was clear
she was the subject of a form of suicide watch and this
gave her some kind of hope, but for what, she didn't
know. She had already seen enough, however, to know
that she couldn't trust everything she saw on TV, and
that she was being lied to virtually all the time. Maybe it
was that.

"Oh, God, oh, God, oh, God, oh, God," Ms.
Haskins moaned, in mock ecstasy, arms flung over her
head, as the chairman pistoned inside her, "I'm coming,
I'm coming . . ." but, of course, she never did. They lay
together, minutes later, in a castle outside of Edinburgh,
her blond head on his sculpted chest, an impossibly
ripped senior citizen prophet à la Michelangelo, and she
talked, as she often did lately, about being one of those
beauty-pageant news readers on CNN or CNBC, or,
maybe, a weather girl on a twenty-four-hour weather
channel. The chairman, who had heard all this before,
simply ignored her, staring out the window at the black
clouds racing over the moor.

The chairman is troubled, but whom can he really talk

to, who indeed, but this silly secretary-prostitute with her simpleton ambitions? He looks down at her, in more ways than one, a dim awareness in a comely body that he gave her, a pretty animal, a living doll, an automaton whose program he purposely forgot in order to be occasionally surprised. He gives her nipple a tweak to get her attention, and then he asks, quite casually, well, as casually as it's possible for the voice of fate to sound, "How about if I gave you breast cancer, for no good reason at all? Would you like that?"

"Huh . . . wha . . ."

"Breast cancer, or some nonsense going on in the uterus, or maybe even a melanoma . . ."

"My God," she says, really looking aghast; you can feel her fear. "You wouldn't, would you . . . please . . . you're kidding, right? I'm only twenty-six."

"Oh, I don't know: a mugger, leaky gas valve, cab jumping a curb, something silly like a bee sting or a common food additive you're suddenly and inexplicably allergic to. An accident: let's say, falling asleep with that fucking gum you're always chewing and choking to death, for instance. Anything can happen."

"Please," she squeaked, helplessly, reaching desperately for his procreative member, and felt him momentarily harden, and then it all went soft again. She was afraid to annoy him or, worse, embarrass him, so she merely cupped him in her hand, like the proverbial sparrow that already fell from the tree.

"Ah, Jesus," the chairman sighed, suddenly feeling exhausted, totally played out. "What's your name, sweetheart?"

"Sofia."

"Yeah, right . . . Sofia . . ."

He seemed to go far off in his thoughts for an instant, light-years away, so far he no longer seemed to be there at all, having abandoned his creation. When he returned from wherever he'd been, a little less of him was there than before.

"Everyone thinks it's a picnic to be God, creating, destroying, calling the shots, but let me tell you, it's a thankless hassle. No one sees the road of blood and broken bones that leads to the pinnacle where I sit, alone, from the beginning of time to the end, or until someone with the brains and balls decides to whack me in the middle of eternity. Oh, there's the newspaper headlines, starlets, front-row seats, tornadoes, St. Valentine massacres, and all that, but what it's like to wear the face I wear, always confident, always in control, even when I'm contracting innocents to their deaths . . . Do you have any idea what that's like? Battlefield commanders, surgeons, pilots, Mafia dons, they understand what it's like never to be wrong, even if you're dead wrong, and how chaos is held off simply by single-minded stubbornness. Fuck it, if it weren't for me, nothing would get done and someone else, maybe worse, would be there to take my place, because one thing is for certain: everyone wants to be me. So be thankful, sing hallelujah, say amen, because it may all be a pile of shit, but this is as good as it gets."

The chairman grinned tightly, madly, and was taken aback himself at how much of himself he had revealed to this whore of an administrative assistant. He really wasn't himself lately. Perhaps that explained the short exchange that followed next.

"Speak honestly with me, Ms. Haskins . . . Sofia . . . You can do that, can't you?"

"I'll try. . . ."

". . . without fear that I will do something . . . something terrible. . . . Are your parents still alive? How old are they anyway? Are you married? Do you have children?" He didn't seem to notice her terrified expression and waved off her choked attempt to answer. "What I really want to know is, have we forgotten parts of ourselves? Is that possible, do you think, sweet Sofia?"

Unsure what answer he was looking for, and knowing that no answer at all was definitely not an option, the secretary managed to squeak out her real opinion on the matter: "I don't know."

"I wouldn't think it possible on the basis of the definitions."

Ms. Haskins widened her eyes, hoping the chairman would read whatever he wanted to read in the ambiguous expression.

"But perhaps the definitions are wrong. It's unthinkable, but let's think it, shall we? Let's put our heads together on this one, Sofia. What if there's a dark half, a forgotten half, a half that doesn't exist? The question is, who can be against us, if we are all that exists? Can we be against ourselves? Does it even make sense to say something like that?"

"It's been said," Sofia acknowledged quietly, and more than a little cautiously, "by parts of us."

"Absurd," the chairman thundered, "those parts are now all dead." Silence followed and the prevailing mood was one of profound regret and loneliness, of one who'd acted rashly and in poor judgment. "I'm afraid I'm left to conclude that there is only one other possibility."

Ms. Haskins had let go of his penis some time before. She had briefly considered doing something with her mouth, but had given up on those thoughts as well. The truth was, the chairman had been entirely impotent for quite some time, and, although they both pretended, it was clear they weren't fooling each other, and they certainly weren't fooling themselves, at least Sofia wasn't, and she didn't think he was, either. Sofia had come to consider what they did a ritual, and let it go at that, figuring the reason he kept her around was to be his high priestess of sorts, but now she knew differently. He had kept her around to hear what he was about to say next.

"The only other conclusion to draw from our dilemma," the chairman said, and Sofia really didn't want to hear what he said next, afraid she would suddenly become one of those people who "knew too much," but she heard it anyway, "is that there is someone else."

You might have thought that, things being what they were, what he said might have given her some glimmer of hope, but instead, it only made her feel ill, but then she might have only been programmed to feel that way.

"God is not alone," he said. "There are two of us."

It was all too much for her to consider, this idea that the chairman was insane. Instead, she asked him the one question that had really been troubling her from the start.

"That thing you said . . . about my uterus . . . You wouldn't really give me cancer, would you? My mom died of uterine cancer at thirty-eight. It was horrible."

The chairman winked. "I'd be getting that PAP smear, darling, if I were you."

But the jocularity was forced, faked, and entirely inappropriate to the current weather. There were dark clouds racing over an empty plain, lightning, distant thunder, all the old clichés, and the thought, or whatever it was, coming once again, again and again, like a troubling dream: Maybe there is another.

"Once upon a time," Io said, telling the bedtime story for a change, "there was a curious race of creatures who just could not say 'no.'" He was dressed in a pink teddy and white thigh-high fishnets, big white stiletto-heeled mules, short blond pigtails. On his back a large and elaborate scene had been tatooed from a Chinese sexual manual circa 1750 B.C. "I want you to remember exactly what I'm going to tell you now because someday you'll write it all down and broadcast my message to the world."

Vince, too terrified, as usual, to extricate himself from Io's dangerous postcoital embrace, felt even more universally alarmed. "Should I get the laptop?"

The boy-vamp pricked Vince's carotid with a long pink nail. "Silly . . . just listen."

Later, much later, after it all fell apart and Vince had been reprogrammed, or deprogrammed, unsuccessfully in either case, and he came upon the document he'd produced from this conversation linked to a site found during a routine search on fraternal twins, he wondered how much of it was really what Io had said, and how much Vince had made up out of desperation, hysteria, and fear, not to mention his own admittedly life-hating pathological neurosis.

"I've seen life," Io said, "from birth to death, over and over again, and it's not good, none of it, not at all. Nothing lasts: and worse, it all ends in pain, disappointment, isolation, and, just before you die forever, a sense that you've been duped. And so you have. 'Do not go gentle into that good night,' the poet screams, and most don't, until you can't avoid it, and then . . . just like that . . ." and Io snapped his fingers and hooted, "You do!

"You're alone at the end, as you've been all along, only at the end you realize your loneliness even if you're surrounded by a roomful of loved ones. Each of them is already moving on with their own lives—lives in which you're not there anymore. You're nothing but a milepost in the lives of others and never more so than when you die. Does anyone really see you? Did anyone ever truly listen to a word you said? Of course not. We are damned to the misinterpretion of others! And the same friend who holds your hand at your deathbed will that night be thinking of where to take his supper. Life goes on. It's just a saying everyone says—until life goes on . . . without you!

"Sssh . . . don't breathe a word about love! People don't love each other: they use each other for a time and then move on, and lucky are those who die in love, for if they had lived but five more years the love of their life would have simply been someone else. Like dried-up husks, sucked of all life and importance, are the memory of lovers, and they lie stretched out behind you like abandoned automobiles taking you on the highway to nowhere. Luckiest of all are those who find a victim who can feed them all their lives. But I've never seen a widow or widower that didn't look somehow relieved. Each man dies alone, in pain and isolation and a panty full of poop and I have seen that knowledge in the eyes of even the graceful dead: I am alone, alone, alone . . .

"No one likes it, but what else is there to do? You must accept the human lot, so the spiritual say, but is it really acceptance when there is no choice, or is it merely a breaking of all resistance? It's rape that mortals suffer and the lovers are those who are determined to smile and enjoy it. What else is there to do? Even the most defiant are broken at the ultimate moment, heave a sigh, and let death pump them with its maggoty jelly.

"What is there to do but enjoy your bowl of ice cream and negotiate for someone to touch your private parts and take a cottage by the sea in the warmer months? You live like animals and call it blessed and then pretend it makes no difference when the diagnosis comes that takes it all away. Ah, but you know it does, you know it does. Show me a man who ever said: 'Yes, make me sick, make me old, make me mortal.' Show me the woman who wouldn't escape the so-called natural life-process if only she could. No matter how holy or enlightened, no one chooses life—life as it is, expect because they have to!

"It's human to want to be young, happy, and immortal. It's human to desire—to survive. We develop egos naturally, after all. To call submission to the law of decay—what? Grace? Now there's a joke. To call the elimination of ego—what? Enlightenment? Ha, ha, ha. Would nature be so absurd as to require man to overcome the very terms of his survival, to suppress the very quality that makes him . . . human? Would God dictate such madness? Oh, but nature and God do not . . . only man, man, that absurd beast, that sick animal! What is there left then to be . . . Oh, I don't know . . . beyond human . . . not superhuman . . . that's been tried and tried to death and failed. Not superman . . . no, antihuman . . . posthuman . . . afterhuman!"

"Let's stop this hopeless game of pain and futility once and for all! Everyone knows the score by now. Why continue to play? Everyone knows what lies in store—and yet, more children, more and more. Even the most miserable bring forth new victims to be lacerated, subjugated, and slaughtered. The world is no different today than it was in five thousand B.C. Every pretty truth known now was known then and look at the world around us: the same violence, poverty, corruption, and wholesale evil. You want peace in the world and yet neighbor cannot live with neighbor, husband with wife, parent with child.

"It will never change . . . never! We will never learn to live in love and harmony with each other. It's impossible. Life feeds on life at every level, in every relationship—it can't be any other way. Life is vampirism and they call us vampires. But we aren't any different from you!

"We *are* you!

"There is no separating man from thirst, no getting rid of the need for blood crying out in his every cell, no getting rid of man without getting rid of his life!

"Children, more children, aren't the hope of the future—they are the problem! Look around you. Look at yourself. You were once a child, too. You were once the hope of the future. Generations and generations of hope—and here we are. Look at the next generation. They are us! No better, no worse: just more stupidity and needless pain. When I see a pregnant woman walking down the street, I want to kick her until she aborts: I want to cut the living fetus from her womb! The bitch! The killer! The slaughterer! The Mother. If you want to liberate the world from evil and pain, kill all the mothers! Start with your own!

"Is it shocking to hear me speak this way? Am I saying the worst thing that you can possibly say? Why? Ask yourself, why? Can it be that I'm touching the greatest taboo of all? Pressing, so to speak, the red button of species annihilation? Why is that people, gathered around a suicide, always try to find a reason: he was sick, depressed, out of his mind? Why is it inconceivable that a rational decision had been made: life has simply been rejected?

"I'll tell you why: we've been programmed to survive. Everything induces us to obey this script: a sunny day, a pretty boy or girl, a pleasant meal, the sound of the surf, a colorful flower, a new morning after a good night's sleep, the very reflex of the body away from pain, everything says, 'Live one more day, one more hour, one more minute'—everything but me! That's why you all hate me, that's why I must be betrayed, discredited, destroyed . . . sacrificed. Because I dare tell you the truth that no one wants to hear. In me, you see the grinning skull that laughs at your dreams, your hopes, your loves, you fears, your desperate clawings after meaning—I am the reductive asburdum of it all, the everlasting zero, the repulsive kiss of death itself.

"Do you want to know the meaning of life? I'll tell you the meaning of life—the meaning. Don't make me laugh. The meaning of life is more life: bodies to carry sperm and eggs to produce more bodies to carry more sperm and eggs, mindless, pointless, endless, on and on, forever and ever. That is why you are alive. That is why you suffer. That is why you die. That is why you create art and philosophy. That is why you worship God or liberty or whatever it is your worship. That is why you go to the gym or get a haircut or paint your toenails. That . . . and that is all. To create more bodies and that is all!

"When I hear of a war breaking out in the Balkans, or some new holocaust, or an earthquake in Peru, or a bomb-blast in Jerusalem, I rejoice. Two planes crash over Germany, a girl is abducted in Salt Lake City, a dam collapses in Bengali, a World Trade Center goes down . . . I'm giddy with delight. I know it's coming . . . it's coming . . . eyes are opening, and you see it, just a glimpse, but you see it, and the more these events are strung together the more of it you'll see, like frames of a film, a little strip, perhaps, but enough to begin to know what you're watching. . . .

"There are only two paths out: enlightenment and extinction. And after all these centuries upon centuries, these endless millennia, who doesn't see that enlightenment is too slow, too impossible, and will simply never come about? One Buddha—for two thousand years of killers. And in the meanwhile, oh, so much suffering! Who's the bad guy? Who wants it to end . . . all the pain, stupidity, and pointlessness? Oh, I'll be the bad guy if that's the way it must be, if I must be the only one with the strength to carry that burden on my fragile, pretty, white shoulders. I stand for extinction: I carry that cross, stone, whatever. Extinction is the shorter, surer way. It is the only way. The extinction of humanity—to wipe him away once and for all, the entire mess, the cancer that is life itself, life with this consciousness that only causes pain, this creature that only suffers, causes suffering, and cannot die. . . .

"Whether you like it or not, I am the only thing that hasn't been tried. I am the answer no one wanted to hear. I am what's coming. I am what's Next!

"I stand for extinction: the one true path to liberation. And I ask only that you exterminate yourself. That's all I ask! I ask that you bring about the end . . . and end yourself! I ask that you make the sacrifice. Your suicide is a prayer to me and the salvation of humanity. Die—but die voluntarily. Die—it's not the easy way out, but it's the only way out. Die not like a man or a woman, not like a human being, forced from life, or stripped of everything before finally giving in with sadness and a sense of, oh, can you believe it, gratitude? Oh, fuck you, not that! There is nothing to be grateful for. Don't procreate: don't cause more suffering. Kill what's here. Kill it all. Leave no trace. Just die. Just die. Kill yourself. Do it, do it, do it. Make way for what comes next. Hail to all that's antihuman, posthuman, afterhuman. Hail to the Afterhuman. Good night!"

And Io had stopped his oration around then, giddy, feverish, having faked a cataclysmic, transmogrifying death-orgasm, or perhaps he had gone on, Vince could not remember anymore, if he remembered even this much correctly, so much trauma, reconditioning, and disinformation having followed. But he was relatively certain that Io, having sunk back on his pillows, calling pointlessly for a ginger ale and crackers, had told Vince to leave a line at the bottom of this document when it appeared on the Nekroticka Web site, so adherents to his rigorous new crusade against the species, death, and even themselves, wouldn't have to trouble themselves with a suicide note, but print out the page, sign it, and, as Io said, waving, limp-wristed, his pale, perpetually boyish hand, say "bye-bye, cruel world."

Nikka had returned to the primordial honeycomb, if, in fact, she'd ever left, and if the whole misadventure hadn't been a dream, but a bad example of astral projection. In a hypostatic coma she stared blankly into nowhere, which is to say, deeply into herself, and by now it should be obvious, that kind of thing can go on forever. The honeybees were droning, some clinging to her beloved features, others moving drunkenly through the heavy smoke, falling into infinity, the bottom of which was already covered by a writhing carpet of hairy black-and-gold bodies.

The inviolable city had been violated, the invaders having surprisingly little trouble breaching the security, especially insofar as there was no security left, or, rather, the security had itself turned against Nikka and the golden city, following the clinical model of the typical autoimmune deficiency disease.

Like black spiders, they strung the walls and hexagonal chambers with their fatal ropes and wires, until the place looked impossibly tangled and out of control and growing ever more so. The comb was burning, the wax tombs melting, and all the Alexandras, hundreds of thousands of them, one for every night and day of her reign, the pretty, naked, neutered Alexandras were burning, and all of it was nothing but an incredible waste.

The last of the bees, the ones that hadn't yet asphyxiated, were clustering frantically around Nikka's ten holy orifices, seeking shelter, if not outright escape, and into her open mouth they swarmed, countless numbers, as she hummed her world-sustaining mantra, hummed until the bees filled her, choking off the sound.

And there Nikka sat, mute, filled with bees, the last refuge, looking past everything as the fire eventually consumed her body and whatever life remained, if such a thing were even possible.

5. nada

On every railway line there is a set of tracks going nowhere, and, as impossible as it may seem, originating from there as well. It's on these tracks now, somewhere between two indeterminate points, that a black train is speeding through the night, all but invisible, and in the seventh car from the engine, amongst luxurious classical English drawing room appointments, Caleb sits on a divan beside Juliet, while Mahoney, carving a piece of genuine ponderosa pine, tries to explain away entirely their lifelong homicidal blood feud.

"It was all a misunderstanding," he says. "I hope we can get beyond all the bad feelings and personal tiddly-twat. We're all much bigger people than that, so to speak."

It had been Mahoney who invited Caleb to this rendezvous, and this time Caleb had accepted because, what the hell, and besides, he sensed the exhaustion behind Mahoney's eleventh-hour overture of peace. And just as the ex-commando had promised, there were no heavily armed guards, hostages, leaking plague canisters, or rigged explosives, not yet, anyway, although it was certainly possible that the whole train was racing straight for some kind of bottomless chasm.

As for Juliet, she looked, well, alive, a little rough around the edges, to be sure, but still more or less intact. Caleb had expected nothing less. He hadn't believed in her execution, not for a moment; there were too many mitigating and extenuating circumstances for her to be killed in a hail of automatic weapon fire, especially in such an offhand and basically peripheral kind of way.

"You're a smart man, Mr. Darr," Mahoney continued, if he'd ever stopped. "I wasted so much of my life hating you, but it was inevitable, I guess. Sometimes the lesson is the stupidity of it all and the only way to learn it is to make one mistake after another all the way to the very end. Not, of course, I add parenthetically, that my bad example will serve as a precautionary example to anyone—it won't. Everyone must fuck their lives up on their own."

Caleb acknowledged nothing. Beside him, Juliet shifted uncomfortably, bleeding lightly from various places, dabbing at herself rather ineffectually. Caleb knew that Mahoney was feeling effusive; he had, after all, heard more than a few of these "deathbed" confessions in his time. It would be to no purpose to rush the ex-commando even if time was of the essence, which it was, because Mahoney would not be rushed, and besides, everything was occurring, as they said, in due time.

"Is it possible to love someone or something that doesn't love you back, that doesn't acknowledge your existence, and about whose nature you are wrong? Is it possible to feel intimacy for a person, or a thing, with which you have no relationship at all, or just a one-way relationship, as in devotee to object of devotion? Is it all an illusion? Isn't intimacy, by its very definition, an interpenetration?"

Caleb continued to say nothing: a man at the end of his rope doesn't need to hear that he's not clinging to anything.

"To what, in the end, did I devote my life? An illusion, I suppose. Everyone turns inward, sooner or later, and

travels their own road to nothing. Never mock those you
love, even in the little things. There comes a point when
you stop drawing cards and you have to play the ones
you have. Woe is the man who has discarded too much.
One night you rise at three A.M. and check your voice-
mail accounts but they are empty: no one has called. You
put the phone down and it rings immediately. You pick
it up in the middle of the first ring and say, 'Hello?
Hello?' but there is no one there, or no answer, and the
irony is witnessed by you alone."

Mahoney pulled a cheap, gold-plated pocket watch,
chainless, from his pocket, flipping open the cover, and
a wind-up rendition of "Greensleeves" escaped. It would
not be accurate, or correct, to call what Mahoney was
doing crying, nor the expression on his face sorrow, or
hatred, or anything that anyone had ever seen before:
it was the look of a man who had seen everything a man
needed to see, including himself seeing it, and now
wanted to see no more. "It's three A.M.," he said. "It's
always three A.M."

The watch in Mahoney's palm, of course, was broken,
and the tune had wound itself down, or would have, had
the ex-commando not snapped the cover shut, and returned the watch to his pocket. The train was rapidly
decelerating and although Caleb kept any questions
from his face and Juliet was probably too preoccupied to
ask and not important enough to be noticed, much less
answered, Mahoney said it anyway: "We've arrived at
your stop."

They stood at the door of the open car as sleepy
porters moved dreamily on the wet platform, bringing
down bags they hadn't had when they boarded the train.
Mahoney was in his shirtsleeves, smoking a cigar, looking relaxed and clear-eyed, like a man whose mighty
struggle with disease, the endless cycles of remission and

recurrence, was finally done and over, and from which he had emerged, not a new man, but not the man he was.

"Good-bye, Mr. Darr," Mahoney says.

And Caleb is like a man whom you come upon inexplicably sitting in your kitchen or at the desk of your home office in the middle of the night, everyone else asleep, and you, alone, wandering the house, having woken from a troubled dream, Caleb was like that man, all in black, sitting there, saying nothing, having come to collect a debt you've always owed, and his presence should be eerie and alarming, but by the time you are able to see him, you've been so displaced, it's not.

"Wait," Mahoney said, and rummaged around in his pocket for a moment. He squatted in the open doorway of the car and held out his arm, the fingers curling open, and in his palm lay the wood he'd been mercilessly carving, now tortured into what looked like a vaguely obscene shape, fluid and insinuating. "I want you to have this."

Caleb took the unspeakably childish and meaningless item, perhaps it was a butt plug, and put it into his pocket, and the general idea is that he'll eventually leave it stuffed between some couch cushions in the home of a soon-to-be-dead fashion designer, which is certain to cause the most confusion.

"Good-bye, Mahoney," Caleb says, looking up from the platform at the man in shirtsleeves, nearly eclipsed. And what passes between the two men is a complete absence of any emotion whatsoever. "It's time to go."

The train starts moving again, minus Caleb and Juliet, and whether through some high-tech military stealth technology or because its apparition was a form of psychic communication from the other side, it seems to instantly, or very nearly instantly, dematerialize right before their eyes (although they had already turned away), as if moving at terrific speeds, which it no doubt was. And along with the miragelike train, as much a ghost as any of it, Mahoney vanished, leaving behind a disembodied and emotionless scream that went on for ten miles or so, fading quickly into silence but returning every night on time, at 3:00 A.M., whenever anyone thought of him, or died.

"What now?" Juliet asked, The platform was deserted and there was no station, no call booth, no one in sight. There was a road, or what was left of one, and it led into the darkness on a moonless night like a road that had already been traveled, or must be traveled now, since it was the only one going anywhere at all. From the smell in the air they might have been in Provence, or northwestern Belgium, on a night following the night of the smouldering of many bonfires.

"We follow the road," Caleb said, sensing, for once, that no one was watching, but only for a time being.

They walked into the night, deep into the clammy night, away from the relative exposure of the train platform and through a kind of inaccessible forest, or densely wooded outskirts, toward what they both expected to be a town, or village, or hamlet of some sort. Juliet, Caleb noted, with his customary lack of urgency, needed immediate medical attention, and there was something sinister about the way the trees by the road were marked with blazes drawn in white bird shit. There was a hermit, or homeless vagrant, deep in the woods, the "vampire" of the place, who'd fed here for centuries, and now he lay dying, having no idea, probably, what had happened to the town. Caleb would pay this lost soul a visit, a simple side matter, in due time, but not now.

"Why didn't you kill him?" Juliet said, breathlessly. She was limping, trying to keep up, falling behind even with Caleb's unhurried pace. She was talking not of the hermit, of course, whose presence she could not have guessed at, but of Mahoney. "He'll follow us, you know. Watch us. He only let us go to find out what's going on."

"There is no need to kill him. He has decided to do it himself."

"When? By the time—"

"Soon." Caleb stopped a moment, as if picking up a warning on the perimeter of his awareness, a branch breaking in a dry creek bed or a satellite surveillance signal. "If not already."

"How can you be so . . . sure?"

Caleb didn't answer. He was never big on explaining himself; and he'd done enough of that with Juliet already, and had a little more to do. Instead he said, "Listen to that."

"What?"

"Nothing . . . not a cricket."

And even Caleb had to admire the thoroughness of the evacuation.

Half a mile, maybe less, the terrain had been entirely misleading, and the road led into a modest municipality that looked distinctly European: brick buildings, narrow streets, a hostel, several pubs or taverns, perhaps rathskellars, whatever, and, of course, a more or less ubiquitous American-style hotel, something exactly along the lines of a Holiday Inn without quite being a Holiday Inn.

The term "ghost town" suggested itself immediately to Juliet, who found herself involuntarily walking on tiptoes, afraid, somehow, to make a sound. She was reminded of a city like Pompeii, people caught in the act of everyday activities, buckling a sandal, washing their teeth, or making love, when everyone and everything was flash-buried, except in this place, not a person, alive or corpse, was to be seen anywhere. Had they all fled in time, or had they been instantly incinerated by one of those smart anti-personnel nuclear devices? Perhaps a cleanup crew had been dispatched with block-long rolling morgue vans, packing away the dead, assiduously scrubbing the town square, compulsively vacuuming up hair samples, obsessively sterilizing eating utensils, steering wheels, and cash register buttons. The town—from its park benches to its hospital to the bathroom of any of its carefully ordered homes—was as devoid of any sign of human life as the planet Pluto.

They took up "residence" at an old brick row house, number 16, to be exact, a neat little place with yellow chintz curtains and flower boxes full of white geraniums: the kind of place an elderly Swiss doctor might let, or a retired civil servant and his wife, although no one was home now, nor would anyone ever be. Out of habit, perhaps, Juliet pulled open the icebox door and found nothing but a hard and glaring emptiness.

"Thorough job they did," Caleb commented. "All the perishables have been stripped away. Maggots."

The whole setup made Juliet feel more than a little uneasy, as if she were on a stage set, and, indeed, everything felt a bit like cardboard. She sat at the small kitchen table, trying not to touch anything too much, while Caleb fixed a package of freeze-dried coffee he'd found in one of the cabinets, along with other foil packages of desiccated foodstuffs, the kind of thing, she thought, that they always claimed the astronauts ate in outer space.

Outside, in the distance, the muted thunder of repeated missile detonations like a dull headache: whatever had been avoided here happening there. Or, perhaps, the bombardment was still to come.

Juliet sipped the scalding black coffee. On the icebox door, held up by a strawberry magnet, was a shopping list on which she recognized the Turkish word for eggs, or, maybe, snails.

"Is this poison?" she asked, indicating whatever was in her cup.

"Not yet . . . it's not likely."

Juliet shrugged, and after a beat said, "Do you believe them?"

"The world needs a new savior; the appearance of one, anyway."

Juliet made an unintentionally abbreviated gesture meant to include her, Caleb, the kitchen . . . everything. "But . . . this . . ."

"Absurd, yes. Entropy . . . the myth is tired, the universe is played out."

"Can it be saved then, after all?"

"No."

Caleb was absently examining the knives hanging on the stuccoed wall: the big knives for separating the joints of whole chickens or slabs of beef ribs, the tiny ones used for coring and skinning fruits, peeling grapes, for instance.

"I suppose we should . . . before I collapse. Something is torn inside me, I think."

"Hmm," Caleb said, thinking of something else. He was temporarily seeing something else: two heads on sharpened bamboo pikes outside a thatched hut being lit on fire by dancing Africans. He came back to the kitchen, saw Juliet again. Leave it to a woman, he reflected appreciatively, not to ask the question, why?

"I think I might be dying," Juliet said, considering that he hadn't heard her, or hadn't been paying attention.

"There's something you don't understand."

Juliet started to laugh bitterly, but it came out as a hard cough instead, and she was embarrassed to have spit up blood, hot and private, all over her chin, the table, the front of her T-shirt. Caleb moved instantaneously to take her wrist, preventing her from wiping it away.

"Ah . . . shit . . ." she murmured. "Ah . . . shit . . ."

"This won't be the first time, apparently. Some fluke, some mutation, some"—Caleb formed the word with distaste—"empathy makes it possible."

Juliet was nodding, but at what, specifically, she couldn't say. Maybe she was only trying to get him to finish quicker, or trying to keep herself from blacking out.

"I've seen the life inside me, what is being called life . . . and it's like a barbarian army, a riot, a lynch mob, a rebellion, a cancer . . . It will multiply inside you without consideration, chaotic, uncontrollable, a mutiny against reason and equality . . . Think of Hitler's speeches, the death squads of Stalin, Pol Pot . . . It will survive at all costs and the first and most inconsequential demand it will make will be your life."

Juliet spoke softly, weakly: "I think a part of me knew that, knew it from the start."

"It will kill you, what I do, the way it killed so many others, only worse, because . . ." Caleb stopped abruptly, staring at a fly in the otherwise immaculate sink.

"Yes . . ."

He looked up. ". . . yes."

And Juliet, who'd been fighting it the whole time, collapsed, slumping over onto the kitchen table, her head at an odd angle, but the neck not yet broken, and the slack mouth wet and messy with blood, lips trembling with the last words she'd managed not to say: "I love you."

"No, no, no, no, no, no." Io stomped a platform boot in mock frustration. "This is all totally wrong." They were rehearsing for the sacrifice, empty refrigerator boxes standing in for the Stonehenge blocks, sheets of paper covered in crayon to simulate the dreary English sky, green mats of plastic patio lawn on the floor of someone's Lower Manhattan loft. The princess seemed lost, and, frankly, a bit out of it, coming down from quaaludes and not yet sufficiently up on Ecstasy, and Vince, doing double duty as executioner and artistic director, was both exhausted and terrified. He still wasn't sure why he'd been chosen by both Io, and, ostensibly, Jason Horn, to kill Alison, even if it was only all pretend, but something about the whole thing truly unnerved him.

Io had not definitely decided on his couture, and seemed to be leaning toward a semimasculine chic: leather capri pants, bolero jacket, midi-T with something suitably arch emblazoned in lavender glitter paint, chokers, anklets, wristbands, etc., but he seemed to be changing his mind constantly, driving Vince to the limits of his ingenuity. How, for instance, was Vince supposed to resolve the paradox of Io's demand in footwear: a clog and something open-toed? Did such a shoe even exist?

"Not like that," the diva said with dangerous petulance, and grabbed the two ends of the suitably passé

Fendi scarf wrapped around the princess's slender throat, "like this, like this, wrists turned out, elegant, you're not trying to twist off the gummed-up top of a Pepsi One, for goodness' sake. Oh, heavens, I'm parched. Will someone get me a Crystal Light?"

The crew, such as it was, pretended to laugh at the obvious joke, at least those who were still alive during the heyday of Linda Evans.

In the meantime, the princess was visibly suffering, straining for breath, her elegant, childish hands clawing stupidly at the scarf embedded around her constricted windpipe, eyes bulging in bored alarm, tongue beginning to protrude, distorted face not yet totally unpleasant-looking, but definitely getting there, already the red color of certain cuts of inferior porterhouse.

"More toe action, darling," Io shrieked, instructionally. "Curl them up, separate them a bit. I want those pretty little piggies emoting sexy agony!"

If the girl heard, she made no indication. Only the whites of her eyes were showing: she looked about to lose consciousness, if she hadn't already.

"Please . . ." Vince said, ". . . you might want to stop. . . . She might die right now. . . ."

"Oh, poof, we'll just get another one to replace her. How hard it is to find a fake virgin princess nowadays, anyway?"

Did that mean, Vince wondered, that the girl strangling to death at the moment wasn't really the princess, after all? Were the rumors, already circulating, true? Did it even matter?

The boy vampire let the scarf go and the princess, or whoever she was, fell over limply, not even bothering to pull away the silk embedded in her swollen flesh. Io had deigned to give Vince an explanation as to why it was to be he, and not Io himself, who was to actually

execute Alison. That explanation was neither flatter-
ing, nor particularly reassuring, and probably was
meant to be neither, anyway. The juxtaposition, Io explained, between the balding, potbellied, middle-aged
Vince and the pretty pop princess would provide for
far more frisson, Io had lazily theorized late one autumn afternoon among forty-three or forty-four staked
victims in the lush garden of somewhere that was supposed to look like Laos, than if she were dispatched
by the dashingly handsome bleached-blond prince
himself.

"It will be so much more grotesque, sweetie," Io had
said, examining, through a monocle, the navel of one
boy, writhing, on a stake, "and that's something like the
general idea . . . I think."

Io was constantly trying to justify the most egregious
and outrageous of actions based on his pursuit of an aes-
thetic ideal he articulated only with the stock phrases
"maximum frisson," "frisson to the max," and "ultimate
friss." But Vince was hardly satisfied with this rationale,
and not only because it was personally insulting and
placed him on the scene, center stage, of a live Internet
snuff simulcast featuring one of the most famous women
in the world as the victim.

No, what bothered Vince most of all, far more, he
was almost ashamed to admit, than the abstract con-
siderations of murder, which he could hardly believe
he would actually commit, was the nagging paranoia
that he was being set up to take the fall in a government conspiracy to take control of the free flow of ideas
on the Internet. Vince couldn't shake the suspicion
that Io was not the wild nihilistic harbinger of homicidal nothingness and purposeless wholesale human
slaughter, but an agent who, working in tandem with
cops like Jason Horn, sought to arrest Vince and so

many like him who were doing nothing more harmful than sharing basically harmless fantasies on the Worldwide Web.

By coercing him into a real-life murder, the government would be able to provide a rationale for a bored public easily manipulated into mass hysteria by make-believe evil, while the sleep poison was mainlined directly into the system: the phony best-sellers, the silly sitcoms, the fake emotions of newscasters, morning shows, talk shows, man-and-woman-on-the-street interviews, the pretend piousness of churches, synagogues, and newspapers, the presidential PR, the reams and reams of polls in which everyone was lying through their teeth.

The idea was to isolate anyone who was different, which was, really nearly everyone, to force them to feel marginal, unloved, and unlovable, as they had throughout the centuries, and thereby render the individual not only ineffectual, but suicidal, afraid of themselves and others, guilty, horrified, driven either to conform or to commit acts of desperation that would, eventually, condemn them, one way or another.

This is the way it had always worked—and this is the way they wanted it to continue to work into the indefinite future. But first, they had to regain control of the imagination, which, of course, was impossible, so they did the next best thing: they made true, unregulated communication impossible. One person in Topeka with an outlaw thought was nothing but a lonely crank—but what if he or she linked up with another person with the same outlaw thought in Oslo, and another in Surrey, and on and on, like crabgrass, spreading, linking, cross-linking all over the world? What if people with "outlaw" thoughts began to think of themselves as . . . normal?

Only when we are free to express the worst, Vince had always maintained, are we free at all.

"Is it possible to know for certain," Io asked the technical advisor, a doctor who specialized in postmortem subjects, "if she will hemorrhage from the nose? It seems there should be some way to predict that. The condition of her nasal capillaries or something . . . Help me, people, help me, I'm grasping here. . . ."

They were sitting in the back of one of those kitchy horse-drawn carriages, one of fifteen hired out by the latest celebrity Manhattan real-estate tycoon, for the cast and crew of Nekrotika, sipping from champagne flutes that someone Vince didn't recognize, someone from the arts-and-leisure section of the *Times*, maybe, kept refilling from a plastic bottle of False Alarms mixed back at one penthouse or other. Vince was shocked at the number of people strolling through Central Park on that early autumn night who seemed to recognize Io, shouting out endearments and encouragements, throwing flowers hastily snatched from surrounding bushes, phone numbers, bras, etc.

Certainly, Vince thought uneasily as the night ground on, and several innocently appealing boys and girls were killed and left in their wake, their sweetly broken bodies tumbled unceremoniously from the caravan of gaudy carriages, all the attention they were getting, could not be good.

It was the ultimate fuck that Juliet had been looking for, perhaps, her entire, relatively short, and soon to end life. But now, at the penultimate moment, she realized, entirely unexpectedly, that what she sought was something far, far greater than that. She was lying on her back, in a surprisingly postmodern bed, a suspended antigravity platinum platform with Victorian elements, including four posters and canopy, but incorporating, although seemingly impossibly, elements from traditional Korean, Scandinavian, and Pocono Mountain honeymoon kitsch.

She had regained consciousness, sort of, although she had no recollection of coming to this bedroom and presumed, logically, albeit mistakenly enough, that she had been carried here by Caleb. She had no memory, likewise, of removing her clothes, what little clothes she'd had left, or having them cut away from her body by paramedics, and now she lay naked atop a coverlet woven of some kind of high-tech polymers into a kind of sacred Himalayan design.

The room was lit, she suspected artificially, by that mysterious melancholy light that only came on certain golden autumn afternoons, between 4:00 P.M. and 5:00, that seemed to deepen the already sweet regret of the coming darkness. But from where that light emanated, as predictable, even cliché, as it might have been, it was simply impossible to say, and one was left with the general sensation of something like this: well, what else would have you have you expected?

In this light, bathed in this light, as if the room itself were illuminated by his total apotheosis, Caleb stood at the foot of the bed, naked, like an angel is naked, without having removed its clothes, terrible, flawless, and yet scarred beyond imagining. Juliet wanted to touch that radioactive body, and yet she was afraid she couldn't, or wouldn't, as she reached up, her fingers hoping to brush against the smooth chest, its curve like a hairpin turn that cost countless lives, the flesh, a thin, taut, translucent carapace of muscle protecting, unnecessarily, a heart forever dead. She hoped to touch him, and yet, although scant centimeters away, she couldn't reach him.

What happened next, each would interpret differently, and even if a camera were running, recording devices saving every second of sound, what would play back would be enigmatic and brutal but it would appear something like this: Caleb, transitional frames deleted, on the bed, crouched there on his hams, like a demon from the old iconography, which he is, at least archtypically, his mouth on the girl's throat, her carotid between his teeth. A low growl escapes his throat, guttural and fierce, and he drags her upward toward the headboard with its depiction of one of the lesser-known landscapes of Edvard Munch, Juliet digging her heels into the coverlet to follow his lead, trying to relieve the pressure on her already catastrophically separating and damaged vertebrae.

Caleb grabs her upper arm and pulls it right out of the socket, and Juliet, in excruciating pain, one arm rendered totally useless and her left hip broken, finds herself thrown, savagely, facedown on the bed, both cheekbones shattered, her face already unrecognizable. Her earlier wounds, desperate as they were, have reopened, if they ever completely closed, soaking the mattress beneath her almost instantly with blood. Her right knee, meanwhile, has been dislocated, along with an ankle or two, rips in her Achilles tendons and one hamstring, and it's hardly even worth mentioning the broken toes, left wrist, and, of course, jaw. Her ribs have been inevitably bruised in this foreplay, several of them shattered outright, splintered really, and it hurts her terribly to breathe, so Juliet does so, upon risk of passing out, only in short reluctant gasps, managing barely to teeter on the verge of consciousness, which, delirious, she clings to for some irrational reason. Her head, lolling sightlessly, is hanging over the end of the bed, and she is staring up, ostensibly, at a sacred medieval maze, painted on the ceiling, which she finds herself trying to solve, hoping to absent herself, by any means possible, from the unspeakable pain of Caleb, who, without preamble or apology, has forced himself inside her, his organ, of absurdly alien proportions, containing death like a shotgun barrel, or an injection full of a new genetically engineered hybrid form of AIDS, and immeasurably more deadly than either.

What Juliet experiences, philosophically, during all this, however, is difficult to ascertain. A text of her thoughts, along with centuries of extensive exegesis and pointless metaphysical debate, has not yet been released, although it has been compiled and edited, and will become available when it is found, accidentally, by an exiled contract killer inside a plastic compact disk case buried along with others, containing recordings of various other confessions, visions, and the like, beneath a blighted no-man's land that was once the remains of an inner-city housing project.

In the meantime, one imagines that Juliet is experiencing something along the lines of the following: that it is through the intense pain Juliet now suffers that she feels most alive, that she apprehends the meaning of her meaningless life, and the meaning, entirely anachronistically, of love: she wants to restore Caleb's belief in the possibility of the human race, and, specifically, of a woman's ability to love and bring love—and life—into this otherwise lifeless and loveless world, and to do so fully, uninhibitedly, giving without expecting anything in return. She wants to show this angel of destruction fucking her, this avatar of nothing, who has passed over the barren deserts and ruined cities of modern life, and searched, in vain, that a woman does, in fact, exist who might be worthy to begin the human race anew.

And, now, being kissed by that mouth, that mouth that she had dreamed of, obsessed over, tried to reform in her imagination and in the mouths of all the other hungry men who'd kissed her, time and time again, that mouth, cruel, sardonic, unpitying, carnivorous, unquenchable, scornful—that mouth, lying open as if it were one's own open grave, revealing nothing but the awful truth, that mouth kissed her now, and Juliet, seeing the future, screamed with a new voice all the horror that Caleb had known, all by himself, since the goddamned beginning of time.

This is something of what one might reasonably suppose Juliet feels at the moment of her passionate dismemberment, her ecstasy and surrender, helped along by endorphins and delusion, and perhaps she does, except for the horror frozen on her face, the face that realizes, too late, that with the kiss she has been waiting for her entire life Caleb has, at the same moment, betrayed her and convinced her and proven to her that he was right all along: there is no such thing as love.

What Caleb feels, dreams, imagines, etc., at this moment is, as always, relatively simple: nothing.

On a plane, any plane, that could be going anywhere, Caleb sits in first class, as usual, not paying attention. When you're tracking down apocalypse you have to do a lot of traveling. He's been in so many planes going to so many places it's all come to run together: Madrid, Sydney, Los Angeles, Hamburg, Trenton—it's all just one big party broken down into different cliques, everyone yammering in bad English. Caleb must have accumulated so much frequent flyer mileage in the last six weeks alone that he's earned a free round-trip to Pluto and back, although, nowadays, who hasn't? His secretary, back at the Antwerp extension office, e-mails him his itinerary three times a day, but Caleb barely consults it, merely jumping into the limos always waiting curbside to whisk him away someplace, wherever.

"Phone call for you, Mr. Darr," the stewardess whispers, in consideration of the other passengers, most of whom are sleeping, as they fly over one dark land mass or other, sometime after two o'clock in the morning of what's shaping up to feel like one of those really cheesy Mondays.

Caleb takes the cordless handheld. "Yeah?"

"I'll bet you never expected to hear from me again."

"Uh-huh, and my refrigerator is running, too."

"This is no joke, Mr. Darr."

"What, are you ten?"

"I mean it, Mr. Darr, this is no joke."

"That's one of the worst impressions I've ever heard."

"It's not . . . for crissakes it's really me . . . Mahoney."

"Idiot." Caleb thumbed the disconnect button and stared down through the dark clouds. Crank calls, he thought, and shook his head, but neither in approval nor disapproval, probably some idiot on X-Rock. People don't have anything better to do anymore. Well, for that matter, did they ever?

Then, while an unscheduled meteor shower flashed to the north, Caleb allowed himself to think of the last seven days before the sack of Alexandria and wondered, but not a lot, if that had anything to do with anything at all, because, really, nothing so far did.

"Cameras rolling, and five, four, three, two, one, and . . . action!" *This is it,* Vince thought, *it's actually* *happening now,* whatever was happening, or going to happen, because nothing had happened yet. In his hands, wrapped around his clenched fists, the cravat, which only the most astute aficionado would note had once belonged to the imprisoned playwright Oscar Wilde, was pulled taut, dramatically. There were, if one looked closely and with a knowledgeable eye, over one hundred and fifty famous artifacts placed around the scene: Carl Jung's pipe, a Bible belonging to Rembrandt's mother, the boots of astronaut Neil Armstrong, a Dean Martin pool cue, Yukio Mishima's pen, one of Madonna's scrunchies, an FDR wheelchair, an eye patch from someone famous who had one eye, stuff like that.

Vince, to his vague relief, had not been costumed to look like a complete moron, but was dressed, semi-respectfully, in military chic: Israeli desert camouflage pants, black-ribbed sleeveless T, bulletproof vest, Civil War cavalry boots, and, of course, the omnipresent kepi, the latter modified in homage to the French Foreign Legion, representative of all lost causes. He was also wearing a pair of white Marine Corps dress gloves and the dog tags of some corporal killed in the Korean War. Vince had not been allowed to disguise himself in any way, although he had been permitted a pair of night-vision goggles, but only to lend him an air of menace, because, as Io put it, "Darling, you have that simpering, furtive, apologetic look like someone caught urinating on the side of the Trump Building."

Io was sitting in a sling-style chair, suspended from a crane, just off camera, holding a bullhorn, from which he occasionally issued extemporaneous aphorisms, stage directions, news headlines, whatever came into his head. The effect, of course, was disorienting, as it was no doubt meant to be. He had chosen, at the very last moment, to outfit himself like Jodie Foster in the old movie *Taxi Driver*, but why was anyone's guess.

"Seven Armenians killed in a shoot-out in Mexico City," he called out, godlike, from his perch high above the scene. "Forty-four drowned in a wave machine malfunction at a Pennsylvania water park. Move that right thigh forward!"

They were at Stonehenge, as planned, the entire crew having arrived yesterday afternoon, but although the stones looked real enough, old, weathered, and all that, the place looked different than it did in the pictures Vince had seen of it, smaller somehow, and, to be perfectly honest, he wasn't entirely certain that one of the stones wasn't actually missing. On the ground, scattered around pell-mell, perhaps to give the entire affair a kind of international flavor, were postcards from all over the world: Manhattan, Dublin, Florence, Geneva, Ho Chi Minh City, Pusan, Disneyworld, Cancún, etc., etc.

"Officials unconcerned about fate of kroner . . ." Io shouted out from his perch, his long legs, clad in fishnets and red platforms, dangling. He was, apparently, still reading headlines from the paper. "London Exodus Follows Fly Infestation. Lips puckered, lips puckered, darling!"

At Vince's feet, the princess was wearing a tiara you might buy in the Barbie section of Toys R Us, and a white gown, supposedly by some retro-chic designer in the tradition of Wang or Wong, but hacked up around the hemline with pinking shears, so that it looked like Alison had just risen from a pile of hurriedly shredded documents implicating important people of something scandalously important, arms sales, fake drug approvals, election fraud, corporate kickbacks, crimes against humanity, the usual nonsense. Her hair was swept up to showcase her throat, and, at the same time, to compensate for the unfortunate fact that she was not graced with what is usually called "a swanlike neck."

"Criminy," Io had said, upon seeing Alison's neck for the first time, shrugging in his faux apologetic way, "how was I supposed to know they'd vote for strangulation? I could have sworn they'd go for crucifixion."

Her breasts, although not much to speak of (the idea of a quickie breast implantation was nixed by someone, Vince didn't know who, but it wasn't Io), were concealed for the time being, or, rather, partially concealed by what amounted to little more than a few handfuls of confetti, based on the theory that their eventual baring would give the viewers something to look forward to between the impromptu beginning of the show and the girl's eventual asphyxiation. She was supposed to lose a shoe, as well, since no one could definitively answer whether foot fetishists preferred their victims barefoot or clad in sexy, very delicate, high-heeled silver sandals, and they finally decided on the one-shoe-on, one-shoe-off compromise, even if it did, as Io seemed delighted to note, represent a lowering of artistic vision in an effort to pander to the masses. And that reminded Vince: he had to make sure that Alison exposed herself during the "struggle," which might take more than a little inventiveness on Vince's part—the girl didn't look like she was up for much struggling. Fact is, Alison seemed almost comatose, the only thing, it seemed, keeping her sitting upright, being the port-colored cravat around her pale, but rather short, throat.

"Sony officials testify in subliminal message scandal . . ." Io said, paused, and added a bit of advice, "Don't worry, be happy."

Vince had no idea what was wrong with Alison. He'd

tried speaking to her three days ago, the last time he'd been permitted access to her, as Io wanted to ensure that today's performance had a "fresh spontaneous edge of desperation and confusion," and although she had been entirely delusional about her upcoming "nuptials" to Io, she was nevertheless animated, even if in a hysterical, schizoid way. Now she seemed to be emotionlessly going through the motions in a doomed, robotic way.

"Estranged wife kills kids, self, postman," Io booms, apropos, as usual, of nothing sequential. "Don't do the crime if you can't do the time."

The princess, of course, had been on mega doses of oddly mixed drugs, Vince knew that firsthand, since he was often the one who administered them to her. But her current state was inexplicable, even for relentlessly drug-induced catatonic shock exacerbated by abuse and sensory deprivation, and that made Vince speculate, wildly and hopefully, that perhaps she was only acting, placing herself in a sort of yogic hibernation that would enable her to survive for long periods without oxygen until Io screams, "Cut." Was that unreasonable for him to hope, was he only deluding himself? Such a thing must be possible, mustn't it, among high-level governmental operatives, anyway? It was clear, after all, that she might not be a princess, that this might not be Stonehenge, that Io might not be the world's annihilating messiah of the afterhuman. The odds were, it suddenly struck Vince, far more in favor of none of these things being true at all.

He pulled the cravat tighter, as if to test his theory, as if to dare someone, and the princess seemed to shrug a little, sort of disinterestedly, but then Vince realized the movement had only come from the knee he'd pressed between her shoulder blades for leverage.

"Celebrity grave robbings haunt Hollywood," Io called out, as if deeply exasperated by something, and, not necessarily, what's going on. "One word people: drool. . . ."

The princess seemed to have forgotten everything she was supposed to do, all that coaching how to die, and here she was just lying there at his feet, as if he were tying up a sack of day-old donuts. "Please," he whispered, making it look as if he were bearing his teeth with savage effort, lechery, diabolical something or other, "remember, we're just pretending, for God's sake, hold on. . . ." Vince ripped away the front of her gown to expose her childish breasts and thought, whose stupid idea were all the spider tattoos, anyway? She was "fading fast" as they say, too fast, in fact, so that Vince was left wondering what the hell was the hurry. She hadn't even lost the shoe yet, and he was desperately trying to surreptitiously kick the sling-back off her foot with his own. She was losing the battle for life, except it wasn't much of a battle, it was more like she had just sighed with relief to finally have the whole stupid thing over with. To think, he thought, that people watching this were actually going to be horrified, or turned on, and the whole goddamn thing was turning into some kind of absurd comedy.

Io called down from above: "Berserk Ape Mauls Ten in Taiwan," and it no longer sounded like some kind of purposefully jarring and surreal soundtrack to the events at hand, but as if he was really reading the headlines from the paper at random, sort of bored, hoping to find something interesting. He had stopped calling down stage directions, stopped offering banal platitudes, stopped, as far as Vince could tell, paying attention to the show, or sacrifice, or movie or whatever the hell it had become altogether. "Scientists Consider Theory of De-evolution."

Vince smells the unmistakable smell of urine and he's looking—he has no idea where he's looking, everywhere and nowhere at once, trying not to see, not to be seen, even though his image is being scanned and sent electronically along hundreds and thousands of millions of strands of the Web, instantaneously, all over the world. *I'm the spider in the web,* he thinks, irrationally, self-pityingly, a lazy metaphor that leads nowhere, *and I'm the one who's caught.* And still it didn't end and Vince was surprised, even though he knew it probably to be true, he was surprised at just how hard it was to kill a person, even when she was making no effort whatsoever to stay alive.

"Stay alive, damn it," Vince is muttering, praying, really begging, hoping, encouraging, promising, trying to tell himself that none of this is real, it's all a fantasy, and Io, calling down from above says, "Secret Genetic Warfare Two Decades Old" and then adds, "Assyrian Doctor Claims Cure for Death," and Vince, so pumped with fear and adrenaline, is unaware that he is now strangling a corpse as he reflects on the last outrageous headline Io has read, not from some tabloid either, but the *New York* fucking *Times,* and he thinks, *Oh, that can't be true,* but how would he know, how does anyone know, for sure?

Crisscrossing the darkness, on any given night, black limousines speed occupants to important rendezvous, and in the back of one such limousine, Caleb Darr, the light above him switched on, sits doing a crossword puzzle. He pauses, for a moment, over one particularly arcane clue, and then jots the answer down, "Euthyprho," one of the dialogues of Plato. Life, Caleb reflects, and rather shallowly at that, for the immortal, anyway, ends up being like nothing more than a cross-word puzzle. Sometimes it was difficult to keep in mind the seriousness with which human beings regarded all this, and, true enough, there was much that needed attending, but it truly needed to be put into perspective: in a hundred years no one here now would even be alive, in half that time the young would be old, and in twice that time whatever happned now would be all but forgotten, and what was remembered fodder for popular entertainment, like movies about World War II or Cleopatra. What nonsense. Only a few would be remembered at all, and not, of course, by anyone who knew them, but from words read in a book, or video shot of some kind of fake performance. And then the whole lot of it, the whole solar system would eventually fall back into the sun. . . .

If you saw things that way, Caleb thought, as he did, then existence was like a crossword puzzle that was solved one day and posed again, with a different alignment of boxes and different clues the next day. And what, ultimately, was the point when everything he figured out today had to be figured out all over again tomorrow? The point, he supposed, was to waste time—after all, what the hell else, under the circumstances, was there to do, and doing, didn't end up being?

They had arrived at the heliport, and the door of the black limousine was opened for Caleb and he stepped otuside onto the tarmac.

Another goddamn helicopter was waiting, going God only knew where, the blades hacking at the air, and everyone running, holding their heads.

Someone fell in beside Caleb, who, of course, was simply walking. He had a clipboard, whoever it was, and he was screaming some kind of report but whatever he was screaming could not be heard over the helicopter racket so Caleb had no idea what the man said and it never occurred to him, no matter how inconclusive the answer might have been, to ask the question, "What?"

"Internet snuff ring busted," Io had called down, and it took Vince some moments of choking on tear gas fumes, tears running down his sooty face, squinting in disbelief at the dead girl at his feet, to understand that what Io had said wasn't just another headline from this morning's paper, or, maybe, it was, but in any event what he was saying was happening right now.

Vince wondered, briefly, if this could all be part of the show, the rolling smoke, the flashes of gunfire, the heavily armored figures appearing and disappearing in the mist, equipped with gas masks, stun-shields, virus canisters, frag grenades, laser pistols, and flame-jelly. The vampires, or crew, or whatever they were, everyone, was being slaughtered wholesale, or so Vince assumed, staggering forward from one scene of shocking dismemberment to another, faces half recognized, slack and uninterested, or sharply focused on nothing, and every face on a head displaced from its usual body.

Could Io really have organized the sabotage of his own extravaganza, or was this sabotage an integral part of the extravaganza?

The time for philosophizing, Vince concluded, bending over to spit out a mouthful of blood and tissue, was over. There were flies, literally, on everything, the air so thick with them, it was necessary to part them with one's hands, and the sound of Danzig or Rammstein, or both together, or rapidly alternated, was blasting at mind-leveling decibels high enough to cause instant amnesia as well as bruising under the eyes.

It was time to get the hell out of here—but there really was nowhere left to go.

What was going on now seemed to be going on for-ever, or, rather, it seemed as if it would never end, nor had it any beginning, and it was happening everywhere at once. Vince had this vague, somewhat protean, idea of escape, all of these ridiculous fantasies of flying, burrowing, becoming suddenly omnipotent, bullet-proof, multilived, and suchlike, everything so clearly impossible and convincing that he suspected he was dreaming, or hallucinating. He was hit over the back of the neck, allowed to crawl away a little, and then a barrage of blows, like a nine-rayed star, fell over him, and he stopped crawling, thinking, dreaming, every-thing. He was cuffed and dragged and further beaten and stood up, sort of, and for a breathless few mo-ments, stared into the hard, no-nonsense face of Jason Horn.

"I didn't do it," Vince screamed, hoarsely, if you could call the raspy strangled whisper he emitted a scream. "You know I didn't do it."

Horn was impassive. "Of course you did. We have it on diskette. On CD."

"Bullshit . . . that's bullshit . . . you told me to do it."

"Mr. Manning, this is unbecoming of you."

"You set me up," Vince sobbed.

Horn said nothing, but put an oxygen aspirator in his mouth, breathed in, breathed out, luxuriously.

"You bastard," Vince gasped, gulping, as if underwa-ter. "You wanted me to kill her. You said so. It was all part of the plan."

"Are you getting all this?"

Horn appeared to be saying this to no one in particu-lar, and without, although it was difficult to be certain, any sarcasm at all.

"Please . . . I have my rights."

"You have no rights."

"My rights . . ."

"We raided everything. Your computer has been seized. You're done. Dead. Off-line."

"You can't do this . . . you can't . . ."

"Get him processed."

And, of course, no one heard a word of this conversation, not a word, because the music was so loud, the smoke so thick, the flies so omnipresent, the disorientation program so complete that it all appeared a dumb show, an absurd pantomime that only later would be dubbed in with the aforementioned dialogue, which Vince would eventually hear read back at the trial. Only by then, he'd come to believe that's what really had been said, just like everyone else, because something like that is always what is said, and, in the final analysis, it doesn't make any difference whatsoever.

Too late, Caleb arrived, as always, exactly on schedule. He stepped down from the helicopter and into the midst of complete pandemonium. The entire place was burning with irrational fires and the ground littered with the dead, the deader, and those not yet fortunate enough to be dead. There were the usual cries of pain, confusion, sorrow, the desperate "why?" of existence you hear in any ICU among those semiconscious, or those due for another dose of pain meds. There was a spunky jazz ensemble piece being piped through the mega-speakers, which had been set up like mini-Stonehenge monoliths, all around the grassy knoll, which could easily have been located outside Chattanooga or Panama City.

The princess was dead, of course; he'd seen her

corpse zipped into a specially monogrammed black body bag, rushed past him by the medical corps, which, upon recognzing Caleb, or rather his credentials, gave him the confidential news, and let him gaze on her now unfamiliar, grotesquely bloated face, although, like anything else, it could have been a lie.

There were arrests and summary executions taking place all around him: beatings, sexual abuses, bias crimes, police brutalities, illegal search-and-seizures, and no shortage of "citizens" on hand videotaping it all. Once in a while, seeming to arise from out of nowhere, and sometimes at the most inappropriate moments, there was the spontaneous and enthusiastic applause of a laugh track. Someone, oddly enough, perhaps confused in the way many with massive head trauma will confuse an issue, knelt before Caleb, embracing his knees, beseeching something or other, mercy, medical assistance, benediction, legal advice? Whatever—Caleb dispatched him without interview one way or another, and kept on walking, past a tank that seemed to be pointed in the wrong direction.

"Colonel, Colonel," a group of reporters, most of them dressed in khaki, were shouting, surging toward him, ahead of camera crews, the hollow eyes of zoom lenses trained on him, looking for reaction shots on a face that betrayed no reaction. "Colonel, Colonel, can you comment on the events of the last twenty-four hours?" And microphones, handheld and boom, were proffered to him, as the reporters surged against the barriers of soldiers and sawhorses that cordoned off the sacrosanct area only Caleb, at this point, had any right to tread.

Caleb remained silent, expressionless, iconographically gaunt. Someone, a spokesperson for something or other, said—with the excruciating predictability of an old liturgical prayer: "The colonel has no comment."

There were flies all over, and Caleb, occasionally, waved his hands in certain precise and priestly arabesques, almost like tai chi movements, to ward them away or welcome them, which was effective, for a time, seconds or so, at a stretch. Huge fans had been moved into position, ostensibly to promote the dissemination of some kind of insecticide, but they had not been turned on as yet, or they had malfunctioned, it was impossible to say, and so know one did.

Somewhere past a side field set up as a field "crematorium," down a gully, and through a shallow rocky stream accessible by a chauffered all-terrain vehicle, Caleb made his way to his mark, where, supposedly, whoever was in charge of this segment was ready to give Caleb his cue. Io was there, of course, having attempted to flee the scene on foot, a modest entourage of Humvees waiting for him above the post road, two entourages, in fact, pointed in opposite directions, one of them a decoy, but everyone in both entourages had already been slaughtered.

"So . . . they sent you," the boy-diva lisped, mock-coyly, ". . . of all people."

Io was dressed in black leather incognito chic: a trench-coat-style jacket, pants, slouch hat, with lavender silk shirt and accompaniments, black boots, gloves, and wraparound silver mirror shades, a stylish scar and bruise makeup accenting naturally perfect cheekbones for that beautiful martyr effect.

"You know who I am then. No need for the lengthy preamble . . ."

"Oh, my pa-pa." Io rolled his eyes, and clasped his hands in mock rapture. "To me you were soooo wonderful!"

"How long did you know?"

"Ever since I was a little boychick. They told me all about you in the underground."

"I didn't know . . . until very recently. If that makes any difference . . . which it doesn't. Nothing would have changed."

"No." Io giggled. "I guess having you for a dad was never going to turn out very well one way or another."

Caleb noted his son's two bodyguards, already dead, lying in two heaps, somewhat dismembered, one by a tree a few yards to the left, the other having apparently attempted to flee into the woods. On a handheld radio by a nearby moldy log, someone, perhaps Jason Horn himself, was encouraging Io to hurry, trying to coax him to the entourage of burning Humvees, where the young vampire could be captured alive.

". . . so you know how this must end," Caleb said.

"Oh, I've read this story a few hundred times, at least. Ho-hum."

"No 'take this cup from me' dramatics then . . ." Caleb said grimly, not unsettled, but not settled either.

"A different question, instead."

"Go ahead."

"Why . . . Daddy . . . why do you bother?"

A fly, momentarily . . .

"It's what I do," Caleb said, and for the first time in a long time, maybe the only time, he was telling something that approximated the truth, although more accurately, it was more that what he'd said was not an outright lie, like everything else. "Whatsoever thy hand findeth to do, do it with thy might."

"Ecclesastes 9.10," Io said. "You . . . ?"

Caleb nodded.

"Oh, daddy," Io squealed and clapped. "One last request, Daddy . . . and you know I never asked anything of you before."

Caleb, charging the auto-da-fé canister, nodded, indulgently, in the true sense of that word: papally. He watched as his son stripped lasciviously to a black lace G-string, and sank, indolently, to a carpet of specially treated pine needs, arms back, elbows up, smooth legs slightly parted, in a position of suggestive surrender. Caleb knew, of course, that allowing the boy this final act was a mistake, but Io was his son, and the message of this perverse young psycho was Caleb's message, too, in a distracted, third-party kind of way—a message the world was not ready for, not yet, like a child that had to be aborted, which, as cameras, presumably hidden somewhere among the foliage, recorded what would later come to be celebrated in art and literature as "Io's passion," Caleb did just that: pressing the button on the auto-da-fé canister having already decapitated his only begotten son without much ceremony or commotion.

Caleb stepped through the crackling burning pine needles to the limousine waiting on a dirt trail that led, presumably, to wherever he was supposed to go next. He slid into the backseat of the refrigerated car, picked up the crossword puzzle book, and put it aside again, but without any particular feelings of regret, or anything else for that matter. From the front seat, his chauffer, one of them anyway, some kind of cross-country killer or other, had the good sense not to look in the rearview when he, or she, asked, "Tough day, sir?"

Caleb paused for just a second, knowing the importance of the moment, and, having considered an improvisation, fingered the navel ring he'd plucked from the smoldering ashes of his son, and said, in a manner much imitated from that moment on, "I've got forever."

Sitting, of all places, in a Starbucks, which could have been practically anywhere, and was, Caleb Darr quickly scans the Book of the Apocalypse V. It had been left for him, partly as a reward, and partly as a warning, disguised in a restaurant supplement in a free copy of the *New York Press* that he'd gotten from a take-box on the corner. There was a lot among the flimsy typescript that Caleb either already knew or could probably have figured out, and the rest of it, he thought, was probably better left unsaid.

The program containing Nikka's replicated image will be destroyed, but not before someone will manage to make a copy, for not everyone will be certain that with a little noodling, a manipulated Nikka VIII could be used to manipulate the masses. There is always, and Caleb nodded understandingly, a market for iconographic nostalgia. The mortal, Vince Manning, had apparently betrayed his lover-mentor Io, as per the powerful old formula, but the whole fiasco of the "double sacrifice" will, more or less, be considered to have been aborted due to the efforts of the Internet spook Jason Horn and his cohorts who attached an impossible virus to the file transmitting the Web-cast, crashing, simultaneously, all the hard drives into which it had been downloaded, whether on purpose or merely accidentally.

Manning himself, the only possible survivor, aside from Caleb, of this whole hellish transition, will be inexplicably released on the grounds that all the evidence of his wrongdoing consists of pixilated images whose ultimate reality or unreality cannot be established on any firm foundation. To put it simply: it will end up a stalemate between those who believe a thought can kill—and those who don't. Manning is guilty, though, of something, that much is certain, since everyone is, and someone like Vince Manning, a man with imagination, is guilty more than most: so why will they let him go? The answer, perhaps, which is really no answer at all, might be found in the few lines of the Apocalypse describing the new secret Web site he will start, protected by someone powerful, maybe Jason Horn himself and whoever he represents, devoted to the slaughtered "vampire" prince.

Soon cults will form: a loosely connected random worldwide network of suicidal maniacs, nihilists, anarchists, wackos, and perverts all devoted to the vague inarticulate concept of the afterhuman and doing whatever they can to speed about the extinction of the human species. It seemed already that whenever he picked up a *New York Times* their work was proceeding pretty much right on schedule. Caleb read that, like the telltale lesion of some new, highly contagious, entirely incurable pathogen, there will be a new kind of tatoo or trademark seen on the naked flesh of mortals all over the world: an Egyptian-style ankh with the catchy slogan, in Bookman Old Style, *dead chic*.

Mahoney, Caleb will insist, had killed himself and, from now on, will continue being dead. But still Caleb will get up to forty-five cell phone messages a week, and twice as many e-mails, from someone insisting that he is the ex-commando, and very, very much alive, in a manner of speaking. Caleb is a little disappointed to read this part, and reads it twice, just to make certain he's reading it correctly. He can, of course, change his cell phone number and e-mail address, and he probably will, but only when the novelty of the messages wears off, which it won't.

Juliet will die: she must, sucked of life from the inside out by the impossibility of loving Caleb. But her image, fresh and so twenty-first century, will be taken

up worldwide by the human cabals who seek to promote the idea that there's a world out there
somewhere. After all, somebody's got to make a buck.
Everything's vampiric. The top talents in advertising,
religion, and digital media, among others, will devise
the fist prototype upon which the face of the new par-
adigm will be based. Like orthodoxies everywhere, they
will be oblivious to her "true" meaning. She will stare
down chaos and in her name and endlessly replicated
image the cults of Io will be hunted down and annihilated, if it takes forever, and this will be the first
hundred years of it. They will call this hot new cyber-
celebrity Juliet II.

As for Caleb's unborn son: he will be sheltered by the
disparate bands of the "vampire" diaspora, passing from
one to the other, one step ahead of the various forms of
assassinations, both human and alien, as Caleb looks on,
helplessly, compelled to help whatever way he can. The
new messiah's message: a pastiche of this and that, here
and there, a nervous frittering on the edge of the utter
nothing that the iconographic ghost of his slain half
brother will continue to tempt everyone to embrace.

So that was it, more or less, Caleb thought, putting
down the Book of the Apocalypse V and finding himself wondering, *Well, is it prophecy or prologue?* He pretends
to sip his iced vanilla chai and thinks of all that had happened and all that hadn't, of Nikka and Io, of Juliet and
his coming son, and he thinks of how people lived and
why and why they didn't and he reflects on how he exists, day after day after day, watching, disinterestedly, how
it all passes away and only that morning Caleb had seen
a man in a shop window folding sweaters and an old
woman walking up the street with two bags of groceries
and he wondered, what in the world could they possibly
be living for, and choosing life, what kept them from

going mad? Perhaps they were mad—mad or dead. But some—there must be some—who were not.

There was a famous philosopher once, who eventually went through the windshield of a car and died, or so they said, and he and Caleb had once had a lengthy conversation after the latter had drowned a pair of children in the Seine, and later, in one work or another, the philosopher had quoted Caleb without attribution, as if the thought, taken out of context, were his own: "There is no fate that cannot be surmounted by scorn." It all had something to do with that, Caleb felt, maybe. And now, thinking of it all, in a Starbucks that could be anywhere, Caleb saw a fly land on the paper he'd been reading and Caleb knew, of course, that he was certainly quick enough to kill that fly and had been all along, and he decided, for the time being, to kill it not again.

And Caleb grinned.

final instructions

Wherever you are right now, stop, take notice of the situation, and try to determine, first off, if you are alive or dead. Try to determine, right now, if anything you do or say is in the least way, or can ever be mistaken as, remotely genuine. If the answer is yes, you've been warned.

You're sitting, perhaps, at an all-night diner, at 2:00 A.M., between one place and another, drinking coffee, chain-smoking cigarettes, divorced, middle-aged, bankrupt, potbellied, going bald . . . or not, at least, not yet.

You're the ex-wife of such a man, possibly.

Or the son. Or daughter.

Are you in your mid-twenties or early thirties, feeling rootless, without direction, as if your life is going nowhere, or, even worse, heading inexorably in the wrong direction, which it invariably is? You're even younger, perhaps, feeling confused, hopeless, lost, trying to fit, talk to people, find that special someone, and you cry sometimes wondering if you'll ever fit in anywhere?

You are old, maybe, and if so, let's say nothing, nothing at all, shall we?

Whoever you are, it's now time to move on.

If you want to speak your heart, don't. If someone wants to speak their heart to you, don't listen. That's how contagion is spread.

Sometimes say "either," sometimes say "or," but not strictly fifty-fifty.

If someone askes for directions, give the wrong ones intentionally, if possible.

Don't take stands, metaphoric or otherwise.

Buy a white lab cat from a uniform-supply store: the idea is to gain access, anywhere, automatically, anonymously.

Have business cards made: false name, cell, and e-mail addy, of course.

On a street corner, any corner, look around, vaguely.

Wear contraceptives one day, but not the next, and always when no sexual encounter is possible.

Post links to nonexistent Web sites.

Model yourself on nature, in particular, blizzards, but in an abstract way.

Discard, unthinkingly, any letter that carries with it the instructions "open immediately." Tune radios, if necessary to have them on at all, hoplessly between stations.

Distrust, and categorically reject, any program, strategy, etc., whose motive, expressed or implied, is a return to whatever might be meant by the term "sobriety" or "recovery."

Take that pill—if you have it. If there is a drink in front of you, drink it.

If things are fake, make them faker.

If things are violent, make them more violent.

If things are dead, make them deader.

Get a tattoo: an Egyptian-style ankh and the slogan, in Bookman Old Style script that says, *dead chic.*

Do whatever comes after whatever comes after whatever is happening right now.

If you believe the script you are reading, do not panic.

This is an emergency: Dial 1-800-SUICIDE.

Dial 911.

When someone answers, wait a heartbeat as if about to say something, and then hang up.

Like this.

More Books From Your Favorite Thriller Authors

More Thrilling Suspense From Your Favorite Thriller Authors

More Thrilling Suspense From
Wendy Corsi Staub

All the Way Home	0-7860-1092-4	$6.99US/$8.99CAN
The Last to Know	0-7860-1196-3	$6.99US/$8.99CAN
Fade to Black	0-7860-1488-1	$6.99US/$9.99CAN
In the Blink of an Eye	0-7860-1423-7	$6.99US/$9.99CAN
She Loves Me Not	0-7860-1424-5	$6.99US/$9.99CAN
Dearly Beloved	0-7860-1489-X	$6.99US/$9.99CAN

Available Wherever Books Are Sold!

Visit our website at **www.kensingtonbooks.com**

More Thrilling Suspense From
T.J. MacGregor